BEST BELOVED

Feb 20, 2020

Paul

I do hope you enjoy the book,
the time of 100 years ago - the time
of my grandparents' youth. So many
things have changed - and so much
has not.

Best, Bob Bissell

For Janet

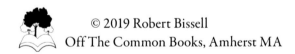
Front cover painting by artist Walter Cudnohufsky
of Ashfield, Massachusetts. http://www.cudnohufsky.com

Back cover photo by James Francis Hurley.
October 29, 1917. Chateau Wood, Belgium.

BEST BELOVED

by

Robert Bissell

But towards evening, when people and things grow restless and tired, there came up the Man (with his own little girl-daughter?)—Yes with his own Best Beloved little girl-daughter sitting upon his shoulder.
Rudyard Kipling
Just So Stories

Death is nothing terrible after all. It may mean something more wonderful than life. It cannot possibly mean anything worse to the good soldier.
Alan Seeger
Letters and Diary of Alan Seeger

Prologue

August 29, 1917

It was hot on the evening of August 29 and the sweltering crowd seemed to drag the heat with them into the stifling auditorium. Women drooped onto chairs ineffectively fanning their red, sweat-stained faces. Men removed their coats and loosened their ties while murmuring about the heat as if worried that more serious talk would increase their discomfort.

I adjusted my blouse and marveled at the attendance. Shouldn't we be down by the Charles River instead—sprawled on the grass, nibbling the remains of a picnic and sipping lemonade and beer? We'd welcome the moon as it appeared in the east bringing the cool night air and chasing the sun and heat and worries of daylight. We'd dip our feet in the water while laughing about the art show or the theater or the latest book or the Red Sox, and we'd avoid any mention of the war. Some would wade in and reach down to cup a handful of water toward their neighbor, and soon the splashing would escalate, and we'd laugh aloud and shout and splash and sputter and fall thankfully into the river, and feel the cleansing water wash away the sweat and cares of the world. And then we'd troop out to collapse on the shore, our wet clothes clinging to our bodies, and we'd make quick work of the cookies and gingerbread, our laughter only slowly receding as if in tempo with the river where our ripples would subside to allow the moon glow to coalesce to a single reflected beam shooting across the water into our eyes.

Instead, we crowded into the old hall like animals crammed in a stockyard, except we entered voluntarily, trying to politely ignore the odors of sweat, alcohol, and belched dinners. The windows stood open but the curtains moved not a whit, and I thought the fanning ladies were only moving the human stench from here to there, and the more vigorously they fanned the more heat they produced thus adding to the smell and discomfort.

i

I wished there was some way to signal the speakers to shorten their remarks, but once given the platform each seemed enchanted by his words and oblivious to the perspiration that dripped from his forehead and stained his shirt. I thought of slipping back to plead with Marshall, to let him know of the audience discomfort, but I knew this night was special; he hoped to register his one thousandth recruit.

I tried to ease the heat by ignoring the droning talk, and dreaming, instead, of a winter dusk at home in Birkett Ferry. There is no sound save for that of my snowshoes swishing through the fresh light snow as I return downhill from the knoll, cooled to the core. I detour from my homeward path to the river, where a winter breeze is both refreshing and chilling. The stark trees are silhouetted against the surrounding fields. The waning light accents their dim blue shadows lengthening across the frozen river. The ice and snow are so inviting that I stretch out on the riverbank, lying luxuriously back in the snow, to watch the last touch of crimson disappear from the sky.

My fantasy worked; I must have briefly dozed until my dream was interrupted by movement beside me. I opened my eyes to see my brother, Matt, settling into the adjacent seat. Then I wondered if I was really awake as I tried to make sense of his left eye, swollen and bruised, and his disheveled shirt torn at the shoulder, and his sickly scent of alcohol. Marshall was speaking now and Matt put his finger to his lips to stop my questions. "Shhh, Gwen, I'll tell you about it later," he whispered and then he smiled.

And all I could do was silently ask him, Why does this keep happening? Why do you allow it to continue? And, I suppose, as much as I wanted to ask Matt, I wanted to ask myself those same questions.

And then Marshall's voice, rising to evangelical heights, asked for recruits to come forward, and several men made their way to the central aisle. And in a moment Matt was in that line. And I didn't know what to do as competing thoughts hammered my brain. Just how drunk is he? Should I pull him back? But another thought held me in my seat. Maybe it's all for the best.

As was his fashion, Marshall clasped each man at the shoulders pulling him in for a manly hug before steering him to the recruitment table as the crowd stomped and cheered. When he saw Matt next in line, he frowned and looked quickly to me, and in that second I nodded. Marshall raised both his arms to quiet the audience. I thought he might honor Matt with a public acknowledgment of his bravery, but then explain that Matt was not quite seventeen, and that, in spite of his willingness, he must wait for his eighteenth birthday. And then Matt would return proudly to his seat next to me.

But, no. With his hands in the air and sweat drenching his shirt, Marshall waited for the cheers to taper. "Ladies and gentlemen," he dropped his arms to Matt's shoulder and then turned him to face the crowd. "Ladies and gentlemen, I don't believe in self-congratulation, but this is an honor, not for me, but for the people of Boston." The crowd was now quietly curious. Perhaps they wondered about Matt's bruised face and torn shirt. "This fine young man," a few whoops and cheers, "this fine young man, who is also a personal friend of mine, is the one thousandth man I have recruited to serve honorably in the United States Army!" His last words were lost in the clapping and cheering and yelling and stomping, and a few men ran forward to thump Matt on the back as Marshall gave him a bear hug and walked with him to the recruitment table where Matt stood proudly before bending to write his name. In spite of the heat and the odor, the cheers and yells continued in that hall for quite a while, echoing out into the night and down the Charles River and across Boston Harbor finally to die out over the Atlantic Ocean.

Chapter 1
1907

Matt and I lived an idyllic childhood growing up in Birkett Ferry, a small town in western Massachusetts where our father's family had lived for generations. There was hardly a stain of discontent: that was the outward appearance of our family. But that was not our reality. Even at a young age, I knew our rambles to the river and knoll were a way to escape the tensions of home. My parents fought—it was often enough that I remember supposing it normal. But then why did I cry each time? Once, when I was nine, my parents quarreled in the kitchen—she was angry that he would not come with us to Cambridge to visit her parents. Voices rose, something shattered onto the kitchen floor. Matt and I cowered on the living room couch. I remember Matt turning pale and wiping his eyes. My stomach churned. I put my arm around him causing us both to sob. Father yelled something about Mother wasting all her time on painting. A door slammed and then there was quiet, except for our whimpering.

It must have been ten minutes before Mother came in, her eyes red, her face drawn. She sat between us, arms around us, not speaking for a minute or two.

"I'm sorry you heard that," she said. She bit her lower lip. "Sometimes parents fight. It's not good but it happens. Don't worry—we'll be friends again."

I looked away from her, out to the lawn.

"I know," she said, "we'll read a book. How about *Just So Stories*?"

Matt nodded.

She began to read the story of how the elephant got its trunk, but I couldn't listen. My mind was whirling. When would Father be home?

After reading two pages, Mother closed the book and looked at me. "You know, your father and I, we're usually happy." Now she started to sob, then caught herself. "It's just that sometimes we fight." She dabbed her eyes, then blew her nose.

"Our wedding day, it was the most perfect day. Would you like to hear the story again?" Mother loved to tell us about that day. In happier times, Matt and I would curl by the fire, listening while studying the four photos of the wedding, youthful faces of our parents and grandparents staring forth. Now she gave a vivid description, speaking slowly, offering details I'd never heard. As she spoke, my heart slowed and my muscles relaxed.

"It was strange to have the wedding here—usually it's in the bride's town—but your Compston grandparents insisted this was the perfect spot. My parents didn't care, or said they didn't, so Grandmother Joan organized the whole thing." She paused for a moment. "And it was wonderful. A warm Saturday morning in October. Your father and I walked out of the Congregational Church, down the steps, and across the green to the reception here in his backyard. The trees were red and gold, the sky the deepest blue." She sighed. "Every autumn we have a few days like that, and with each one, I'm taken right back to our wedding."

She smiled and I felt better. I trotted over to the desk and brought back one of the framed photos showing Mother and Father posing hand in hand in front of our white clapboard house.

"No one stayed inside for the reception. It was such a lovely day. There was a huge tent on the terrace and white-coated waiters with trays of elegant food and champagne."

"Yuck!" Matt scrunched his nose and pretended to gag.

"And we had a quartet playing Brahms and Dvořák. My parents gave us the perfect gift—it was Grandpa Michael's idea. They gave us the canoe—our red canoe—just like the Cambridge canoe we courted in. I suppose it wasn't very practical but it was our favorite gift."

Matt and I smiled. We were only seven and nine but we'd been in that canoe a hundred times.

"Later in the afternoon, after most of the guests left, we just couldn't wait. We had to try the canoe. Grandmother Compston was irritated—she insisted we not, but for once, your father wouldn't listen to her. Without even changing clothes, we ambled down to the dock. Everyone followed us—everyone except your Compston grandparents." Mother laughed. "But that was okay. The photographer made us wait on the water while he set up his camera."

Matt went to get that photo, bringing it back to the couch.

"Then we paddled down to the island, just the two of us. And we had a lovely time." She paused for a moment as if lost in memory. "I tell you what. I want to show you a secret, but you must promise not to tell your father." She led us through the kitchen, stopping at the bits of china scattered across the floor. "Oh, dear, I'll need to sweep this up." Her voice cracked and I bit my lip. "Watch where you step." As she took us through the gardens and across the lawn, the sight of the river and willows revived my spirits. We entered her studio, a small barn-like structure she had restored. Mother painted—she was quite good, having studied in Paris initially with the conventional artists and then with the Impressionists. She complained that she never had enough time to paint, but sometimes she spent all day in her studio, leaving us in the care of Grandmother Compston who always told us to be still and stay out of the way—perhaps to read quietly on her porch—so as not to interfere with her guests. I preferred escape to the river or woods over such confinement.

"This October is our tenth anniversary," Mother told us that day. "I'm painting a picture for your father. It's nearly done and I thought you would like to see it, but remember: not one word to him." We were rarely allowed in her studio and I was curious, just as interested in the drippings of red, yellow, and blue across the unfinished floor-boards as I was in the painting. I wished I could sit here with her and watch her paint, bring her a drip cloth or a glass of lemonade—whatever she needed. I could not understand why it was a problem for us to be there while she painted, though I remembered the year before, a bright summer day, when I chased Matt across the lawn and he sought refuge in the studio, dashing in to grab her dress folds, surprising her, upsetting her balance, and bringing the easel and the palette to the floor. Her shrieks chased us out the door and down to the river where we curled in the hammock under the willows, frightened and crying. Grandfather found us there still sniveling a half hour later and calmed us with a quiet story.

She must have hoped to soothe us with the anniversary painting but it was hard to be calm when I saw more tears trickle down her cheeks as she brought the painting from a closet.

The painting was quite beautiful—I thought so even then. It offered me a tiny bit of hope, and as the years went by there were many occasions when I stood at the mantel staring at it, wishing I could will that lovely scene to replace the reality of my parents' marriage. It showed our island—at least we called it ours—the island two miles downstream where my parents canoed on their wedding day. It was an autumn landscape in late afternoon, our beached red canoe tipped off to the side. The glowing amber light reflected from the calm river to the canoe's cedar ribbing and then upward to the mix of gold and red and green in the island's canopy.

With a quick glance, the painting could easily have been mistaken for a still life, for it was the canoe that one noticed first. But then the angle of the canoe and the direction of the light drew the eye onward to a background point just off center where a barely visible, darkly suited arm emerged from the foliage holding up a bough to allow passage of a woman into the thicket. She blended into the forest, her form bent slightly forward, her chestnut hair skimming just below a limb of similar color, and her long white bridal gown partly obscured by the brush and easily mistaken for sun-dappled undergrowth. One did not at first notice the people—my parents. The artistic deceit was so masterful that when visitors came for the first time into our living room, we would watch for their predictable response. At first there would be a look of polite admiration followed, in seconds, by an exclamation, "Oh!" And as they looked more closely to be certain they had it right, "That is clever!"

When I was fourteen and sixteen, I would study the painting and

4

wonder what else might have happened the afternoon of their wedding, my parents retreating back into the brush of the island's interior. And then I'd shudder, repulsed, not allowing my imagination to go too far, not wanting to connect the fact of my birth—just about nine months later. Even as an adult, this was not a scene I wished to contemplate, but last October on their anniversary, on a golden day similar to that portrayed in the painting, I canoed to the island and lay in the grass, thinking, trying to make sense of my family's mistakes. I don't believe I succeeded in that, but when I found myself thinking of their wedding day, it suddenly occurred to me that my parents were in love then, they must have been—at least for a time.

I found solace in the thought, my imagination drifting back to that day thirty years before, perhaps the day of my conception.

The painting showed the landing beach, and from there they would have followed the trail past maples and chestnuts and through a grove of birch, the white trunks beckoning them forward into the small grass meadow, a hidden surprise in the island's interior. Perhaps it was, for them, just like the day I visited: the lush field, the trees of red and gold, the calls of birds, the lapping of river waves, and the warmth of October sun. I smiled to myself: it would have been a shame to waste such a moment.

Starting in love. Why then, did it all end as it did?

So yes, Matt and I escaped when we could, when we were old enough to hike to the knoll and canoe the river. We escaped Mother's bored resentment and Father's melancholy. It was hard for us to imagine Father with a different personality, but Mother sometimes told us how different he was when they met, he a student at Harvard and she working in her parents' bookstore, in the time before his war. After graduation, he had spent a year in Labrador working in a medical clinic. He returned to marry Mother, and his plans to return to Labrador, perhaps to settle there, were thwarted first by her pregnancy and then by the war with Cuba. Mother, just a few months pregnant, did not want him to fight, but his father, Grandfather Compston worried at his son's lack of direction and pushed him to enlist with Teddy Roosevelt. Grandfather, forever frustrated that he was too young to fight in the Civil War, did not want his son to miss this opportunity. So he wrote letters to gain his acceptance into the exclusive Rough Riders (25,000 applied with only 1,000 accepted). Soon Father left his tearful wife and proud parents to train in Texas and fight in Cuba where, as I learned so many years later when Father finally could talk of it, he witnessed the mutilation and death of his friends and agonized over his inability to help them.

The Rough Riders, their daring adventures lovingly covered by the press, were welcomed home as heroes. I've kept Grandmother's scrapbook with the newspaper clippings. There was an energetic welcome on the docks of New York where Roosevelt spoke, describing himself for the press, "I am feeling disgracefully well . . . I feel positively ashamed of my appearance when I see how badly off some of my brave fellows are. Oh, but we had a bully fight." Roosevelt appeared exuberantly robust, in contrast to his men, who, as the press reported, disembarked with such astonishing weight loss and weakness that they could barely manage the one-mile walk from the docks to their camp.

A month later, we were waiting to meet his train, along with the rest of the town. I had been born while he was in Cuba—in fact, on the day of my birth the Rough Riders were standing victorious on San Juan Hill. Mother waited until I was an adult to tell me how, at three months old, I was so frightened by the station hubbub that she retreated back to our carriage where she could sit and nurse, shielded by an umbrella. She told me that, while she was relieved to see him step from the train uninjured, she was so startled by his gaunt and hollow appearance that her milk stopped flowing. I looked up from her breast in a panic, wailing and squirming until Mother turned me sideways to see, for the first time, the bearded, willowy man who was my father. He paused a few feet away and finally allowed a smile before gathering us in his arms. So he returned home to his own proud parents and to a glorious small town welcome that included a parade from the depot up Ferry Street and around the green to end with a party on our lawn.

He never recovered the exuberance that Mother said she found so attractive. Matt and I knew him as a weary, melancholy man, though we would sometimes see a spark of enthusiasm when he talked of his Labrador days. After the war, there seemed no prospect but to join his father in the law practice. Father accepted some of the drearier cases while his father, benefiting from the decreased caseload, felt renewed vigor. Grandfather agreed, almost on a lark, to represent the Northern Pacific Railroad in a local land dispute. The successful outcome of this suit led to further railroad cases throughout New England, expanding the practice and swelling Grandfather's income, but leaving Father the bulk of the town practice, consisting of estate settlements, family disputes, and land sales.

Chapter 2
1908

My parents separated for a while when I was ten and Matt eight. Father came roaring down the attic steps yelling about a trunk. Matt and I trembled in the living room, staring at each other with wide eyes, not wanting to hear but taking in every word, not able to move. Mother's words were dry and sparse, and each time she spoke Father shouted an interruption. Finally he remembered we were there and ordered us next door to our grandparents, but still we could hear their quarreling until Grandmother took us into her kitchen and shut the door. She wiped my tears and sliced some blackberry pie which I picked at, surprised that Matt was able to eat one piece and ask for more. Later she fed us dinner but I noticed she and Grandfather ate little—instead they watched the kitchen door as if they expected company at any moment. Matt and I curled together on the living room couch, and I hid my face against the back cushion letting the tears soak into the fabric. We fell asleep there, listening to Grandfather read Shakespeare, *Macbeth* as I recall. He often did that, read us Shakespeare, and when we asked what it was about, he said not to worry, we would understand if it was repeated often enough.

We stayed at our grandparents that night, and the next morning Mother came for us, thanking Grandmother but not speaking much with her. Mother stood straight. Her eyes were dry and focused, her voice was steady. On the way home she told us we would be going to Cambridge the next day, to visit her parents—as we did every summer.

"But we can't leave yet. We'll miss the July Fourth party," I paused, "and my birthday!"

Each July Fourth, my grandparents hosted a huge family celebration on the back lawn. Cousins, second cousins, third cousins, aunts, uncles, friends—often two hundred people or more—attended. The gardens were not yet at full production, but Grandfather arranged for a load of vegetables and fruits from the south. The aromas of grilled meats and baking breads were intoxicating. And because this event closely followed my July 1st birthday, there was always a cake and a few presents, briefly making me the center of attention.

"Yes, well, we'll be doing things differently this year." Now there was a quiver in Mother's voice and she looked away from us. "I'll need you both to help me pack."

"But the fireworks! We've got to see the fireworks!" Matt tugged at her dress.

"Matt, stop that this instant. This is not a game. Please start getting your things together."

That night, Father tucked us in and told us a story, not the usual pattern in our home where we often saw him only at dinner. That night he talked about Labrador. These were our favorite stories partly because when he spoke of Labrador his melancholy left and he became animated, talking in funny accents and gesturing with his hands. But now he was subdued and spoke slowly.

"I enjoyed my time in the clinic, working hard, hauling wood and water. Sometimes, if I was lucky, one of the doctors or nurses asked me to help with a patient and I would lift an old man while his sheets were changed, or help with fresh bandages. There was always something to help with." He paused and looked out our window. "But my favorite times were when we were called out, usually a nurse, Lynne, and I to a hut. Isolated families sent word down the lake, by snowshoe or dogsled, when medical help was needed. I still remember the first time I went. It was December and I had only driven the dogsled a few times. Luckily, Lynne knew about medicine and dogs both, and she knew the way to the hut. I remember how happy I was to be traveling across the ice, riding on the sled, sometimes walking when there was a difficult patch of ice. We traveled for three hours. We weren't cold—not with our warm clothing and the sun reflecting off the ice, but we pulled into a little cove off the lake, protected from the wind. The dogs needed rest. Lynne showed me how to get a fire going in a hurry, using spruce boughs, and soon we had a pot of tea ready. I remember sitting there in the sun, some kind of tiny ice crystals filtering down from the spruce, falling through the steam of our mugs. It was just so beautiful to watch."

"How about the story?" Matt sat up in his bed.

"It was probably two more hours to the cabin, and by then it was nice to see smoke curling out of that chimney. The father was off trapping. It was the mother who met us at the door, saying she was sorry not to have a meal ready for us but she had no time with the kids being sick and all. There were two kids a girl and a boy—about the ages you two are now."

Matt and I smiled at each other.

"It was something about coughs and fever; I don't really recall. Lynne showed the mother how to use steam vapors to help with the cough and surely gave them some medicine or other. I chiseled ice out of the water hole in the lake and brought several buckets and then carried wood to stack next to the house. Then I sorted our supplies, getting dinner ready."

"You cooked dinner!" I was surprised.

He paused as he looked toward our bedroom door. "Yes. In those days I did. I had some kind of meat—probably caribou—and carrots and potatoes. Quite a nice stew as I recall. There was not much food in their kitchen so I stocked their shelves with our extra supplies—corn meal, flour, vegetables, and such. After dinner, I brought out a sweet cake—a fruitcake—and I remember how wide those children's eyes were. They had never eaten such a thing! And that's not all that was new for them. I know you won't believe this—remember they were your age—after I had cleaned up from dinner, I brought out a book to read to them."

"*Just So Stories*!" Matt exclaimed. This was our favorite book.

"Well no, believe it or not, Kipling did not get around to writing *Just So Stories* until after you two were born. Anyway, I brought out the book—some children's book or other. And now that I think about it, it must have been a book supplied by your mother's parents, from their

10

bookstore. They gave me a whole load of children's books to take with me. I wonder if they had any idea how useful they would be."

"Go on with the story, Father." I had nearly forgotten we were leaving tomorrow.

"Well, what was so amazing is that those children had never had a story read to them before! They had never seen a book!"

"Not even in school?" Matt asked.

"They had no school—just their parents to teach them. I read them a chapter or two. I didn't think they would ever settle down. Lynne and the mother were sitting in the only two chairs, watching how I would handle things. The kids were at my elbows looking at the pictures, asking questions, wanting to know how to read the words. Finally I made a deal with them. If they would stay in their blankets, I'd find another surprise for them. And then I'd read until they fell asleep— no matter how long. And I would give them the book to keep. They were in the blankets in a second and I gave them each a piece of hard candy—I do believe they'd never had that either. I was sure to give one to the mother too, who may have enjoyed it as much as the kids. I must have read an hour more before they winked off. They looked so cozy curled in their blankets close to the woodstove. Then it was strange: the mother started to cry a little, nestled her face into Lynne's lap.

"'What is it?' asked Lynne.

"'The story for the children,' she said. 'It was so wonderful. They'll want me to read it. I don't read.'

"Lynne was quick to answer. 'Sweetheart, don't worry. They love the pictures. All you need to do is make up a story for them as you go along. Use the pictures. Or ask them to make up a story.'

"But I don't think that was what was really bothering her, because she kept on crying.

"'We've got so little. You saw our food. And my husband is away— trapping all the time. He's been gone four weeks now. Every day I worry that he is hurt, alone in the snow. It's just me and the kids.'

"Well, wouldn't you know it, but at that exact instant, in he comes, snow clinging to his clothing, his dogs yelping outside. You wouldn't believe how those two hugged each other—and the kids were awake in an instant, the four of them dancing around that tiny cabin." Father sighed. "In spite of all the troubles they had, I don't believe I've ever seen happier people."

We were all quiet for a moment.

"Father," I finally ventured, "why are we going to Cambridge tomorrow?"

"It's complicated," he said. "But I'm sure it will be fun to spend more time with Grandma Becky and Grandpa Michael. They'll be so happy to see you. You must tell them the story I just told you about how happy their books made those Labrador children."

"But their father made them happier," I whispered.

"When will you come to Cambridge?" asked Matt.

"Don't worry. We'll figure it out," said my father as he kissed each of us, straightened our covers, and left the room.

The next morning he had left for work by the time we rose to finish packing for the journey.

Chapter 3
1908

After we boarded the train and settled into our seats, Mother handed us some books and began to read her novel, obviously intending to avoid conversation with other passengers and perhaps with us.

At breakfast I had hazarded asking about their fight. "Why was Father yelling about the attic trunk?"

"Ah . . . that was a parent conversation. Finish your biscuit. We've got a long day ahead of us."

I wondered if it was the same locked trunk Matt and I discovered a few months before. We played in the attic on rainy days, exploring all manner of baskets, suitcases, and trunks. Much of Mother's art was stored there, paintings and drawings from her year in Paris. The best work was hung in prominent places in our home and in each of our grandparents' homes. My favorite painting, by her friend André, hung in a corner of Grandmother Compston's sunroom, her salon. It shows my Mother standing in the grass beside the Seine in dappled sunlight, dressed in a prim white dress closed at the neck, an opened parasol resting on her shoulder. A strand of her chestnut hair has come loose, and she replaces it with her free hand. Her youthful green eyes stare out at the viewer, and her smile asks for company on her walk down the riverside path.

But there was a lot of other art in the attic: rolled up canvases and sketchbooks stored in old steamer trunks. Matt and I delighted in looking through them, the old styles of Paris in the 1890s, some sketched in Mother's hand, some drawn by others. At times, we carried the sketches down the dusty attic stairs and Mother paused in her chores to look through them. Some were by Pierre, or Marie, or George, quick studies of a café, the sunlight sparkling across the tables, or of the river, a man fishing from a punt in the shade of a willow.

When we tired of the drawings, we opened other trunks to find generations of discarded clothing. We pulled out hats, coats, dresses, and suits, and slipped them over our clothing. We paraded our costumes downstairs to show Mother and she laughed and told us how her great-aunt wore this hat or that dress at some long ago wedding.

Matt discovered the mystery trunk. It rested under an old wicker basket near the solitary window. We clamored downstairs to ask Mother if she had a key. She turned away, continuing to check pantry supplies before carefully saying no—that trunk held private things and we had best leave it alone. We returned to the attic, lifted and shook the trunk, each holding a side clasp. Papers rustling, or books. Perhaps some clothing. As we replaced the trunk under the wicker basket a memory flashed into my mind, a scene from my earliest childhood, an image of her sitting by the window, the dim, filtered light encompassing her trim frame, highlighting her sharp chin. She studies the item she has pulled from the trunk and then she places it gently on her lap before turning to the window staring for a long time down toward the river. Maybe she had brought me with her. Maybe I was napping and woke to capture this memory. Or maybe I've imagined the whole thing.

That day on the train, Mother was so somber that I feared interrupting her. She sat for long periods staring at her book but not turning a page. At times she'd look toward the window until she saw me watching or until I asked something about the land or the river, and then she'd say, "Hush, now," and return to her book.

I guess we were all too upset to enjoy the train as we usually did. Other years Matt and I loved to gaze from the window, initially surprised by the speed at which outside objects passed. We went south through the fertile bottomlands of the Connecticut River where nearly every acre was cultivated. The hayfields sported yellow buttercups and red hawkweed awash in the intense greenery of June. Families were busy in vegetable gardens hoeing and weeding; and when we returned in late summer we'd see the harvest in full swing. We passed through small towns, like ours but with a unique blend of homes, shops, and churches.

The river looked strong and prosperous and, on other trips, Mother explained its importance in providing energy, transportation, water, and rich soil. It also provided, for Matt and me, the most marvelous vistas. Sometimes we saw a punt stopped to fish in a cove or, on sultry July afternoons, swimmers cooling in the shallow waters or sitting on the shaded banks. From the angle of the train we gazed downriver, past the long barns and homes, past the sheep, cattle, horses, and people, to the comforting mountains in the distance.

On other trips, I played at inventing stories about the people, the animals, and the river. Sometimes I dreamt quietly by the window; sometimes I shared the stories with Matt and he added details while Mother gazed out the window, a smile playing on her lips at our chatter.

At some point in every trip we'd move up and down the aisle, jolted first to one side, then to the other, laughing at our inability to maintain balance, trying not to hold on to the seats. If we jostled against the legs of a stern-looking man, Mother apologized for us, but most of the passengers seemed not to care, and some engaged us in conversation. Matt, eyes cast downward and face red, responded with one-word replies, turning to me for help while drawing his hand over his lightly freckled cheeks. But I was always willing to talk; when I was six I could relate a multitude of family yarns, embellishing when I thought it necessary, until Mother intervened. "No secrets in this family!" she'd say as she led us back to our seats.

Sometimes, she induced us to sit still by producing a new book from her bag. "Grandma Becky and Grandpa Michael sent this to help pass the time. We had best read it so you can tell them how much you liked it."

But it wasn't difficult to enjoy the stories they sent. As bookstore owners, they had access to all the recent children's books, and always made good choices. We read *Peter Rabbit* on one of these journeys, long before our friends. By the time I was six or seven we had read Kipling's *Just So Stories*. It became our favorite book, and we read it dozens of times, quoting whole passages to each other, and using *"Just*

So" nonsensical logic to gain a foothold in family debate. And on our eastern visits, the five of us, Matt, Mother, Grandpa Michael, Grandma Becky, and I, used Kipling's phrase, "my Best Beloved," to address one another.

When we were young, Mother restricted us to our coach, but later we were allowed to go the length of the train. Mother charged me with the responsibility of watching Matt, but I think that would have happened anyway. His shy nature kept him close and inspired some protective instinct in me. We wandered from car to car falling against each other as the train wobbled back and forth. My favorite spot was at the very back where we stood on the outside platform and watched the tracks magically recede. There, we had a wide view of the passing fields and towns, and we felt superior to the other passengers who were content to stay in their seats looking vaguely forward from a sooty window.

We also explored to the front of the train, passing beyond the dining car and kitchen. The year before our current somber trip, when Matt was seven, a conductor, relaxing with coffee in a small chamber just in front of the kitchen, stopped us. I thought he was going to send us back to our seats but he only wanted to talk. Where did we live? Where were we going? His children were about our age.

And, after a thoughtful pause, "Just a moment, now. Come with me." We followed him forward, past the notices that restricted passengers, outside to the rear of the locomotive and on into the engineer's compartment. The two engineers turned to look at us.

"What have you brought us here, Tom?" They had to yell over the noise of the engine and the clatter of the tracks.

"I thought they would enjoy the view from the front."

"Well, come here then."

They showed us controls, knobs, and levers, and we stood on a wobbly old wooden crate to see from the forward window. As we approached a small town, one engineer asked Matt to help with the braking. And we both pulled the cord to activate the steam whistle, which blasted with a shrillness that sent pain reverberating from one eardrum to the other.

Then, from a small closet confused with all manner of clutter, the conductor pulled an old trainman's cap, a bit tattered and dirty. "This will do you proud, lad!" The cap covered every strand of Matt's sandy red hair and descended over his ears and forehead. The conductor tilted the visor up so that he was able to see. Matt's huge grin and his sparkling green eyes reflected pure happiness. Mother tightened the headband and he wore that cap for years.

This year there were no such triumphs. I was tired of sitting with my book. I wanted to explore the train. Or I wanted to be home. I knew Mother was sad and I knew it had to do with the argument with Father. But the rest seemed too complicated.

Matt had been busy with the same silly book for an hour. I told him it would be fun to go to the back of the train but he had no interest. Mother nodded permission and I walked several cars back, coming out onto the rear platform just as we slowed for a station. I imagined inching down the rusty steps and then, before the train had fully stopped, jumping to the platform as I'd seen the conductors do. The thought of sneaking through the crowd hoping Mother and Matt would not see me, of wandering through an unknown town, was thrilling. My heart beat faster as I wondered how long it would take Mother to begin a search, and what they would do when I was not found. I imagined the train people putting me on the next train to Boston and my proud arrival, Mother, Grandma Becky, and Grandpa Michael all relieved.

I began to worry that Becky and Michael would not meet the train as they did every year. Had there been time to tell them of our early arrival? Mother was always anxious in the crowded Boston station but she would calm once we found them. I supposed it wouldn't be like last year when Matt sported his trainman's cap. Then, he gripped the visor lest it slip down over his eyes while, with his other hand, he clutched Mother's dress. She had engaged a porter to lug the trunks down from the train and we exited the coach, straining to see Grandma Becky and Grandpa Michael amid the chaotic bustle and clamor. Passengers rushed by, bumping and jostling from every direction.

"Keep close to me." Mother searched for her parents. It felt as if we had left the safety of our quiet swimming cove on the Connecticut River to flounder in the pandemonium of the ocean surf. But we found Michael and Becky, waiting near the front exit, and now, years later, I understand Mother's relief. Her parents were like fortresses of calm, standing against the bedlam. Becky, only five-foot-three and elegantly stout, stood with a firm matronly air, her gray hair pulled back in a bun, her face crinkled up into a huge smile at the sight of her grandchildren. I tried to tell her about the journey and the passengers and the conductor, but it was hard for her to hear in the noisy station. But she did hear Matt when he said, "Thank you for the book, Grandma." Yes, she was pleased that we enjoyed the stories.

Michael sported muttonchops that had begun to turn white at the edges and a mustache that must have tickled his bulbous nose. His soft blue eyes widened in admiration of Matt's trainman's cap. "And where did you find this, young man?" Matt shyly looked at his feet while I told the whole story of the cap and Michael bent to my level so as not to miss a word.

This year would be different. I stood at the back of the train, watching the rails recede. I kicked at the railing and went back to my seat. I stared out the window, offering no response to the children who ran alongside the tracks shouting and waving.

Michael was at the station but Becky had to remain at the bookstore. As they embraced, Mother's face reddened, and when I thought she might cry, I started to sob and Matt joined in. Michael frowned and gathered us into his arms.

We felt better by the time everything was stowed in the carriage he had hired. The enclosure felt secure, and we brightened watching the bedlam of the Boston streets. It seemed impossible that the driver could find his way amid the confusion of the intersections. Other drivers bawled at pedestrians and at each other. Jumbles of unloading delivery carriages blocked streets. Shoppers squeezed by obstructions of reeking garbage piled next to produce markets. Dust rose from the carriage wheels, covering people, windows, and produce. The scene was full of life, danger, and splendor.

Michael and Becky lived above their bookstore, three blocks from the Harvard campus. The white frame building stood just off the sidewalk without space for yard or garden, but Becky had adorned each of the three levels with window boxes that, by the time of our arrival, had grown into an unkempt jumble of color. Each summer, Mother said they looked magnificent positioned below sets of green shutters, and Becky always laughed and said she didn't have time to tend the tangle of plants. This year there was none of that banter, just a tearful embrace with Becky and the three of us.

At other times, Matt and I found the intimate bookstore delightful. Irregular rambling aisles ended in hidden corners. Michael emptied out lower shelves and stacked books and boxes to create nooks, just the right size for a young child. By squeezing into these snug spaces, Matt and I felt hidden yet still able to hear the chitchat of Mother and Becky. Then we'd played hide-and-seek for hours, hiding in empty crates, or under a desk. When I detected Matt's impatience at never finding me, or at always being found, I allowed him an unexpected coup, announcing loudly to Mother and Becky, and to any curious customer, that Matt was simply not to be found. We heard suppressed giggles coming from his usual corner, but I still could not find him. Finally he emerged, running to Mother and hugging her, eager to play a few more rounds.

That day we were not up to hide-and-seek, but by the time we had finished dinner I did feel a little better. After all, this place was like a second home to me. As the days went by we fell into a routine, almost like our ordinary summer visits, which always lasted a month or more. Father never came to Cambridge for more than a few days, so after a while I did not much notice his absence. The adults must have tried to mask their worries, but I did overhear anxious conversations.

Sometimes in the evenings I found Mother sitting by herself staring into the kitchen window and then I'd feel sad.

In the mornings, I often went with Mother and Becky to buy groceries and browse in the fabric shops. While we were gone, Michael watched Matt and managed the shop. Sometimes Michael read to him or showed him card tricks until customers required attention. But Matt's preferred activity was to hibernate in his cavern, an empty lower shelf, around a corner at the end of an aisle. He took a pillow and a stack of his currently favored books. He could stay there for an hour, especially if he enticed Byron, the aging motley cat, to curl up beside him.

Mother had not brought her painting supplies with her, but two weeks after our arrival she pulled Becky and me into an art store and bought an easel, paints, and brushes. In the afternoons when heat began to build, she would carry her painting supplies to the flowery park nearby while Becky minded the shop and Michael took us to the Charles River, only a few blocks away.

On the riverbanks there was a sense of freedom even though it was all so civilized compared to our Connecticut River. Here, there were bridges and well-trodden paths along the banks, and we always encountered people out in numbers not found along the Connecticut. They walked in the shade of elms, stopping to admire the wild iris. They sat on riverside benches, reading and talking. Even the canoes were sedate, gliding aimlessly upstream and down. And the canoeists were sometimes dressed well enough to be at a wedding.

But, as we passed under bridges, Michael kept us close, for often people were living in the damp and filth, unshaven men, sitting with meager sacks of possessions, gazing out at the river as if lost, or sometimes accosting us with pleas for food or money. Then Michael walked more quickly past and avoided their eyes.

I remember when we first saw the family. There was a young woman and a man with only one arm and a boy of seven or eight. The man knelt by the river, rinsing some ragged clothing, while the boy stood next to him, wading in the shallow water, gingerly testing the bottom with his toes. A rudimentary fishing pole was staked nearby, the line limply pulled by the current. The woman sat on the bank a few feet above them, rubbing her hands together, an anxious look in her eyes. As Michael slowed to return her gaze, Matt and I stopped, fascinated by the boy in the water who was near Matt's age, and by the father with the missing arm. We stared at his scarred and swollen stump, trying to imagine what might have happened. But when he turned to smile at us, we quickly pretended to be captivated by the mud at our feet.

"Please, sir," the woman pleaded.

"Of course." And Michael dug into his pocket to put a few coins in her palm.

The man turned from us to Michael, "Thank you, sir. Your children are lovely."

"But they are my grandchildren." Michael was flustered.

"All the lovelier, then," he smiled. "Thank you again, sir."

Michael motioned us and we walked on, around the next river bend. Finally Matt spoke, "Why was that man's arm cut off?"

"I don't know, maybe the war, maybe an accident." Michael didn't seem to want to talk.

"Was he a Rough Rider, like Father?"

"Well, maybe he was."

"Why did you give them money?"

"I think they were hungry."

"They didn't catch fish today!"

"No fish today."

This was the first time I realized that some people did not have enough to eat. Occasionally, in Birkett Ferry, a vagrant—it was said they arrived in railroad boxcars—came to the door and Grandmother or Mother gave him some bread or food scraps. But I hadn't thought much about the meaning of their begging. To think of this boy, hungry each day, was troubling to my ten-year-old mind, and I'm sure it bothered Michael, too. The walk home was uncharacteristically quiet. That evening after dinner, Matt and I were in the living room, dangling yarn in front of Byron's nose. In spite of our laughter, we heard part of the kitchen conversation as the three adults lingered at the table.

"A little boy, Matt's age . . . I'm sure they've not a cent to their name."

"Yes, of course, but really, Michael, they can't come back here."

"And his arm somehow torn off." At this Matt and I tried to listen more carefully, even as the voices lowered.

The only other voice we heard was Mother's, "And Father, we don't know what they may have. Don't let the children play with him."

On our afternoon walk the next day, Michael carried a sack. When we reached the bridge, the family was still camped underneath.

The boy watched some ducks gliding upstream. The father and mother sat side by side on the bank a few feet away. As the boy took a step into the water his mother called to him, "Hezekiah, please stay out of the river." He stepped back without protest. The father recognized our approach and gave Grandpa a smile.

"A good day to you and your grandkids, sir!"

"Thank you. I've brought a bit of something for you and your lad."

As Michael handed them the bag, the eyes of the mother grew large. "Bless you, sir, you have no idea what a help . . ."

"Now, now, we just thought," Michael paused, at a loss for words. His face, already warm from the windless summer day, reddened further.

"Your kindness will be repaid in one way or another, sir," the man said.

As I watched the woman open the sack and smile to the man, I felt a twang of jealousy. This family was together.

"Well, we must get along, now. Good luck to you. Come on now, Gwen and Matt, time to go."

After we had gone a ways upriver, Matt bent to pick up a stone. He studied it for a moment and then threw it out over the river where it landed with a single plop. As he reached for another stone, he asked, "Grandpa Michael, what was in the bag?"

"Some food."

"What kind of food?"

"Some cheese and bread, and a few of those oatmeal cookies your mother made yesterday."

"They liked us, Grandpa."

"Yes, my Best Beloved, they did."

"And they are really nice!"

"Yes."

"Why shouldn't we play with the boy, Grandpa?" I asked.

A very long pause ensued. Matt and I could see that some answer was coming so we remained quiet, watching a faint haze rise over the river, the hot August air drawing moisture up, right in front of our eyes. Finally he quietly said, "Gwen, I cannot really say why not."

I'm sure there were more kitchen discussions we did not overhear. But the next day and the next, we brought them a bag of food, engaged briefly in conversation, and then walked on.

One day Michael rented a canoe. The cooler weather had chased the heavy humid air, leaving such crispness and clarity that walking was impossible; Matt and I raced along the riverbank toward the boathouse. Later, as we floated under the bridge that served as shelter to our friends, Hezekiah waved tentatively. Matt and I waved merrily back. Hezekiah was always just by the river or wading about, but really, where else was there for him to go? His parents looked up from sorting through their belongings.

"Grandpa, I think Hezekiah would like to canoe with us," I ventured. Michael merely waved blandly to the family as we drifted by. We silently floated another hundred yards downriver, Hezekiah's eyes locked on ours until we disappeared around the bend. Matt was looking down, perhaps about to cry, when abruptly, Michael swung the boat about.

"Just why not?" he muttered to himself.

As we approached the family, he called across the water, "Would

Hezekiah like to come out with us?" I don't think there was any doubt as to the answer.

His mother, smiling, placed him in the vacant area between my bow seat and Matt, who was sitting on the floor of the canoe. As his father steadied the canoe with his one arm, Hezekiah turned around to ride backwards, facing Matt and Grandpa. I don't recall that Hezekiah said much on our voyage. I just have this image of turning in my seat to see the two boys grinning at each other. Grandpa, trying to fill in the silence that was awkward to no one else, murmured about being steady in the canoe. He pointed out some of the sights along the bank but I suspect these landmarks were well known to the boy who had spent so much time by the river.

Only a week later they were gone. We had passed the day before, leaving a food sack but pausing only briefly, the boys spending but a few moments together. They had not spoken of leaving. Michael was stunned, looking about for a hint of their fate or a remnant of their stay. We lingered at that spot longer than ever before, sitting on the bank, watching the river, and eating Mother's cookies.

Just before we left, Michael turned to us, "Gwen and Matt, you do know that I too was once just eight years old. You know that, don't you?"

Matt and I spoke of Hezekiah for years. He became our imaginary playmate, the boy with the funny name. Often we saved him from catastrophe, pulling him half drowned from the raging flood, or leading him back to safety after he became lost in the blizzard. Less often he rescued us from the designs of some wicked witch or troll.

Chapter 4
1908

We had letters from Father, at least Matt and I did, so I assume Mother must have too. When Grandma Becky insisted, we wrote him. Short notes that seemed to take me an hour: "It was fun to watch the rowers on the river." "A friend of Grandpa Michael's has a new automobile! We went for a ride!" That sort of thing. As I recall, Father's letters were not much different.

Then, in mid-August, Mother told us he would arrive the next day. She made us bathe that night and she took extra time ironing our clothing. I think we were ready two hours early, but she wouldn't let us play outside. "Don't you want to look nice for your father?" she asked. She wore a pretty blue skirt, a frilly white blouse, and a large hat with feathers that she bought the week before.

"Now," she said. "Listen to me. Your father and I are leaving for three days—we're going to Hastings Beach."

"Can we come?" Matt interrupted.

"No. You two need to stay and help Grandma and Grandpa with the bookstore."

Matt began to cry.

"Oh, Matt, it'll be fun. You'll see." I said. "I'll be here with you, and we can play hide-and-seek. And Grandpa will take us to the river." But I was worried. Mother had never left us before. She seemed happy, sort of. Not entirely happy—more like happy and nervous at the same time. She kept pacing the kitchen and looking toward the window.

Matt and I ran to Father as he entered. He hugged us and I snuggled in, surprised at how I enjoyed the cigar scent from his jacket. He straightened and faced Mother.

"I'm sorry, Marge."

"I am, too."

That was all they said but when they embraced, Mother did not seem to want to let go.

They left after lunch, Matt and I waving nervously from the door. Two days later they sent word that we should join them. Becky and Michael closed the store, the first time they had done so in their thirty years of ownership. Michael worried, "No telling how much business we'll lose."

But Becky reminded him that with the students and professors away, they didn't do much business in August anyway. And the next day he raised his eyebrows in a funny way when Mother mentioned that most of the Paris shops closed for all of August, not just for one week. Our beach trip became an annual ritual. Early each August Michael jubilantly hung the closed sign in the shop window and locked the door. We always went to Hastings Beach, renting the same cottage.

Years later, I learned that Grandfather Compston, thinking to rescue his son's marriage, had procured the use of the beach house through the goodwill of a railroad client, a fact that explained the discomfort that seemed to initially afflict Michael and Becky. "But it is so grand, Will. Just look at the view . . . and each of the children with their own room . . . I'm afraid to cook in the kitchen for fear of making a mess." These comments were repeated each year, but my Sherwood grandparents calmed after unpacking, and after the first beach walk they were mellow for the remainder of the visit. I believe that Father was equally uncomfortable in their Cambridge home. He never stayed there more than a night or two before we traveled to the beach, and most years he came directly to Hastings Beach.

The cottage sat on a bluff, looking out over the dunes to the ocean. Matt and I burned easily so, in the heat of the day, Mother kept us on the wide porch where we played and read, pampered by the ocean aroma and cooling breezes. But in the early morning before breakfast, we raced to the water with Michael and Father. Father had more energy at the ocean; even I noticed that. When I was older I reasoned it was not just because he was away from his office, it was also because he was away from his father. He rose at dawn for an hour's walk alone, for no one else was awake that early. When he returned, the adults were up, but often he needed to rouse Matt and me for a glass of juice before our swim. We raced across the damp sand to the water's edge where Father dashed ahead, not slowing until he plunged into the deeper water. Michael followed but Matt and I stopped to test the water with our toes. Father returned to the shallows and then cupped his hand across the surface to send a cascade of water over us.

"Come on in. It's quite warm," he said each morning. As we stood in the chilled morning air, the splash of ocean water did feel warm against our skin, so we entered and returned Father's splashes. Sometimes there was a dense morning fog and, as we lay back in the water, we saw nothing, save a small bit of beach and the swells around us. On those mornings, we walked slowly back, wondering when our house would appear through the mist. The murmuring voices and quiet laughter of Becky and Mother, and the smell of baking muffins, bacon, and coffee, carried to us across the sand before we could see the house.

In late afternoon, our favorite time, we walked along the beach watching the fishermen and playing in the sand and the shallow water. Since our beach was nearly south facing, we could walk east along the water's edge, starting an hour or so before sunset. The slanting light came from behind, skipping off ocean and beach, gradually stretching our shadows as if to point ahead to the red-orange glow painted across the eastern horizon in reflection from the west. When the sun had fallen sufficiently to dull the glare, we turned around to walk west, the full magnificence before us and lasting, it seemed, for miles as we walked in the cooling saltwater air, gulls squawking anciently overhead. It felt as though we were the only people on earth.

I often think back to that first beach vacation, Matt and I discovering the wonders of the ocean, my parents reunited and seeming content. I wish that time had frozen, keeping us there forever. But, soon enough, it was over.

Chapter 5
1908

That year, I returned from Cambridge still enchanted by the beach, unprepared for the loss of my wistful summer days. School would start in a week and I wanted to make the most of my freedom. Those early September days of deep blue sky and clear air: I knew they would soon be gone, so I lay on the grass pondering the heavens, the autumn sun shifting leaf shadows across my face. Matt would have missed that magic had I not forced him away from the couch where he was content for hours, books stacked around him. But I insisted and he followed without much protest. We lay on the grass, at times in quiet thought and at times telling stories imagined from the cloud figures above. And when our parents resumed their fights, there was good reason to escape the house and the yard.

I remember racing Matt through fields and forests, following my favorite trails. Many farms were abandoned during the 1800s when families migrated west. The best bottomlands were still farmed, but in the less desirable hillside pastures the woodlands encroached. It was here that I most loved to wander. We explored the fields of tall grass following vague trails made by deer. We climbed the huge solitary pasture trees, which the settlers had left for shade; some were more than a century old, dating to pre-Revolutionary days, with branches stretching outward to such extreme that they could have provided shade to one hundred sheep. Stone walls, over fifty years old and seeming ancient, advanced in straight lines over hillocks and through wetlands, only occasionally forced by the course of a road or stream to meander more agreeably. We lingered in the overgrown yards, sitting on the old stone foundations, which cooled our skin on the hottest days.

In these low hills less than a mile west of town was our favorite spot. I bragged that we had discovered it, but when I described it,

Father told us, "Everyone knows that spot. It certainly is wonderful . . . Have I never taken you there? I've been badly remiss."

And we found, soon enough, that others did come to that place—alone to gaze and ponder, in groups to picnic and swim, and in pairs to stroll among the old apple trees. Situated on a plateau near the stone foundations of a house and barn was a small natural lake, which the farmer had enlarged by damming the outflow. The earthen dam still stood, resulting in a lake well over an acre in size. The area around the lake had been cleared for grazing except for the southern shore near the deeper water at the dam, where a few maples and oaks provided shade. Brambles and juniper now advanced into the meadows but the eastern side remained open, the grassy pasture sloping down to the river valley of our town.

Matt and I munched tart apples while lounging on the soft grassy dam or we spun tales of adventure while straddling a wide branch, facing one another high up in a spreading maple. When we tired of the stories, we dared to lie back lengthwise, balancing precariously along the limb and pretending interest in the sky and the clouds, while our palms gripped the branch beneath and became slick with sweat. Finally one of us would bluster, "I wonder if Mr. Whitman has begun to plow the lower field," or, "Is the ferry running today?" Though we knew the ferry ran every day, and though we had not the slightest interest in Mr. Whitman's fields, any excuse was adequate reason to inch back up to the safer sitting position to study the sweeping vista below. From that ancient maple, we gazed east down through the high pastures to the white clapboard buildings nestled beside the sparkling river and the fertile fields. We recognized the buildings, including our home. We named the roads radiating outward, and we identified carriages belonging to neighbors.

Matt's friends found him awkwardly shy, but here on the knoll, with just the two of us, his green eyes sparkled and his freckles shimmered. When he laughed at my stories, he rocked back and forth, so that bits of grass and bark shook loose from his hair. The passage of a carriage on the road below drew from us astounding tales of travel, deception, thievery, abandonment, rage, and love. We were spies, voyeurs, insightful beyond our years. At times, sitting high up in our maple, we were real spies, witnesses to a solitary walker, or to a couple seeking to escape notice in the village.

I remember the appearance of one young couple on a warm afternoon—I can picture them now as clearly as if I were still watching from the tree. The pair, perhaps sixteen or seventeen years old, strolled toward the lake through the field of high grass, white daisies, and orange devil's paintbrush. They were not talking and they held hands stiffly, their bodies a foot apart. But then the boy suddenly swung their joined hands upward as if to crack the stillness. When the girl looked at him, surprised, he dropped her hand and cartwheeled ahead, then waited for her, a lopsided grin crinkling his face. They sat on the old stone foundations and gazed east as if fascinated by the view. She pointed to something and they smiled, but there were long pauses between their words. The breeze increased, lifting her long brown hair from her shoulders.

Matt and I were twenty feet up in the tree, well hidden by the green canopy. I had urged quiet at the couple's approach and Matt obeyed, as eager as I to spy. I suddenly remembered that friends had told me couples sometimes stripped and swam naked in the pond. I had not believed them, but now I worried that this might happen. It would be a weird thing to see, and I seriously doubted that Matt—or I—would be able to suppress laughter. I was relieved when they left. Matt and I were stiff from sitting in our awkward perches and thankful to climb down. We hung by our hands from a low branch and dropped the final six feet to roll on the ground in laughter.

"They were running off to Vermont and Canada," Matt started the story.

"But they had no food or pack, no extra clothes," I questioned his premise.

"They had to leave quickly after her father found out they were in love."

"And she was to have a baby." This made us giggle. "They'll stay in one of the abandoned houses until friends bring them food and clothing for the journey."

"One of the friends will tell and her father will find out and he'll come with a gun."

"They'll be warned and escape just in time. They'll go west instead of north to confuse him."

"They will go to Buffalo!" We always liked that name, Buffalo.

"They arrive in Buffalo hungry and tired and wet. The girl is crying and weak because of the baby."

"But a kind old woman takes them in. They live with her and help with her farm. The baby comes and they are all happy together." Matt liked joyful endings.

I considered myself more realistic. "But soon they have a second child. The old woman dies and her wicked son forces them to leave the farm. They return to Birkett Ferry to find that all is lost. The two fathers went north to search for them and were killed by Canadians. The mothers and little children and the farmhouses were all washed away in the spring flood."

Matt kicked at a stone. I thought he might cry and I smiled to myself.

"Skipping contest!" I yelled. We each found some flat, round stones and took turns. This was the only competition that Matt always won. He bent to the water and threw hard. His stone struck close to shore and then fairly skidded across the surface, leaving eight, nine, ten ripples, maybe more. I was more awkward. My stone caught an air current, sailed out too far, and fell into the water with only a couple of skips.

On our homeward walks, Matt stopped in the oak stands, stooping to collect acorns. He stuffed hundreds in the pack. I was content to study the trees and watch for birds while he worked, but I admired his diligence. Once home he delivered the nuts into an unused basement storage bin next to the potatoes and carrots. By late November it was full. After each winter storm, he brought nuts outside to scatter for the squirrels, which, he imagined, would otherwise starve.

"Such foolishness," Grandfather groused. "Such a waste of time."

"Don't discourage him. It shows compassion." Father took Matt's side.

"They wouldn't waste their time on acorns and walks in the woods if they had farm chores like normal children."

"Father, they are lucky to have the time. Think of all they learn from the outdoors, the same things I learned at that age. You will recall, it was those experiences that made me a Rough Rider."

"Well, yes, but Rough Riders didn't worry about squirrels."

Matt continued to store acorns until the fall of his fourteenth year when he stopped without giving an explanation and no one asked.

Four days before school started, Mother was in the yard picking flowers for a bouquet. "For your teacher," she said.

Then I remembered. She had told me Miss Robbins would be arriving on the afternoon train. "Wouldn't it be fun to meet her there?" she had asked a few days before. But now it turned out that Mother couldn't go with me. She had a meeting or something. So I was to greet Miss Robbins alone. Well, actually, I'd have the flowers—and Matt—with me. But I was still pretty nervous about the whole thing.

Matt and I were eyeing penny candy in Carson's store when we heard the train whistle.

"Race!" Matt yelled, zipping out the door, holding on to his trainman's cap. It was not a fair race since I was carrying the flowers, but I caught him as he charged onto the platform just as the engine lurched to a stop. We collapsed on the station steps, our breathing rapid, the bouquet rumpled.

The school principal and mayor, both middle-aged men, met Miss

Robbins's train. She descended the train steps, her wind-blown black hair offsetting a light olive face with high cheekbones, dark eyes and a poised smile. Both men were reduced to stuttered introductions after bumping one another while reaching to help with her luggage.

"I can manage nicely, thank you both." She held on to her suitcases, stepping between them and to the side of the platform, clearing the way for other passengers. The men turned inward, heads nearly colliding, their eagerness punctured by her poise.

Matt and I held our hands to our mouths, hiding our laughter.

"We have a carriage outside," the mayor said.

"Oh, but I have been told it is only two blocks to my rooms—at Mrs. Highton's boarding house, and it is simply delightful outside after being confined to the train. I shall walk, if you will direct me then. To Mrs. Highton's, please."

"Well yes, of course, it is two blocks to the right, at the corner of Ferry and Whitney. Let us carry your bags to the carriage and escort you."

"Oh, that would be a help. Here are my trunks now." She pointed to a porter pushing a cart. "And I suppose it would be nice to be free of these." She handed the principal her two small suitcases. "Please take care with the small brown case—it holds my viola."

I inched forward, Matt hiding behind me.

When Miss Robbins glanced at me and smiled, I held out the flowers. "These are for you," I stammered.

"Why, they are lovely! Thank you so very much." She paused. "I think you must know I am Cynthia Robbins. Do tell me your names."

"My name is Gwen—Gwen Compston. And I am in your class—fifth grade." I added this because she was to teach both the fifth and sixth grades. "This is my brother, Matt." I stepped aside so she could see him.

"That is a wonderful hat you have!" she exclaimed to Matt. He looked at his feet.

"Mother fixed it—sewed it so it would fit." Everything I said sounded dumb, but I so wanted to impress her.

Miss Robbins thought for a moment. "I suppose you must know the way to Mrs. Highton's boarding house. Will you guide me there?"

I walked beside her and Matt scooted ahead, ducking behind a hedge now and then, waiting for our approach, laughing at Miss Robbins's surprise. She asked where we lived and about our parents.

"My father plays the cello." I offered. I remembered her viola and I thought this fact would interest her.

"I shall have to speak with him about music, then," she said. "What did you two do this summer?"

I chattered away about the beach until Matt interrupted, "But we had to miss the Fourth of July party—and the fireworks."

"My goodness, a July Fourth party with fireworks! What a pity you missed it."

"Grandfather Compston has a big party, all our friends and relatives," I explained. "Will you come next year?"

"We'll have to see about that. It would be great fun, I'm sure." We arrived at the boarding house. "Gwen and Matt, why don't you come in with me and we can ask Mrs. Highton for a vase for these lovely flowers."

Mrs. Highton met us at the door and bustled about finding a vase, talking the whole time about dinner hours and such. As she was showing Miss Robbins the rear entrance facing the carriage house, her luggage arrived. The principal insisted on helping the porter carry the bags, but he seemed more to slow the process, stopping and smiling to Miss Robbins, blocking the doors and hallways as the porter tried to pass. Soon the commotion ended as Mrs. Highton left to see about dinner and the principal waved good-bye. Miss Robbins frowned at the trunks stacked in her living room.

"Such a task to unpack," she sighed. "I suppose you two should be leaving soon but, Gwen, please put the flowers on the side table. She pointed to the opposite side of the room where a chair and table sat next to the fireplace. It looked as though her living room had been remodeled from a study, one wall covered with bookshelves and a writing desk with matching chair nearby.

Matt bent to examine the fireplace as I placed the vase on the table. I wondered what could be so interesting about a fireplace.

"Come on, Matt." I said. "We should go."

Miss Robbins pulled a photo from the top of her suitcase. "Oh, I must show you this before you leave," she said. "My sister and brother." There was a woman, close to Miss Robbins's age, and a boy of high school age. "Everyone says she looks just like me."

I looked from the photo to her face. Maybe, I thought, but in a way, you look more like your brother.

My cousin Anna, a year ahead of me in sixth grade, tested Miss Robbins early. As Miss Robbins was explaining our weekly schedule, Anna spoke up, "But last year we had our spelling contests on Thursday."

"We'll be doing a few things differently this year, Anna, and it may take a little getting used to. Monday is a good day for spelling bees since you can study your words on the weekends. Thursday is needed for theater rehearsals. And don't forget to raise your hand to be recognized."

Later, Anna complained, "But we need to have recess right after lunch. Everyone does. And that's when I see my sister and the seventh graders."

"Well I'm sorry about your sister, but recess after lunch isn't a very good idea for digestion, and exercising before gives you healthy appetites. Anna, please stay with me for a moment. The rest of the class may go outside now." I felt badly for Anna and embarrassed. I expected Miss Robbins didn't know she was my cousin and I hoped Anna wouldn't tell her.

School rarely closed for weather. When children from the outlying farms did not attend after winter storms, they were derided as "too soft and lazy to walk through the snow!" Matt and I never missed, save for illness. Most roads were not shoveled and, instead of carriages, the horses pulled sleighs; but at times it was too deep for horses. Matt and I used snowshoes. It was easy to track hare, deer, and fox across the snow, and with the leaves gone from the trees, we would sometimes spot them, if we were quiet and patient. We walked atop the deep snow to the knoll to gaze across the frozen valley to the eastern hills. The frigid temperatures scrubbed the air to a splendid brilliant clarity, and we lingered at the view. We could see houses, barns, streambeds, and rock formations, obscured by trees in other seasons. We returned home filled with excitement, cheeks aglow from the sun and the effort.

Mother repeatedly warned us of the treachery of winter. She required that we be home well before dusk. Once, when we had ventured up beyond the knoll, Matt's binding snapped. Without snowshoes he sank in to his waist. We stripped spruce boughs to tie a new binding, but repeated breakage slowed our homeward trudge. We knew the trails and had no doubt of safely arriving home even as dusk progressed to moonless darkness. But Mother and Father and our grandparents were organizing half the town into a search party by the time we plodded in. Relief (and fatherly appreciation of our ingenious repair) was tempered by rebuke, mostly directed at me as the eldest. Mother threatened to keep us in for a week, and that night we listened to stories which had been repeated since we were old enough to leave the yard: stories of children and adults perishing in winter, lost in blizzards, confused, disoriented, hungry, and cold. Grandfather's cousin, age twenty-four, at the height of his vigor, set out one winter morning in search of a wayward horse. A storm blew in, obscuring his tracks and confusing his sense of direction. Two months later his frozen body was found in the hills west of the knoll with his snowshoes still on and his face pecked over by birds. His example was used for generations as a warning to wandering children. But we were certain we knew the trails too well to ever become lost.

The thick river ice creaked and moaned, but, while a sudden loud snap could startle us, we knew there was no risk of a dangerous gap. On clear black ice the cracks looked like a road map, fissures meandering randomly, finally meeting in a central locus to radiate outward again. Black ice was so beautifully clear that in proper sunlight one could see several feet to the river bottom where autumn leaves of red and gold were preserved. Matt and I would lie flat to witness the huge fish sullenly swimming below, appearing to be just inches away, their size and distance distorted by the lens of the ice. The cracks gave perspective allowing one to judge the ice thickness, but the judgment was accurate only at that spot, for we could stand safely in a quiet shoreline cove on eight inches of ice and look just a few feet distant to where the current ran strong under less than an inch of covering. And any amount of snow would cloud the black ice, making such judgment impossible.

The safest winter passage was at a calm stretch just above the ferry crossing. Only at that spot were Matt and I allowed to cross, and then only in the company of an adult. Mother was uncompromising about this rule and, for the most part, we obeyed. But it was tempting to use the flat frozen river for travel, so much easier than tramping up and down steep, slippery banks and tripping over fallen trees hidden in snowdrifts. It always seemed safe starting close to shore and venturing out slowly, cautiously testing the ice. And it was an adventure to visit the island in deep winter snow. We followed the trail on our western bank until we were out of sight around the bend, then we descended to the ice, keeping close to shore, giving wide berth where hillside streams merged into the river. We crossed in a straight line to the island, keeping a distance from one another and testing the ice with a pole.

One gray December day we were on the island, exploring the inner field, when we saw a man on horseback approaching from the south, staying close to the western side of the riverbank. We crouched down to hide behind the snow-covered bushes. When he was opposite the island, we recognized Mr. Moore, a farmer from two miles downriver. He stopped to study our tracks and then gazed out to the island. He hesitated briefly before starting across the ice, a route that would provide a shortcut to the eastern farms and roads. Matt and I bent lower, though we knew our tracks could lead him straight to us. We were terrified that Mr. Moore would find us and tell Mother.

He was halfway across, following our tracks, when the ice collapsed. We saw the horse's wild eyes search frantically for safety as it tumbled sideways, trapping Mr. Moore's leg. And we could hear the frenzied piercing whinny mix with Mr. Moore's startled cry as the horse tried to right itself, but instead slid further down into the icy water, submerging its hind legs and flank. Mr. Moore was able to squeeze out from underneath but he limped as he walked round trying to calm the desperate animal. The horse thrust its neck back and forth, plaintively neighing and looking to its owner for help. Mr. Moore bent to study its legs, and then we could see the right foreleg bent at an impossible angle. His shoulders stooped, Mr. Moore freed his saddle and gear. He bent down to look in the horse's face and spoke softly for a moment. He succeeded in calming the animal before taking out his rifle and shooting it in the head. He looked off to the distance as the shot echoed across the snowy river to the white hills and back again. Then, while kneeling beside the animal and stroking its neck, he bent his head as if in prayer before gathering the saddle and pack to hobble back west, the way he had come, away from the horse and away from us.

Matt would not stop sobbing. With feeble light penetrating the thick clouds, the horizon blended seamlessly into the snowy dim hills, further accenting the dark tree silhouettes that all pointed down to the river tragedy. I could not take my eyes from the horse, lying still and half submerged in the silent icy flow, a grotesque patch of deep red outlining its head. There was no other color in that sweep of river and land.

Matt's snowy mittens rubbed at his cheeks, absorbing the tears. I put my arm around his shoulder and tried to soothe him. It was obvious we would not go back the way we had come. There was the break in the ice and there was the horse. We could have made a wide circle around the bloody stain, but it seemed wiser to head to the eastern bank, walk upstream and re-cross at the usual town site. We had agreed to remain silent, but the moment Mother greeted us at the door, Matt burst into tears and the whole story came rushing out. Mother was furious that we had violated her strictest rule. "That horse could have been you," she kept repeating.

Father had other concerns about our behavior. By the time he returned home, Mr. Moore's story had spread through town though no one knew the part we had played.

"So those were your tracks Benjamin Moore saw!"

"Yes, Father."

"If those tracks had not been there, he wouldn't have attempted to cross; he said so himself!"

It hadn't occurred to me that we could be blamed for the horse's death but I knew better than to respond. Matt began to cry again. The thought of causing an animal's death was too much.

"Will, I'm sure they're not responsible for that." It was a mystery why Mother offered any defense when, an hour before, she was mercilessly scolding us.

"And did you give any assistance to Ben Moore? He was injured, you know, and cold and wet. He could have used some help to carry his gear. He left his saddle by the riverbank."

At the time, I had not thought to do anything but stay hidden and pray that Mr. Moore would not come to the island. But I'm sure we would have helped if he had been stuck under the horse or unable to walk. I hung my head, now angry that Matt had told the tale.

The most difficult part of the punishment was apologizing to Mr. Moore. Father took us to his home where he graciously accepted our words but refused to blame us for his decision to follow our tracks. "No, that was my own stupidity." His leg had recovered—"Only a muscle sprain"—but he said it would take a while to get over the loss of his horse. As the oldest, I did most of the talking; Matt, at my side, gave nodding support but spent most of the time looking at his shoes. Father was silent on the walk home; perhaps he was satisfied.

The story was known throughout town, and repeated to children, both to teach safety and deliver a lesson. Cousin Anna gloated at my shame, repeating the story within my hearing, "And she didn't even help him." As if there were anyone in town who did not know the whole tale.

A few days later, at the end of the school day, Miss Robbins motioned me to her desk. I stood there while she sorted through papers until everyone had left.

"Gwen, how are you doing?"

My face drooped as tears spilled down my cheeks, the first tears I had shed.

"Oh dear." She rose to shut the door, then gathered me close as I wept into her lap, sobbing for ten minutes or more, her soothing murmurs finally quieting me.

"Dear Gwen, everyone makes mistakes. You're a strong person. You will learn from it."

I started to sob, again.

"Here then." She lifted my head and used her handkerchief to wipe my tears.

She looked into my drained eyes, "I tell you what. I have an assignment for you. I want you to meet me at six thirty tonight, by the ferry crossing. Bring your skates."

"At night? But I don't think my parents will allow . . ."

"You tell them it is homework." She straightened my clothing and my hair and gave my cheeks a final wipe.

There was no one in the school yard, save Matt who waited by the front gate. He did not ask about my red, swollen eyes.

Just above the ferry crossing, a shallow cove was sheltered on three sides. The river pooled, making the ice predictably solid. Many of the townsfolk helped to clear snow from a large circular area, and sometimes the high school boys brought buckets of water to smooth the rough areas. Most winters, the snow confined the skaters to this cove, although there were certain windswept river stretches where the daring could glide for miles. And there were no skating boundaries in those winters when the river froze before the first snows; then the black ice was clear and smooth.

I told Matt he couldn't come because this was a school assignment, but Father insisted on accompanying me. "You can't walk alone at night." I think he also welcomed the opportunity to mend fences; his quiet chatter about the beauty of the night was his way of letting me know I was forgiven. And that night was beautiful. Hard-packed snow crunched underfoot as we walked across the green, passing our neighbors' homes where winter curtains were drawn against the chilly night, allowing only a vague light to escape through the frosted windows. As we continued down Ferry Street past the darkened shops, we faced the moon, nearly full, just now rising above the eastern hills. The snow-covered valley and river reflected the light to color everything white save for the shadowy tree silhouettes that haunted the riverbank. Mounds of snow surrounded the skating rink to give the appearance of a giant bowl and, once within, the high sides reduced my view of the outside world to a solitary barren tree, its branches eerily moving against the moonlit sky. Within this magical bowl the moon appeared all the larger.

We arrived at the same moment as Miss Robbins and I introduced them. Father could be shy, but Miss Robbins had no difficulty. She told him she enjoyed having me in class . . . I was an excellent student . . . Perhaps she would teach Matt in a few years time . . . It really was too bad about Mr. Moore's horse. At this we were silent, but she quickly resumed, "I understand you are an accomplished cello player, Mr. Compston."

He looked at me in surprise. "I could once have been considered accomplished, but only if judged by persistence rather than ability. I played for many years, starting when I was younger than Gwen is now. But I don't have much time anymore; I haven't played in several years."

"But it would come quickly back. Things learned in childhood last forever, you know. I have always played the viola."

There was only the moon and sky above, only the smooth white ice below, and only Father and I and Miss Robbins within. We skated through the wispy moonlight, at times together, then separating, each seeing the others as ghostly beings gliding across the winter ice. We were cozy in our snow-rimmed bowl but, if the river were not impassably drifted, it would have been daring to escape, to skate far out onto the river, straight into the moon, and then turn and sail back, our shadows racing in front of us.

After a time, Miss Robbins stopped and flattened a seat in the snowbank. Father skated a few more laps before pausing to talk with her. I saw her pat the nearby snow, gesturing for Father to sit but he remained standing, gently moving on his skates forward and back. I heard patches of conversation as I skated by, "And look at your snow seat, even with a backrest!" And later something about chamber music, but mostly I was out of earshot. There were pauses in the conversation, too, when I could sense them watching me.

Finally, Father called, "Gwen, we had best head home."

"But I'm not tired yet."

"I told Marge we'd be home by now."

And gaily, from Miss Robbins, "And you must leave time for your homework!"

"I thought this was my homework!" I tried to sound indignant and they laughed at my effort.

Miss Robbins turned to Father. "Mr. Compston, I am going to look into this chamber group."

"Well, I really don't know . . ."

Chapter 6
1909

A couple of weeks later, Father resumed his cello practice. At Harvard he had played in the orchestra, and when home, Grandmother would coerce him into solo performances for gatherings of friends in her home—she liked to think of it as her salon. But shortly after Matt was born, work and family forced the cello aside.

Miss Robbins recruited a fellow teacher, Mrs. Stiles, and her sister, Mrs. Newberry, as the two violinists. Every Wednesday evening the quartet practiced in my grandparents' sunroom where comfortable seats and tables were scattered among tumbling plants. Grandmother was certain there was enough space for thirty chairs, enough for the performance. Father, worried that he was outclassed by the others, retreated to his study nearly every evening after dinner, and we'd hear his deep resonant notes for an hour or more, Mother smiling as she read in the living room, sometimes nodding to the music.

Grandmother, a rather formal hostess, could not have been more pleased. Her son in a classical music group! Why, this was much healthier than working in his dark office or tramping alone through the damp woods. She pressed for an early concert but the group resisted, insisting on adequate practice time, and finally agreed to an April debut. Grandmother found it appealing that the audience would be seated, listening contentedly, while gazing out over her gardens (certainly the violets and crocuses would be out and perhaps the tulips). The guests would look past the lawn, adorned with the blossoming redbud and dogwood, to the rippling river, alive with heavy spring flow. And, afterward, coffee, tea, and cake. Perfect.

We all enjoyed the reprieve from Father's melancholy. He emerged from his solo practice joking and laughing, often ready for a bit of play with Matt and me. And I remember a few remarkable mornings when he entered the kitchen dressed in his dark suit, teased Mother about her dowdy beige bathrobe, hummed through breakfast, and whistled a gay tune as he headed for the door while glancing back to entice Matt and me to run after him. He tossed his bowler hat into the air as we skipped beside him, and then he snatched Matt's trainman's cap and hid it behind his back. We ran to keep pace with the long strides that replaced his usual trudge to work.

To Grandmother's dismay, the day before the concert brought dark gray clouds, cold gusty winds, and a foot of snow to cover the iris and tulip buds and to spoil, in her mind, the view of the freshly raked lawn. The snow melted quickly, forming gooey roads and paths. In spite of the careful removal of boots and galoshes, in spite of Grandmother's admonition of "mind the mud tracks" (this warning directed to the children in such a manner that every adult understood the message), there was a coating of dirt extending into the sunroom, a progression that she eyed in a disapproving way as she greeted the guests, controlled the children, and directed the high school students who ushered and later would help with refreshments.

We dressed, of course. I remember wearing a pale yellow dress (which Mother had copied from a Cambridge window the summer before). Matt wore a white shirt and bow tie. The younger women shivered into the house in their lightweight spring outfits; the older matrons, bowing to the weather, retained their comfortable winter dresses, shawls, and sweaters.

Grandmother, still frowning at the grit on her floor and the muddy snow in her yard, was the last to take her front-row seat, signaling the entrance of the musicians. I felt proud of Father as the group began to play. But I had trouble paying attention to the music, instead sinking into pleasant daydreams (while still careful to maintain my posture to avoid a grandmotherly stare). As I looked across the snow-covered yard to the swift flowing river, the music lifted my imagination to summer picnics and canoe trips: those long July evenings when Matt and I paddled to the island, skimming over the calm water, a single stroke propelling us a dozen yards. Once, we stopped to watch a heron standing motionless in the shallows, eyeing its prey. We waited for fifteen minutes until, finally, the heron's neck flashed forward to snare the frog, and then we saw the lump slide down its long throat.

My attention returned to the musicians and I watched Miss Robbins, her smile tight-lipped, her dark eyes focused on the music, and her black hair, tied loosely back, bobbing with the rhythm. After the final notes, the audience applauded as the four musicians exchanged smiles and bowed awkwardly.

"A great success!" proclaimed Grandmother after the guests had departed. "Thank you, Will. We shall do it again in the autumn, shall we not?"

"Well Mother it is a bit early to . . ."

"Yes, well, I envision a warm October day—perhaps out on the terrace."

"Truly, Will, it was quite good," Mother said. "You all looked poised and comfortable, almost professional."

"Well, I, for one, felt not the least bit calm, not until the last piece, anyway," declared Miss Robbins.

The quartet took a few weeks off but then they resumed practice, perhaps aiming for an October date.

Father did not travel to Cambridge that summer, nor to the beach. "Too much work," he said, though in other years he would bring work with him and spend a few hours a day in a makeshift office, a small room attached to my parents' bedroom. He was cheery on our return to Birkett Ferry, saying he was happy to see us and that he had missed us. The fights with Mother seemed a thing of the past. I was eager for my sixth grade year—again I was to be a student of Miss Robbins.

The quartet had practiced much of the summer using the space

Grandmother Compston called her salon. Each week Grandmother prepared a sweet and tea for the company and often I helped her in the kitchen, watching the musicians through a crack in the kitchen door.

"Well now, ladies," Father placed his bow on his music stand, "that's enough for tonight. I can't resist the smell of those cookies a moment longer. Mother has come through again!"

I brought in the tray of cookies and cream and sugar, beaming when Miss Robbins smiled at me.

"Your April performance was so well received. The whole town talks of it. You simply must put on another show this fall." Grandmother had a way of repeating her ideas until they became accepted.

"You mean the Great April Blizzard Concert of '09? Perhaps our music brought in the storm." Miss Robbins engaged us with her lively brown eyes as she reached up to replace an errant strand of hair. She always seemed at the center of the conversation.

"In that case we need to be careful with the scheduling of our next concert. Do we really want a blizzard in October?" Mrs. Stiles joined in.

"Well, it is just that I have this image completely painted into my mind," sighed Grandmother. "The four of you on the terrace in the October sun, trees gloriously colored, river flowing, music rising tenderly to the sky . . ."

"But either the musicians or the audience will be facing into the sun," Father glanced toward the terrace.

"Why, no," his mother frowned. "The audience is seated under the shade of the big maple, now red and orange. There is the calmest of southern breezes stirring the branches to drop their gentle crimson offerings to the people below."

"Why, Mrs. Compston, your 'gentle crimson offerings' and your 'tenderly rising music.' I must recruit you to help my students write poetry."

There was light laughter here, but Grandmother responded, "I would be honored, at any time."

I cringed, hoping this was not a serious offer.

I always wanted to walk with them as Father accompanied the three women to their homes, but usually I was told it was too late.

They continued to rehearse weekly, aiming to the mid-October performance date designated by Grandmother. There was no snow this time, and the setting for the afternoon performance was just as Grandmother imagined. The tranquil river, in lyrical autumn flow, reflected the red, orange, and gold of trees in full bloom, the terrace was adorned with the fading earth-toned flowers of chrysanthemum and hydrangea, the declining sun still delivered warmth. But the performance was deficient, even to my untrained ear. It was well rehearsed and solid but tightly controlled and lacking in energy. The bows, however, had been perfected.

And then things fell apart. My parents' fights resumed with arguments starting over any old thing—the starch in Father's shirts or the time Mother spent in her studio. Father often left the house in anger to walk by the river. Even when they didn't fight he'd often miss dinner, working in his office evening after evening.

In November there were some days that Miss Robbins appeared pale and ill; occasionally we had a substitute teacher. And when we returned to school in January, there was a new teacher standing at Miss Robbins's desk. We were told that Miss Robbins had to leave school due to sickness and we accepted this, though I wondered why we were not asked to write the usual get-well letters. I felt so attached to her that I asked Father and Mother if they had her Springfield address. Father said that the school must have it, but no one followed up and I never wrote a letter, feeling guiltier as months went by. But then, she never wrote to us either. I imagined Miss Robbins suffering with some horrible illness. Perhaps she was dead and the adults had decided not to tell us.

Chapter 7
1913–14

As I grew older I pretended to care less about my parents' fights. I'd be away from home as much as possible, and I'd take Matt with me, hiking to the knoll or canoeing the river. And when home I'd stay in my room, or sometimes I'd take my schoolbooks and study in the attic, sitting in the old rocker by the dusty window, my feet stretched out on the locked trunk.

When I was fifteen, Jonathan Spencer asked me to sit with him at the July concert on the town green. On that warm evening as I waited by our picket fence, I watched Matt and two cousins careen across the green, chasing each other through the lingering light. Dogs barked, romping after the boys and nearly toppling the lemonade stand that was doing business under a towering oak. Families positioned blankets and chairs and emptied hampers of sandwiches, fruit, and pies.

I carried a basket with rolls and cheese, and Jonathan brought an old green blanket that we spread on the grass. Matt came to sit beside me, but one "Matt, get lost" drove him back to Mother who was sitting by herself near the edge of the green. Later, Matt climbed the lemonade oak and when I glanced up he gave me a wide grin. Jonathan and I sat two feet apart but every few minutes he repositioned himself, first lying back on his elbows, then sitting upright, then shifting to his side, each time ending up a few inches closer. He gradually crumpled up the blanket on his side to make it appear as if there was nowhere else for him to sit save just by my side. I heard hushed chuckles from nearby blankets and wondered if he had any idea we were watched.

At intermission Jonathan went for lemonade. I straightened the blanket, wondering if those seated nearby would find this amusing, too. Jonathan eyed the new arrangement as he sat, the bread and lemonade between us. As the music blared across the green, the crowd settled.

Only a dog's bark or a baby's cry could be heard above the brassy clamoring. Jonathan stared ahead, his legs crossed, his back straight and his arms extended behind.

I looked around the green at our house, a cozy white clapboard house—the same house that Father and Grandfather had been raised in, the same house that generations of Compstons had lived in since 1707. And next door, with its formal gardens sloping down the lawn to the river, was the mansion Grandfather had built with his railroad money. I suddenly felt sad for my parents. Now I moved closer to Jonathan, caught his eye, and smiled, offering a cup of lemonade. After the concert he folded the blanket onto the picnic basket, carrying both in his left hand. He walked close on the way home, sometimes brushing against me, but he failed to take my hand. So, as we neared my home, I shrugged. Why not? I thought and reached over to take his.

That summer, worried that his interest wouldn't survive my absence, I wrote Jonathan several chatty letters from Cambridge. I was thrilled when he wrote back, especially since I knew my cousin Anna, a year older than me and the same age as Jonathan, was attracted to him as well. That fall on the first day of school, I made some excuse to walk partway with Father, thus approaching school from the opposite direction, Jonathan's route. I poked along until he found me, and soon we were walking together to and from school every day, much to Anna's irritation.

On the way to school one day the following spring I convinced Jonathan we should meet on the green that evening—I told him I walked our dog Swampy most nights around eight o'clock. I hadn't expected to feel so flushed as we entered the schoolyard, and I found it difficult to focus in class. My mind kept wandering forward to the evening. I had trouble reconciling my stress with what would surely be an insignificant event. I was simply meeting a boy on the green.

But that evening I couldn't concentrate on homework, either. I was back and forth to the kitchen a dozen times. Finally, fifteen minutes earlier than usual, I called Swampy to the door. While slipping on my jacket, I turned away from Mother, certain she was suspicious. Swampy clawed at the door, then charged back to stand on two hind feet, front paws on my thighs and beseeching eyes urging me to hurry.

"Patience is not an attribute of the canine species. But then, you're a bit restless yourself tonight," she said.

"Just school and homework, I guess."

Since I was early, I was surprised to see Jonathan's dark silhouette idling near the baseball field. Swampy, now released, raced frantically across the green, only slowing to a cautious trot as he neared Jonathan who bent to offer his hand. Swampy sniffed and, tail now wagging, jumped up to place his muddy paws on Jonathan's shirt and lick his face.

"Swampy, down!" I called, trying not to be too loud.

"It's okay. Hi Swampy. Good boy."

As we started to walk through the green, Jonathan took my hand in his. The touch made me gasp. My whole arm felt tingly and awkward. But I was able to turn my head to him and return the hand pressure. There was a breeze from the south bringing the scent of narcissus and the encouragement of spring. A few dark clouds skittered across the moonless sky shrouding first one constellation, then another. We walked across the green in one direction, then diagonally back, talking of school and teachers, of friends and family, trying to fill in the awkward pauses. My hand felt warm and pleasant in his, and it was almost natural to reestablish contact each time Swampy forced us apart by bounding up to insist that Jonathan throw a stick. We paused under one of the giant elms, the new spring growth shutting out the dim starlight.

"This is longer than I'm usually out. My parents will start to wonder where I am."

"Okay, we should be off then. It was fun to meet you." Then he quickly bent forward for a deliberately aimed and speedily concluded kiss to my lips. My first kiss was over before I could think about it.

He must have noticed my confusion. "I hope that was okay." He looked at his feet and, even in the dim light, I could see the flush of his cheeks.

"Sure," I tried not to stammer. Having nearly missed my first kiss, I decided to secure the experience before there was any chance of retreat. I caught his eye and leaned forward for a longer kiss, at least four or five seconds. It was a rather bland experience, I decided. My closed lips put pressure on his closed lips and there was an embarrassing smacking noise.

We continued to meet two or three evenings a week, and the balmy breezes of late May made us linger on the empty green. We gazed at the stars and paused in the shadows of the trees. Jonathan tossed sticks and Swampy galloped after them, skidding across the damp grass and into the freshly hoed flowerbeds, trying to grab the stick in his mouth without stopping.

Jonathan never had trouble getting out, and Mother didn't question why I was out for ten minutes some nights and thirty minutes on others. We became more practiced at kissing, but I still had doubts that we were doing it correctly. I enjoyed holding his hand as we walked around the green, and soon we were strolling with an arm around the other's waist, laughing as we attempted to match strides.

"Friday night is the full moon," he had seemed distracted that night. "I was thinking we could meet down by the river."

"Maybe, but I can't stay out too long."

"I meant we could sneak out late, after everyone is in bed."

"How late do you mean?"

"Maybe eleven thirty, or midnight."

It took some convincing, but I couldn't resist the drama of a midnight escape and the romance of a riverside meeting.

I pulled the covers up to hide my fully clothed body in case Mother came in to chat before bed. I usually enjoyed that time when we would talk about school or my friends, but this night was different. I decided to stay awake and read until it was time to meet Jonathan. Around ten thirty, I heard them prepare for bed. Mother murmured to Swampy as she clattered the dinner plates into the cabinet. Father tapped down the living room windows against a possible storm. I darkened my room and waited. She stopped at my door; I could hear her breathe as she hesitated for some seconds before proceeding down the hall. I relaxed, but still detecting movement in the house, I did not resume my reading.

Somehow, in spite of my anxious alertness, in spite of the discomfort of my clothing, I fell asleep. I woke at twelve thirty, one hour after our meeting time. Anguished shock replaced drowsiness. My heart beat wildly. What to do? I leapt from bed to find my shoes and bumped into my nightstand. Careful now, I must be quiet. Jonathan surely would not have waited this long. But I should go check anyway. I left my covers bunched up to foil a casual inspection. The floorboards creaked as I made my way through the living room. Swampy padded down the hall and whined softly as he sniffed my hand. I was careful with the door latch.

I should have been afraid to be out alone at night. But I was filled with such self-contempt that I abandoned caution and ran to the river. What would he think of me now? I fell asleep while waiting to meet him! Asleep! Our meeting spot was deserted. I hoped he might emerge from the shadows as I quietly summoned him, "Jonathan." Kicking at a rock, too irritated for tears, I could only imagine how we would have sat under the stars and the moon, our embrace enveloped by the river's soft murmurs. Shame and disgrace were still clouding my thinking. My heart had not slowed. Perhaps he had gone to my house, but then I would have seen him on my way here. Perhaps he had waited for me long enough that he was just now on his way home and, if I ran to his home, I could catch him. My steps roused a dog and his sharp growls made me shudder. A lightning flash in the west was so distant that I had nearly forgotten it by the time I heard the rumbling.

There was no sign of Jonathan as I approached his home. His second-story window and indeed the entire house showed dark against the moonlit sky. I slowed to a walk. The run had eased my stress but had not altered my humiliation. I spent ten minutes staring at his home willing him to emerge, knowing that my best course was to head home and face him in the morning with my pitiful explanation. Best to head home. But now my anger surpassed prudence. I tossed a pebble up to his window, fully expecting his father to appear at the door with a gun. After the third ping of pebble hitting glass, the noise seeming as loud as a gun blast, I saw a figure peering from the window.

"Psst, Jonathan! It's me."

Even through the darkness I sensed his caution and confusion. "What are you doing here?"

"Come down here." I imagined my stage whisper could be heard back on the town green.

"Okay."

I thought he could have been more enthusiastic after everything I had just been through for him. I retreated to the shadow of a giant elm. But it must have been five minutes before I saw movement at his side door, the latch catching audibly.

"What took you so long?"

"Me! Where were you? I must have waited hours!"

"It couldn't have been hours; I was only one hour late." At this, his mouth flew open in protest, but as our eyes locked, he slowly smiled and we were both reduced to giggles.

I took his hand to lead him away from his home. "I'm sorry Jonathan, I fell asleep. I don't know how it happened. I'd been so excited about meeting you. How could I have gone to sleep?"

"Don't worry, now we're together and we have a better story." I wondered whom he might tell the story to.

"What did the pebbles sound like?"

"I think I had gone to sleep, or almost. At first I thought it was nothing, just the wind or a bat. But then, when you kept it up . . ." He began to laugh. "I can't believe you did that."

I grinned at his response. "Where shall we go? It's too late for the river."

"But eventually we have to go back that way anyway. I won't let you walk home alone."

Hand in hand, we ambled down moonlit country lanes overhung with grand old sugar maples. An owl hooted nearby and now the occasional barking dog and the distant thunder were peaceful and reassuring. A soft southern breeze rustled the maple leaves and pushed us along. I brought my arm around his waist and he put his hand on my shoulder, but we found this an awkward position in which to walk, and, with a laugh, I returned my hand to his. I felt the warm air ease through our entwined fingers and I felt his warmth as I gripped his hand more tightly. I was surprised, when we paused near the green, to be able to hear gurgling river sounds carried so clearly on the night breeze. We were drawn down to the damp grassy bank. I thought of the river, rushing by this spot each second of each day, and it was strange to realize how the flow continued whether I was there to watch or not. How many couples, how many of my ancestors, how many of my descendants would sit at this very place gazing at the river? I looked at Jonathan. How romantic it would be to glide over the water with him in our canoe. We would hide under the trees that leaned out over the river, nestling together in the night shadows that smoothed the water surface.

Jonathan put his arm around my shoulder and drew me closer. We sat in silence watching the river and it seemed natural for me to turn to kiss him. Our kissing, previously so perplexed, became more relaxed and even enjoyable. I lay back and he followed to lie by my side. It was lovely to feel the whole length of his body against mine, and I tried to squeeze closer, draping one leg over his. Between kisses, I studied his face, and I could see the moon reflected in his gray-green eyes. I smoothed his tangled hair and then brought my hand to his cheek to touch each of his freckles. His hand rested on my hip but now he brought it up over my abdomen and brushed lightly against my breast. I hesitated a moment before taking his hand to position it back on my hip. Then, with a quick kiss, I gently spoke. "Not yet, Jonathan."

"I'm sorry."

"Don't worry; it's okay, just not now."

We lay there until three thirty. Jonathan escorted me as far as the middle of the green, where we paused for a final kiss under a massive old oak. The tree's shadow had lengthened far out into the green, driven by the setting moon now huge and orange on the western ridge. There was no other light, not from any home or street. Words seemed irreverent.

As we parted with a final hug, I managed only, "Bye."

"Bye, be careful when you go in."

It seemed unfair that my inner calm could now be replaced by anxiety. As I unlatched the door, my heart was beating with the same force and speed which I experienced on departure three hours earlier. Swampy did greet me at the door, tail eagerly a wag but without a whimper. As I tiptoed into the kitchen I saw them there in the darkness, my parents sitting at the empty table, not speaking, just staring at me.

I stammered a story of restlessness and a need to walk, but Father just shook his head, looked at his watch, and said, "Gwen, you know it isn't wise to walk alone at night."

Except for school, I was thereafter not allowed to leave the house without one of my parents. I worried that Jonathan would tire of this and take up with Anna or someone else.

I spoke with my parents as little as possible, refusing Mother's after-school cakes, and stomping up to the attic where I'd churn out my homework and then read for hours. So it was that one day that June I found the trunk unlocked. I'd been brooding by the window when I noticed the trunk lid slightly askew—a piece of cloth had wedged in the lock. I eased it open. I paused to listen for footsteps on the stairs; it would be just like her to choose that time to try to soothe my anger. But there was silence from below. I cleaned my hands on the folds of my dress before pulling out the top item that had wedged open the trunk, a silk blouse, pastel green. I held it up against my chest; it would fit me nicely. A small box contained a finely worked silver necklace. And underneath were sketchbooks, a few larger drawings, and a painted canvas, which had been rolled up. And at the bottom was a journal, dated 1896–7, the year she spent in France.

The sketchbooks seemed similar to what I had seen in the other trunks. But then I realized most of the drawings were by another hand, André. Sketches of Mother by the Seine. She sits on a riverside bench in the shade of a large, brooding tree, an unopened book on her lap, the wind rustling the feathers of her fine hat. She looks to the viewer, eyes twinkling and a half smile on her lips. In another sketch she bends to touch a tulip, her face in profile, her dark hair stuffed under a bonnet, strands loose at the edge. I sighed, astonished that my mother was once so beautiful.

And then I found the series of nudes, all of Mother, all by André. The second I realized it was her, a wave of nausea rushed from my stomach to my head. I grabbed the chair for support and then dropped to the floor, leaning against the trunk and shutting my eyes. What was she doing? I stayed like that for five minutes, my heart racing all the while. I tried to calm my breathing. I wanted to see the sketches; that much I knew. But my mind kept churning, trying to process my mother's nudity. What did it all mean—these drawings locked away in an attic trunk? I forced myself to look again, biting my lower lip as I studied each sketch. Many seemed to be in a sculpture garden, a background stonewall perhaps affording privacy. The sculptures are of human figures, nudes, their images blurred in the drawings. Mother sits on a bench among the statues, reading a book or gazing to the distance. Her pose is thoughtful rather than seductive. But in one, she stands on a pedestal as if to mock the statues. Her arm rises straight out, pointing to the distance where her gaze is focused. Her face is serious and heroic. Her hair is pinned up, her chest thrust out. Her breasts are firm, her nipples pointing in the same direction as her finger. I think I would have laughed had this not been my mother.

When I unrolled the one large canvas, I gasped at her beauty. She has just emerged from a bath; the water drips from her limbs and rolls down her abdomen. She bends slightly to reach for a towel which covers her lower half. The sunlight streams through translucent curtains, coating her front and leaving her shadow in the tub. Her youthful breasts tilt downward as she bends forward. But it is her face that captures the viewer. The smile is just forming, the lips starting to turn up with a mixture of surprise and pleasure at the unexpected intrusion. The eyes invite the viewer forward. There is no coyness here; the welcome is irresistible.

"Gwen, are you all right up there?" Mother's voice cut through my daydream.

"Yes, I'll be down in a while."

I quickly glanced through the journal: Mother's writing, interrupted by an occasional sketch. I wanted to read it cover to cover. I considered keeping the journal, but how would I ever return it to the locked chest? I wiped sweat from my brow. Finally, I replaced everything but left the blouse blocking the latch as I had found it. Apparently Mother did not revisit her trunk for several weeks that spring. But I went back every day.

Weeks later, I found the trunk relocked. Perhaps I had replaced everything well enough to avoid suspicion, or perhaps she didn't care to raise the subject, for she never questioned me. In those intervening weeks, I had examined each drawing in minute detail. And I had read her journal.

With the winking approval of her cousin, supposedly serving as her chaperone, Mother and André had quite a year. They met six months before she returned to Boston in one of the cafés frequented by the young Impressionists. There were several sketches of him in the journal, often in profile, showing his lean face. Dark, unruly hair intrudes on his brow, creased with concentration. His thin lips are partially obscured by a drooping mustache.

Mother recorded details of the romance, more details than I wanted to know. It was like reading a thriller. At times, my heart beat wildly as I skipped ahead a few pages, anxious to know what happened.

She wrote of her hesitation, of his persistence, of her cousin's encouragement. There were visits to the cafés and clubs—with a group of friends. She wondered whether it was proper when he asked her to stroll, just the two of them, along the Seine where they stopped to browse through the bookstalls and where he bought her a bouquet of daffodils. She claimed embarrassment when they sat in the square at Montmartre and he moved to the bench opposite and asked her to remain still, looking at him, while he sketched. She had folded his drawing into the journal—it was so detailed I felt I was there. I felt the warmth of the sun as it touched her dress and bonnet, I smelled the damp spring soil and the lilac, and I heard the chatter of the children as they skipped home from school. And, in her face, I saw the impish gaiety that played about her lips and eyes.

Another journal drawing shows Mother sitting on a bench, holding a small volume which she has put to her lap while she gazes out just to the side of the observer. Well-tended beds of tulip and iris grow nearby and, in the background, a boy of four or five bends over the stone embankment of a pond, launching his toy sailboat. Mother records this while André was sketching:

> The wind dropped and the boat stalled in the basin, twenty yards from shore. The boy grabbed a few stones and threw them, trying to create a wake to drive the boat to shore but the boat stuck to the center, bobbing about in the spring air. His mother knelt by his side, speaking quietly to him; she was concerned about the time and wanted to return home. André put down his sketch pad, removed his shoes and socks and rolled up his pants. The young mother smiled at him and

the boy jumped up and down and then skipped back and forth as André entered the shallow pond. He let go of the stone edge and cautiously stepped forward over the slime covered bottom. He nearly lost his balance several times, tottering back and forth, and unexpected depressions in the pond's bottom wet his trousers above the knee but the boat was safely retrieved. André bent to hand it back and the boy hugged him. As he was rising, the mother kissed him on the cheek and then her face reddened as she glanced over to me and then quickly back to André. I was pleased that she might consider me jealous.

This was thrilling to read—thrilling, but somehow nauseating, too. I couldn't stop.

Mother agonized over her engagement to Father, repeatedly asking herself if her time with André—a walk by the river or an afternoon in the café—violated Father's trust. But they were not married, only engaged. She and André talked for hours over wine and dinner. They laughed with the waiter about her accent.

She wrote that, one night, the wine carried them back to his apartment and, though here she did not record the details, the implication is clear. I felt blood rush to my cheeks. I put the diary down and went to the window where I stood for a long time, looking down to the river. She had two months left in Paris and it was at this time the nude drawings were done in such relaxed and casual poses that anyone would assume intimacy even without the diary.

She traveled back to Massachusetts with her cousin, who was returning to visit family and who continued to provide the illusion of a chaperone on the ship. But no chaperone was needed now. Mother described her time wandering the decks, staring out to the ocean, and sitting by herself, pretending to read. One journal entry recorded "my contentment at returning to my intended life," but these words were crossed out.

Had Father seen all this, read all this? Was this what caused their fights? I tried to imagine his reaction if, after years of marriage, he discovered what his fiancée had been doing in Paris while he labored through the Labrador winter.

By the end of the school year I didn't think I could stand another minute in my stifling home.

"I'm bored here. I need to do something else this summer. I want to be in Cambridge. I can't just sit here again." I pushed aside the plate of sugar cookies Mother offered and placed my chin in my hands. Swampy nudged his nose against my knees.

"What's brought this on, Gwen?" Mother seemed more amused than worried. But Matt mumbled something, stalked to the door, and let it slam. He hated our parents' fights and now I was adding to it.

"Becky and Michael will let me stay with them; I can help in the bookstore."

"They can't supervise a fifteen-year-old girl and run the bookstore, too." Father's quick dismissal increased my anger.

"Father! I'll be sixteen next week. You can't keep me here forever."

"I think our usual visit with Becky and Michael will be sufficient this year but, I tell you what." Mother's soothing tone was grating, "While we are there, we can discuss the possibility of you staying with them next summer. Maybe, if you work regular hours, they will pay you a salary."

"Next summer! Wonderful, but what am I to do this summer!" I marched to the door.

Father started toward me but Mother gripped his arm. "Let her be, Will. She'll be all right."

Swampy pranced to the door wagging his tail, but I slammed it before he could escape with me. I ran to the edge of town, then up through the woods until winded and sweaty, both the climb and the June heat taking a toll. I looked back, feeling some disappointment that no one followed. I headed toward the knoll still angered by their refusal. Imagine! Stuck in this town another summer. Now I decided I was glad to be alone as I stomped uphill and glad to find the knoll deserted. I didn't want to explain my fury to anyone.

I slowed my pace but did not allow the view to calm me. Even from this distance I could see that the river had given way to a sluggish summer flow, its banks constricted through fields of freshly sprouted greens. The blue sky was dappled with high wispy clouds that floated across the sun to briefly ease the heat. And there, in the center of the valley, was our town. I thought if I listened closely, I would be able to hear the horseflies buzzing on the green. Why had my parents ever chosen to live here? I would not make that mistake.

The sun, near the solstice, emerged from the clouds, forcing me to squint against the harsh light and finally driving me to the shade near the pond. I looked up. It had been years since Matt and I had climbed this maple, our favorite spot to weave intricate stories. I climbed twenty feet up, to the same broad branch, a fairly comfortable perch where convenient gaps in the canopy offered views to both the lake and the valley. There was no breeze in the sultry air and I considered climbing down for a drink. I imagined a plunge into the deepest part of the lake. The chilled water would clear my sweat and boredom. Matt and I used to compete to see who could swim underwater the farthest, who could stay under the longest. I won by swimming until my lungs ached and, at that point, picking a spot five or ten feet further ahead and forcing myself there before allowing my head to surface.

I reflected on the fight with my parents. I was rather pleased with the scene I caused: Father's anger, Mother's attempt at compromise, and Matt's bewilderment. I nearly laughed aloud. But it's good that I didn't for I would have been heard by the figure approaching from behind. I didn't see Jonathan until he was directly beneath me. I almost called out his name but held back. I was not in the mood.

What was he doing here anyway? I was taken aback when he paused but a moment, surveying the lake perimeter, before stripping off his sweat-drenched shirt and trousers and standing naked in the shallows facing away from me. The sun was slightly to his front so that the muscles of his shoulders, buttocks, and legs were accented by shadow. Both repulsive and interesting, I decided, grinning and wondering what he'd do if I called his name. He brought his hand to his brow to wipe away the sweat as he studied the lake.

The only proper way to enter cold water is to dive quickly in before the mind has time to consider. But Jonathan dawdled, first wading in to his ankles, then backing off, then stretching his arms backward and then above his head, then grabbing first one ankle up and then the other, then bending to touch his toes, movements perhaps intended to limber his muscles. But I knew he was simply delaying. Of course his ballet-like flexing was both funny and interesting so I did not much mind the wait, except when I considered what it said of his character.

Now he paused for a moment as if to warm his front to the point that he would have to dive in. Finally he entered, not instantly as he should but deliberately, each step forward followed by a pause while gently splashing water over thighs, abdomen, and chest. Finally he was in, and then he swam about for some time, braving the cold water longer than I would have expected, going to the far shore and back a couple of times.

It was long enough that my legs and back became cramped and my buttocks sore. I readjusted my position, but it is difficult to be comfortable on a tree branch. I considered descending to pretend I had just arrived. It would be fun to see how he handled it, naked in the lake while I teased him from shore. I decided this would not be as much fun as remaining in the tree, and I didn't act quickly enough anyway for soon he was approaching shore. I'd now get my first view of his front— the first "mature" male I'd seen though I couldn't imagine it would be any more interesting than Matt or other boys I'd seen when they were small. And I was correct—the view from sixty feet away was far from exhilarating. He lay chest down on his clothing, chin in hands, facing the water, letting the sun dry his back. Soon he turned his head to the side as if to sleep. His body was now cooled; mine was not. The heat seemed to shimmer off the lake, saturating the air with hot moisture. If he had been more directly under me, my sweat would have dripped to his back. I had little to do other than watch his relaxed, cooled body and think about my predicament. I had been on this branch for a good hour. My muscles were stiff and numb. My mouth became drier each minute. If he was asleep, surely I could readjust my position. The resulting limb creak echoed across the pond. But when he did not stir, I again thought I could perhaps climb down without his notice. I was considering this option when he moved, turning his head to face the other way. No, it was too risky.

My thirst and cramped discomfort soon led to irritable musings: What gave him the right to lie naked in the sun when anyone might happen by? Or, I crossly thought, perhaps he thought it of no concern, even if others did appear. He would simply laugh and cover up. And perhaps it was of no concern. But I found this thought even more infuriating because certainly I couldn't lie there alone and naked without fear of embarrassment, gossip, or attack. Perhaps I should confront him with these facts! How dare he cause me such discomfort, driving me to madness with thirst and cramped muscles.

Soon he woke to stretch his arms and legs. He rolled to his side briefly before standing to look dreamily about, making certain, I suppose, that he was still alone. Then he dove back into the lake.

This time I scampered down. I had reached my limit. He was still swimming away so I supposed he'd not seen me. I considered a run for the woods but then thought better of it. First things first. I walked to the lake and cupped my hands to drink. Then I stood waiting, arms across my chest. He had turned and was halfway back when he saw me. I smiled, waved, and sat next to his clothing. He stopped and then gradually came to shallow water, keeping his waist submerged.

"Hi, Jonathan." I waved again as if he might otherwise miss me.

"Gwen . . . what are you dong here?" Then, alarmed, "When did you get here?"

I nestled my chin into my knees, weighing my response. "I had a big fight with my parents. They won't let me stay in Cambridge this summer . . ." I rattled on, cheerily giving him the whole story.

When I began to talk about Swampy, he interrupted. "Gwen, I'm getting cold. I'll need to come out soon."

"What's stopping you?" I smiled.

"I forgot my bathing suit."

"You forgot your bathing suit! Well, isn't that sad?"

"Gwen, please. It's getting cold."

"Well it's not cold out here!" I wiped the sweat from my forehead, grabbed his pants, and stalked toward him, close enough to see him shivering. "Here!" I threw his pants to him. He tried to grab them but they plopped into the lake two feet in front of him. "That'll keep you cool on the way home."

I turned and marched away past the empty stone foundations and down the woodsy path.

He caught me as I arrived at the edge of town where the trail widened to a dusty lane.

"Look Gwen, I don't know why you're so angry." He breathed unevenly, winded from the run. Moisture from his pants had migrated over the lower part of his shirt.

I was still mad at him, mad at the situation, mad at myself for being mad. But I was flattered that he'd chased after me. "I'm mad I couldn't swim, too. Okay?" I started to turn away.

"Gwen, it's strange, but before you got there, I'd just been thinking of you. I dozed off, asleep under the tree. Then I had this dream all about you."

"You dreamed about me? What about me?"

"Well, as a gentleman, I cannot say."

He turned as if to watch my embarrassment, but I didn't color. I simply smiled and kissed his cheek. And then I took his hand to lead him down the lane.

Chapter 8
1914

A few weeks later Mother, Matt, and I were again in Cambridge. Age was slowing Becky and Michael and they were happy to have our help. Matt and I moved stacks of boxes from the cramped storeroom. We scurried up ladders, stocking and dusting the upper shelves. Mother suggested it might be time for an employee.

Becky sighed, "That time will come but really dear, we are just fine for now."

Mother was thoughtful. "Gwen has talked of spending the summer here and helping in the store, maybe next summer."

"We'd love to have her," Becky answered. "She would be a tremendous help."

"Actually, I wanted to come this summer, but Father and Mother said no."

"You know, dear, even one year can make a huge difference. Why, look at your brother! Last year he couldn't have carried three of those boxes. I suppose he's grown a foot since we last saw him. And you, dear, you've filled out nicely."

Matt and I exchanged looks and I saw the flush of his cheeks which must have mirrored mine.

Mother remained thoughtful, "There would need to be some ground rules."

"What?"

"Rules. If Gwen stays with you next summer, there would need to be rules."

"Whatever do you mean?" Becky still seemed to be admiring our growth.

"Rules about her hours here. She needs to be serious about work. She can't just work when she feels like it."

"I'm sure we can handle all that when the time comes."

"And she needs some supervision," Mother pushed on. "Going out at night, seeing boys. That's all starting now."

"Dear, you forget we've done this before," Becky smiled at her daughter, "and the results, I think you will agree, are quite admirable."

"Well said, Grandma. Really, Mother, anything I can do here, I can do in Birkett Ferry." When Grandma frowned at me I bit my tongue and turned away to move a stack of books.

Matt came from the storeroom. "Grandpa, canoe trip this afternoon?"

"Why Matt, my Best Beloved, you leave me aghast! I don't know how we can desert this important enterprise leaving these three female warriors to guard the riches! They'd hack each other apart to claim the spoils!" His eyes bulged with perplexed horror, releasing us to laughter.

Becky put her arm around her daughter. "Your father and I have thought for years that, when they are old enough, we'd love to have Gwen and Matt for a time. It would help us old codgers reclaim our youth."

"I know, Mother, but it's a difficult thing for me."

That afternoon, with Matt and Michael out exploring the Charles River, I walked the Cambridge streets while Mother and Becky continued to stock the bookstore shelves. Outfitted in a beige dress, I was pleased that I attracted notice from college men. They sought eye contact, exchanging smiles and summer liveliness. Here I am, a provincial girl, able to turn the heads of the city men. Birkett Ferry was dormant compared to the vibrant activity here: produce markets clamoring, newsboys touting the latest editions, and shopkeepers rearranging their windows. There were still many horse-drawn carriages cobbling down the streets of Cambridge, but now they were losing out to the automobiles whose noise and fumes represented freedom to me. In Birkett Ferry a passing car was still cause to stare and discuss; here they were ordinary.

When I returned, Becky and Mother were chuckling over

afternoon tea, their feet resting on unpacked crates. Mother seemed unable to contain herself. "Gwen, I really should talk with your father first, but Becky and I were just wondering what you would think . . . what would you think of staying here to help your grandparents for a couple of weeks after we leave?" She smiled at my speechlessness and then gushed onward. "You don't need to be back until early September so we figure you could spend three more weeks here, if you like."

"Well of course I'd like to! Thanks Mother and Grandma."

"We still need to convince your father."

We were settled at the beach when Father arrived, luggage, brief-case, and loads of books in tow. I think there had been some reconciliation between my parents that summer, or perhaps it was a façade—for Michael and Becky's sake.

"Will, you've brought your whole office, I see."

"There are a couple of cases to finish, some bills to pay. But it's really not that much. Just a few hours' work."

Mother didn't broach the subject of my extended visit until the second day. "It's best that he have time to relax first." But he had no objection; his only concern was my homeward journey.

"She'll be alone on the train," he worried.

"Becky will see her onto the train in Boston," Mother said.

"But she needs to change in Springfield. Perhaps I'd best meet her there."

"I can do it, Father. It's just switching to the next track. It's not confusing."

"But if you get on the southbound train by mistake . . ."

Michael chuckled. "By George, he's right. If my Best Beloved gets on that southbound train, she's in New Haven before she knows it, commingling with those Yale men, no doubt. We surely can't have that!"

Father, giving up, joined the laughter. "Right, if it's to be anyone, it should be a Harvard man."

Mother embraced him from behind. "That's always been my thought, too." She gave Father a theatrically adoring look. "I've tried to set a proper example with my choice."

Michael had the last word. "It's all happened just the way Becky and I planned."

A few days later on one of those simmering August afternoons when even the ocean offers no breeze to dry the sweat, we wilted on the shaded porch, lounging and reading, hoping the evening air would cool enough to allow sleep. Earlier, Matt and I walked the beach searching for shells, and competing to see whose feet could tolerate the hot sand the longest before dashing into the water. The ocean waters gave relief, but when I emerged the water droplets cascading through my hair and over my trunk seemed instantly transformed to sweat.

Becky and I brought out a tray of lemonade and cookies as the rest of the family drooped, incapable of any movement save for Mother's languid fanning. As I passed the lemonade, Becky returned to her seat and placed her feet in a basin filled with cold water. "You know this really does work: cool the feet and you cool the whole body." We eyed her listlessly. She did appear perkier than the rest of us but so far she had no converts. Maybe it was just too much effort to fetch a basin and fill it with water.

"Gwen," Father said, "I've left the newspaper in my study. Can you get it for me . . . as long as you are up?"

Upstairs, the heat mounted. His study was really a small dressing room off their bedroom. When we were little, Matt and I carried our blankets into this room to be near our parents after we woke to a thunderstorm or a bad dream. On rainy days, we had spent hours in that room, building tents from sawhorses and blankets. Father, using the same sawhorses with some boards, had fashioned a desk which he positioned near the window. Papers and books were spread out haphazardly across the surface, spilling to the floor nearby, the whole scene as wilted and indolent as the day itself.

I reached for the newspaper resting by a stack of letters ready to post. For some reason I started to look through them but the third envelope stopped me cold. It was addressed to Miss Cynthia Robbins! I was so surprised I nearly called her name out loud. But I thought he had said, years ago, that he did not have her address. I grabbed a scrap of paper to copy the address. I could not imagine why he was writing to her. Perhaps she had some legal question to which he was responding, or there was some unfinished business concerning her contract with the town. Father handled much of the town's legal work. Or perhaps she was to teach again in Birkett Ferry. That would be wonderful. I couldn't ask about the letter without revealing my snooping even though I wasn't exactly snooping. I didn't think much more about it although it was nice to have her address. Perhaps I would write to her. But what would I say after all these years?

The newspaper I carried downstairs headlined news of Europe's increasing conflict, one country after another declaring war on her rivals. Actual fighting began the week of our beach stay. As we strolled on the hot beach sands and dove through the curling waves, as we drank lemonade on our summer porch and dozed in the August heat, soldiers died in Europe. They joined armies and died for, as far as I could tell, some confusing set of alliances. Father claimed they fought simply because they had raised the armies and the weapons, and once in place, they had to use them. Much to his own father's dismay, he advocated neutrality. He said it was his combat experience with the Rough Riders that led to this position. He admired the writing of peace activist Emma Goldman, and soon he was in regular correspondence with her.

"Europe is making blunders sufficient for the entire world. We must stay out of this war," Father said.

Here at the beach cottage, he had general agreement. Mother and Becky were more surprised at his worry than concerned for the future.

"Surely, Will, the war won't last. It will be over in a few weeks; I'm reading that everywhere." Mother put down her knitting and reached for the front page.

"I wish I could believe it, Marge. Perhaps it's true . . . and I hope it is. But the rage and stupidity intensify each day. And now Germany has marched into Belgium."

"But that doesn't affect us. I don't even know what they are fighting about."

"It shouldn't affect us but we will be drawn in. If our trade is affected we will be drawn in." He slumped down in his chair and chased a housefly with the back of his hand.

"Trade! We are talking about exchanging lives for trade?" Mother looked up from the newspaper.

"Such has always been the case."

"Wilson will keep us neutral." Becky seemed sure of this. She stood to reposition her chair and then returned her feet to the cool basin of water.

"I hope that's so but he'll be pressured by many. The longer the war lasts, the harder it will be for Wilson to avoid. I expect that old war monger, Teddy Roosevelt, will soon call for our involvement." Father spoke with disgust.

"But Wilson is President." Mother resumed her knitting. She was making a dark blue woolen sweater for Matt but a need for wool seemed unlikely in this heat.

"Don't ignore Roosevelt's following or his power. He squashed his old friend Taft in the last election and, given sufficient chance, he'll squash Wilson too."

"If Taft had been intimidated, he would have bowed out of the race."

"Yes, and then Roosevelt would have won. We would already be in the war, no doubt, and our free speech and liberty would already be diminished."

"Really, Will, your worries are extreme. How, precisely, does war, combined with a Roosevelt presidency, decrease our civil liberties?" She pointed her knitting needle at Father.

"Any war will cause the government to limit free speech. It always has. And Roosevelt, especially, will not tolerate dissent. During Roosevelt's tenure, actually in 1902 at a time of peace, it was Emma Goldman who said that advocates of free speech shall soon be obliged to meet in cellars, or in darkened rooms with closed doors, and speak in whispers."

"And I don't think our free speech has diminished a whit since 1902. You worry too much, Will. And besides, this is the radical Emma Goldman, the atheist and anarchist, is it not?"

"I don't agree with all she has to say. But you should read her writings and letters. They are inspirational."

Becky intervened. "Emma Goldman or not, Teddy Roosevelt or not, we should all enjoy our time together and be glad that we're a long way from any war."

Michael, quiet through the discussion, now eyed Matt and me. "I'm just thankful these two are not four years older."

As I rode back from the train station with Becky, my thoughts were on the farewell to my family. Matt had leaned from the window, a station breeze ruffling his hair. "But you'll miss the best time, the last free time before school. Canoeing and hiking and swimming."

I pulled myself up to his window and lightly kissed his cheek. "Matt, I know it sounds trite but one day, pretty soon, you'll want to be away too. It's not you I want to be away from. It's everything else: the town, the people, our parents, even," I winked at him, "even Jonathan."

Mother grew teary with her last minute advice until I protested, "Heavens Mother, I'll be home in three weeks." Father reminded me to be certain of the northbound train in Springfield.

But in the carriage my eyes grew misty and my throat tightened.

It was the first time I had been apart from my entire family for more than a single day. Becky put her arm around my shoulder. "You'll be such a help to us."

And I was determined to demonstrate my helpfulness, realizing that my plan to spend next summer in Cambridge might hinge on this. I was ready in the bookstore before opening, checking the displays, unpacking boxes, and clearing trash. At slack times I dusted or washed windows.

Michael instructed me of the skill involved in knowing which customers to approach. "A lot of them just want to browse on their own, they don't want the chitchat. For others it's a social event: they want to discuss the weather, neighborhood gossip, politics, war and peace, and their mother's apple pie, anything except the latest book, and that's the one thing I know something about."

Michael and Becky both noticed one change. "We're getting more repeat customers than usual," Becky grinned.

"We're getting more repeat browsers anyhow. I'm not certain they're really customers," Michael added.

"Yes, they might become customers if only they would browse through the books instead of staring at our granddaughter." I turned to straighten some books on the back shelves, trying to conceal my embarrassment and pleasure.

It was true. There were a couple of Harvard men who came into the shop on a regular basis, eager to search the shelves in the corner of the shop where I was stocking or cleaning, eager to talk. Douglas Turner, of medium height (Matt, I thought, was already taller than Douglas), tan complexion, and straight brown hair, had an easy smile and manner. "I'll be a junior this year." He seemed to want me to know this fact, though I hadn't asked. This made him, I supposed, four years my elder.

"Classes don't start for a few weeks yet. You're back quite early." I tried to continue unpacking the book crate but I was distracted by his brown eyes, which followed my every movement.

"I've been in Cambridge for the summer, working in my uncle's law office."

"You'll be a lawyer, then?" As I turned to face him, a strand of hair tumbled down over my brow and I reached up to wedge it behind my ear.

"I suppose—eventually. I'd really like to travel before settling, but Europe is impossible now."

We were then interrupted by, I flatter myself, Douglas's rival. Kevin Durham was taller, slimmer, and more awkward; he had a habit of bumping into displays and tripping on doorstops. "Have my books come in yet?"

"No, Mr. Durham, but I expect them any day."

He flushed on seeing Douglas and stammered, "Well, uh, well, maybe I'll check again tomorrow."

"Do you need them soon?"

"No, uh, well, I just wanted them before classes." He looked about self-consciously.

"Can I help you find anything else?"

"I'll be back tomorrow." He sideswiped the counter in his rush to the door.

I turned to Douglas. "Mr. Durham has been here the summer, too, helping his Greek professor with translations."

"What books did he order?"

"Two volumes, both poetry. A book by the new poet, Robert Frost, and an anthology—he wanted to read Edna St. Vincent Millay's *Renascence*."

"Both books are so obscure that he must have known they'd take forever to arrive."

"What?"

"Just an excuse to come in to see you," Douglas sputtered.

"Well I don't think . . . I mean Millay, as well as Frost, they're both making a mark. We've had other requests for their work."

A few days later, when Douglas asked me to come with him on Saturday night to a lecture about the European War, he must have been surprised that I needed to turn to Becky for permission.

"She has just turned sixteen, you know. I think an evening excursion is not a good idea, Mr. Turner."

But Douglas was persistent, and I'm sure Becky was aware of my silent appeal. They agreed on an afternoon canoe outing on the Charles River, quite the fashion, followed by café refreshments and a return home by six o'clock.

Michael teased my preparations when I appeared in a white dress that covered my body, ankles to neck. "You know, Best Beloved," he paused as I tested my matching parasol, "it has never made sense to me, dressing for a canoe ride!"

"But it is the style now." Becky straightened the bows holding my hat in place.

"When I used to take them on the river, Gwen and Matt and I, we wore the oldest clothes we had. We were perfectly comfortable, too."

Douglas, also elegantly attired in a cream-colored suit, handed me down into the bow where I sat facing him. Etiquette required the use of the parasol though I would have otherwise welcomed the sunlight after spending so many hours in the shop. I felt pampered and useless, my only task to make conversation as I watched his unpracticed efforts to steer. We seemed to veer directly into the path of any nearby canoe, abruptly turning at the last moment or sometimes knocking into the other boat with exclamations of apology. We managed a slow upstream course, curiosity drawing us around each bend, our progress aided by a modest wind. We talked of families, schools, friends, and futures.

The Charles had only dreary current here but we were scarcely making headway. This was a good choice, I thought, to go upstream first so we could drift on the way back. The breeze built, mostly pushing us forward but becoming a devilish crosswind when the meandering river shifted direction. Douglas, jacket off, tie and shirt loosened at the collar and sweat beads falling from his forehead, was doubling his work, zigzagging from one bank to the other through waves and wind. But I should not be bothered by our erratic course, I reminded myself as I settled down in my seat, the parasol now flapping in the breeze. It didn't matter what distance we covered.

As I gazed out to the couples strolling on the bank, I brought my finger to my lips while extending my legs as far as the thwart would allow, my idea of a relaxed seductive pose. But it was difficult to remain calm as we routinely came within inches of the muddy bank, only veering off at the last second.

"Douglas, that spot on the left, why don't we stop there?" I pointed to an inviting trio of maples that stood guard over a hummock covered with thick matted grass, decorated on one side with wild iris. The embankment rose steeply from the edge of the water before leveling. Douglas brought us alongside the bank and held fast. I jumped forward, my momentum pushing the bow back but allowing me to scramble up to the plateau. Douglas, stern line in hand, tried the same maneuver but didn't compensate for the outward thrust of the boat. He teetered on the edge of the slippery grass and then fell, his knees squishing into the mud from whence he slid backward into the river. To his credit, he held tight to the rope.

I stood on the bank marveling at his disheveled appearance. I couldn't suppress laughter. But he refused to acknowledge his shattered dignity, looking up to me in the same manner as a cat which has missed its jump nonchalantly rights itself and licks its paw as if to say, "I intended that all along."

"I think we'll need these." He offered the blanket and basket up to me but still would not smile.

"Douglas, are you all right? Get out of the water. You're wet to your waist."

I gave him my hand to pull him up to the bank where he stood surveying the damage to his suit.

"You should get those wet pants off."

I turned around while he hung his dripping slacks on a limb and then wrapped his lower half in the blanket. He offered to sit me on his jacket since the blanket was now unavailable. I refused at first until he insisted, "The pants will need a thorough cleaning, that is, if they're not ruined, so why not the jacket, too?"

We spread the bread, cheese, and fruit, and he brought, from the bottom of the basket, a bottle of red wine. I had never had more than a taste from my father's glass, but I accepted the full cup. We broke the bread off in hunks, topping it with cheddar and washing it down with grapes, oranges, and wine. But I could only manage small sips of the wine, finding it bitter. I managed to pour my glass into the ground undetected and declined the second cup he poured for himself. I lay back to survey the rustling of wind-driven leaves against the cloud-streaked sky.

"Gwen, turn your head while I get my pants back on."

"They couldn't be dry yet."

"Almost, the wind has done a nice job. And we'll be more comfortable on the blanket."

He had trouble straightening the blanket into the blustering wind, finally sitting to hold it in place and inviting me next to him. "More clouds now and wind too. You must be cold." He positioned his jacket over my shoulders, leaving his arm around my waist. From that point of contact, chills radiated up my back to coalesce in a body shudder. He looked surprised. "You really are cold, aren't you? Maybe a bit more wine would do the trick." But instead he leaned over to plant an inquisitive kiss on my lips.

"Nice," I murmured as my mind dashed about for escape. I abruptly stood, looking out at the river. "Oh my. Look at the river and the wind. We should go."

"But," he was reaching out, beckoning me back.

"No, we'll have trouble getting back as it is. And it might get worse." I scanned the clouds and the whipping tree branches.

The parasol would have been ripped open by the wind. As I stowed it beneath the seat I grabbed the extra paddle and, without asking Douglas, I positioned myself in the bow ready to help. The current was of no help against the wind, and it took all our power to move into the white-capped waves, the bow cresting up to a height from which my paddle could barely reach the water, then slamming down with a forceful splash. Douglas paddled ineffectively, switching sides back and forth, frantically trying to keep the boat on course. There would have been no progress had he been paddling alone. At the first river bend the wind grabbed the lighter bow, swinging us ninety degrees in a matter of seconds and putting us broadside to the waves. Douglas's reaction was to try to force the bow back with the most powerful strokes he could muster.

"Let it go," I yelled over the wind.

"What?" He looked confused and alarmed.

"Let it go, we won't get the bow back around now. And the waves could capsize us."

"But . . ." He brought his paddle in across the gunnels.

"Believe me, I've done this before. And keep your paddle in the water. It'll keep us steady."

I helped the wind bring us about so that our stern was now facing directly into the wind and we were looking back upstream toward our picnic spot and away from the direction in which we hoped to go.

I took over. "Now just turn around in your seat to face back into the wind."

"What!"

"Trust me. Turn around." I tried to keep my voice steady. I turned around too, and we began to paddle through the squall. Now I was in control of the steering and all Douglas had to do was paddle forward. As we neared the corner that would bring us within sight of the boathouse, he suggested we turn the canoe to proceed bow first again. I agreed since the wind had slackened. We turned in our seats as I added, "Maybe I'll just stay here in the bow to help get us in, if that's okay with you,"

"Here you are!" We were greeted by the dockhand. "We almost sent a search party!"

"We were delayed by the wind." Douglas gestured to the river.

"The wind was monstrous. I didn't think you two would make it!"

"We did make some adjustments," Douglas said.

"I see you've got the lady paddling. You must be fine canoeists to have come through that weather."

Douglas beamed as we left the dock, not bothered by our ignoble appearance: our clothing hung damp and limp, my hair was tangled, and both the back of my dress and the front of his trousers were suspiciously muddied. We chose to skip the café.

"You've had a bit of weather," Becky greeted us doubtfully, but she said nothing about our appearance. After Douglas declined hot tea and hurried off, I told Becky and Michael the whole story. Michael enjoyed the spectacle as much as if he'd been there.

Douglas continued to come round to the shop, and we did manage to get to the café for tea and cake. Afterward, walking along the Charles, he had enough gumption to comment on the steering ability of some canoeists who had become snared on a sandbar.

Kevin, too, visited each day, attracted by motives other than those of simply procuring his books. I suppose his shyness prevented him from asking me out that summer, but I enjoyed his awkward company enough to be pleased for him when his two volumes arrived on the same day.

I saw him approaching the shop and I threw open the door. "Kevin, I'm so glad to see you. They are here, finally!"

"Both at once?" He tried to smooth his frazzled black hair.

"Well," now my mind churned. "Actually, uh . . . actually just the Frost volume. But that will keep you busy for a while." I thought he might be socially inept enough to have missed my signals and I worried that if he left with both books, he would be unable to find an excuse to come back.

"Have you enjoyed the Frost poetry?" I asked on the day before I was to leave.

"I've only read a little of it. I've been so busy with the translation. And now classes will begin next week."

"Well, perhaps you'll make time for Millay; I hear she is fabulous." I pulled the hidden anthology from below the counter.

"Wonderful!" Kevin beamed.

"I ordered another copy for the store. But now I think I'll keep it for myself. I would be curious to know what you think of her writing." I paused, but he did not take the hint, and only smiled attentively, waiting for me to continue. "I know . . . perhaps we can write back and forth about Millay, and then I can get a copy of Frost, or we could read other things and correspond." Without waiting for his response, I printed my address on the back of the store business card.

"Yes," he grinned. "That would be grand." And then, with reddening cheeks, he blurted, "I'll miss seeing you."

"Wait, Kevin." He had noticed that other customers needed my attention, and had abruptly turned toward the door, knocking against a glass display case. "Wait, I'll need your address too."

A few hours later, Douglas sauntered in. "The last day arrives. I'll miss you and I'll even miss your canoeing lessons!"

"Douglas! Our outings have been wonderful." I smiled cheerfully.

"Any chance you'll make it back here soon?"

"Not before next summer, no, I don't think so."

"In that case we'll just have to write every week. Here's my address." He handed me his printed card and smoothly leaned forward to kiss my cheek. I blushed when two customers smiled, but at least I did not have to endure the teasing of Michael and Becky, who had disappeared to the kitchen for afternoon tea.

But what I wished for was a prolonged kiss on the mouth accompanied by a passionate embrace and a wrenching, tearful good-bye at the train station. I would pull myself away from Douglas (or Kevin) only as the train started to leave, barely grabbing on to the last car. Or I would be standing on the platform alone and weepy and look up to see one (or both) sprinting toward me with breathless adoration, urging me to stay one more day.

Instead it was just me and Becky on the platform. Michael stayed at the store but had offered his thanks. "You know, Best Beloved, we always hoped to have our grandchildren help us like this, but it's been better than I imagined. Thank you. I hope you will come next summer. And study hard! Just watch out for those boys; they're sure to be after a girl like you! If you have any sense, you'll save your heart for me."

Becky was more subdued, holding her advice until the train approached. "Only two more years of high school. Only two more years at home. Cherish the time. I know you sometimes can't wait to be free but cherish each minute. It all goes so quickly. Remember, parents aren't perfect. We certainly weren't; just ask your mother. But at least consider their advice. And give them some freedom, too."

I only half listened as I stared over her shoulder, almost expecting Douglas or Kevin to appear, dashing toward me through the locomotive's steamy haze. I did not then appreciate that this gushy grandmotherly guidance was more valuable than anything either of those boys could have offered.

I wasn't particularly upset to leave Becky and Michael, but I was upset to leave the stylish shops, the lively streets, the theaters, the artists, and the interesting Harvard men. After changing to the northbound train in Springfield without the difficulty feared by Father, I realized how close I was to home. I would waste the next two years of my life in desolate Birkett Ferry, wallowing in the drudgery of small-town life among provincials lacking any appreciation for the arts, culture, or romance. Grandmother Compston, of course, tried with her musical and literary salons. But still, there was not much to look forward to.

I was tired of Birkett Ferry, tired of my family, and tired of Jonathan. As I continued to brood, I realized that Jonathan was the only thing I could change.

Chapter 9
1914–15

Ending my relationship with Jonathan left me lots of free time. On the train I had begun to read Millay's "*Renascence*." I found it tough going but forged ahead hoping for insight that would intrigue Kevin, who now faithfully wrote to me. He discussed little save his classics work and our mutual reading. "I am so lucky," he wrote "to have this time to read and study and think. My only other obligation is to continue the Greek translations with Professor Dayton." I told him my chief joy was to take our current book to the river, or the knoll. I tried to describe those idyllic country settings, their beauty now intensified by the autumn colors.

Douglas's letters were hurriedly written and only sporadically received. He wrote of the drudgery of his courses and the boredom of the lectures, saving his enthusiasm to describe his social life. He spoke of parties involving flouted rules, missed curfews, and illegal alcohol. He sighed that he had badly ripped a suit, the same one he had worn during our canoe misadventure, while climbing in his dorm window at three in the morning, "but the thrill of eluded detection was worth the cost of a suit." He said he missed me intensely and asked if I would be able to come for a visit. I was not disinterested. I told him I had pleaded with my parents to allow a visit, but their denial was firm. We probably would not see each other until the summer.

"You charge in here every afternoon like a bloodhound on a scent," Mother joked about my eagerness to check the mail. "I see there are two different hands that write you. How many boys have you snared?"

"Mother! I've told you they are just friends. Kevin is a very serious student."

The letters were of no interest to Matt. He liked school and studied long hours. Saturday afternoons he would likely be found curled up on the living room couch, reading. Jumbled stacks of his books cluttered the porch, living room, and his bedroom until Mother took the time to straighten them. But sometimes I would insist on his company on my jaunts to the knoll. I decided this was for his own good for he surely needed more exercise. It was also true that I needed companionship.

That fall it became my favorite activity: Matt and I would wander up to the knoll, our packs containing fruit, cheese, and bread, but also books, journals, and letters. We lounged on the old stone foundations, still warm in the autumn sun. Matt would eagerly dive into his books, hardly stirring for hours, save for a bite of bread and cheese. I could not be as still nor as single-minded. I'd stare off to the east, over our quiet town and its tree-rimmed green, past the soothing river and the autumn fields, to the distant hills that blocked my path to Cambridge. Thoughts of Cambridge, and then of Kevin, would lead to an attempt at the poetry we had agreed to study, but it was hard to concentrate on such undecipherable material while sitting outside where there was much to distract. I would return to daydreams of Cambridge as I gazed at the view and watched the geese honking their way south in tidy migrations. I would begin a letter to Kevin or Douglas, sometimes dramatically tearing it up after half a page. At this, Matt, remaining silent, would look to me, eyes quizzical, before quickly returning to his book.

It didn't disturb his reading when I turned to study his handsome face. The chubby cheeks had given way to sturdy prominences, still freckled, below his deep-set green eyes. His brow furrowed in concentration. I saw the fine hairs sprouting to extend his sideburns, and I wondered why he was not pursued endlessly by female classmates. I knew he found social interactions perplexing, but still I wondered.

After a time I would wander around the perimeter of the lake, glad for solitude, but at the same time wishing that five of my friends would appear, chattering up the trail. I'd sit for a time on the dam and call out to Matt, "Turtle!" or "Frog!" He'd glance up briefly, smile absently, and return to his book. Finally, I'd call out, "Matt, quick, you've got to see this!" He'd trot over to view the tadpoles, or the three ducklings trailing their mother. He took the hint to sit with me for a time.

I playfully rubbed his cheeks. "You'll need to start shaving soon."

"I've already started. Twice now. Father showed me."

"Oh? And how was it?" I felt left out for not knowing.

"Fine. No cuts."

"What will you do after high school?"

He laughed. "Well I've got a ways to go yet, but college, I suppose . . . that's what everyone expects anyway."

"And then law?"

"I don't know. Father doesn't seem particularly happy with law."

"But Grandfather does."

"Grandfather seems so sure of everything: the law, his life, our lives, and now the war."

"And Father seems so uncertain. Maybe he would have been better off in Labrador. Or he should have left Birkett Ferry, to practice law somewhere else. Like Cambridge."

"Or not law at all."

"Once I overheard Becky and Michael and Mother talking about Father, about how different he was before the Rough Riders."

"In what way?" Matt plucked a long stem of grass and held it up, viewing it against the sky. The seeds sparkled in the sunlight.

"I guess he was happier, more carefree. The war made him too serious, too thoughtful . . . and sad."

"He never talks about the war."

"I know, and Grandfather talks endlessly about it, and the Civil War."

"Which he was never in."

"Which he was never in, but you'd never know it to hear him speak of the 'glorious fight,' and the 'bravery in battle.'"

"And he is so proud of Father and the Rough Riders in Cuba, but Father won't talk about it and Grandfather finally gives up." Matt paused. "And what about Mother?"

"I don't know. Sometimes she doesn't seem so happy either."

"She seems happier in Cambridge."

"It's like she's stifled here. I mean she loves us a lot; she's so merry when you and I are happy. But in Cambridge she's different. She's playful and cheery. It's like she's sixteen again. She wants to resume her painting. Maybe that will help."

"And what of you, O sister of mine?" Matt's syntax sometimes made me wonder what he had been reading in English class.

"What?"

"What are your noble plans for the future?"

"College for sure. I've seen how much fun it is in Cambridge—both the academic part and the social part. I'd like to live with Becky and Michael—and work in the store, too."

"And what of the Cambridge romances?"

I was surprised at this question. Matt knew I had broken off with Jonathan, but we didn't discuss my relationships. "You mean with Douglas and Kevin?" I didn't wait for his reply. "They're not romances." He looked doubtful. "Really, they're not. More like good friends, older good friends. They're both three or four years older than me. Oh, maybe they are somewhat interested in me, but I know it won't work." I was gushing now—maybe I needed to talk about this. Matt listened patiently. "Actually, Kevin is like you, not that he's interested in botany or science—he wants to teach classics—but he's a serious student, interested in translations. He also likes poetry, and that's what we write back and forth about. Douglas, on the other hand, studies as little as possible. He's fun to be with, though; he likes parties and always has a scheme of some sort. I'm not sure what his plans are, maybe law or banking or something. They're both appealing in different ways." Matt was dutifully watching my face, but I had the feeling his thoughts had wandered.

There was still hope, that fall and winter, for a short European war, but debate about American involvement was becoming more strident across the country and in our home. Matt and I listened to the discussions, but Europe seemed so far away. It was hard to be interested in events that had no impact on us. Grandfather and Father were able to discuss their differences, but it took an effort to hold their anger in check.

"The world is changing, we'll be drawn in." Grandfather thought President Wilson naive to believe the United States could remain neutral.

"We will be drawn in only if we allow it," countered Father. "Why should we fight this war?"

"The problem is that we couldn't fight, even if we needed to. We have no troops ready."

"We have one hundred thousand men in the army; surely that's sufficient . . ."

"Sufficient to fight Belgium or Mexico perhaps. But Germany and France each had armies of eight hundred thousand at the beginning of the war, certainly much larger by now. Our country should be a true world power; we need the force to reflect that."

"Building such a large army would almost guarantee our entry into the war. There are many in this country already itching to fight."

"And I count myself among them, as does your old commander, Teddy Roosevelt. He's saying we need to prepare for war."

"That's not a surprise. But for what reason should we fight?"

"New alignments and new power will come out of this war. If we are to have a credible seat at the peace table, we must now fight."

"And for what reason do we need a seat at the European peace table?"

"My dear boy, it all comes down to trade. If we wish to have overseas markets for our goods, and to buy from others on favorable terms, we must be in position to protect our interests and our citizens and our trade."

"I know you're right—that trade is the hidden reason for war. But that's not sufficient. We cannot justify exchanging the lives of our sons to protect our trading rights."

"It has always been so, and always will be so. But remember: by protecting trade, we also protect our country, our property, our people, and our way of life."

These conversations and arguments were repeated endlessly, finally becoming more bellicose after the sinking of the Lusitania, by a German submarine, in May 1915. Over one hundred American lives were lost.

"And your President Wilson still has not done a damn thing!" Grandfather grumbled.

"He has put huge efforts into maintaining our neutrality." Father wrinkled his brow. "People don't want war. He has warned the Germans."

"Warning?" Did you hear of his speech? He as much as told the Germans we would not fight—ever: 'There is such a thing as a man being too proud to fight. There is such a thing as a nation being so right that it does not need to convince others by force that it is right,' or whatever it was that he said. That is no way to stand up for ourselves!"

"You think Roosevelt's 'Big Stick' is a better idea?"

"I do! Roosevelt did an admirable job of building our navy. He would have done the same for the army had there been a need. There is now a need. Roosevelt sees that; why can't Wilson? We can't even defend our shores with the current force."

"Defend our shores? From what?"

"From invasion, of course."

"Father, you believe that one of the combatants would siphon off men, and somehow transport them across the Atlantic Ocean, to invade Boston? That is simply preposterous."

"Not likely perhaps, but not impossible. My point is, that if we do not have the manpower to defend ourselves, we are even further from being able to join the Allies in Europe."

"Join the Allies?" Now Father blustered, "Join the Allies? We're supposed to be neutral!"

"Not after the Lusitania. And Wilson had better realize that quickly. There isn't even a plan to mobilize."

Grandmother and Mother sided with Father, but mostly they tried to calm the belligerents. No one stalked away from the table mid meal, but the lingering anger could not have helped their digestion. And the increased hostility of their remarks gradually increased the interest for Matt and me.

Matt judged Father correct. "I don't understand why we should go to war. No one threatens us."

I agreed with him. "Well, the Germans have attacked our ships, but I don't see why we just don't keep our ships at home until after the war."

Kevin and I were still studying the bookstore anthology. Poetry was so involved and intricate when subjected to his analysis. Our high school English studies seemed rudimentary in comparison. I felt inadequate in responding, but he always treated my comments with respect.

At the end of one letter, in which he described our Frost selection as "irresistibly haunting and sad," he closed by asking,

> Have you seen the writing of Alan Seeger in *The New York Sun*? He's an American who was living in Paris and writing poetry when the war started. He joined the French army and is now at the front; somehow he finds time to write, and he sends articles to the *The Sun* for publication. I think the paper sells out when they publish his articles and, on campus, each copy passes through ten or twenty hands, inspiring much debate. How can we justify living here in our comfortable rooms while the atrocities continue in Europe and people like Seeger are living life to the fullest? Some of my friends talk of joining the

French or British armies. You really must read him. I would send you the clippings, but I've passed them on. If you cannot find them there let me know . . .

I couldn't find copies of *The Sun* in Birkett Ferry, and neither my parents nor my Compston grandparents were familiar with Seeger. I wrote back to Kevin, but also sent a request to Becky and Michael. Becky responded first. "Seeger has created quite a stir here in a way I don't fully understand—the students talk of fighting in Europe as some sort of heroic ideal."

The articles she sent did not fire my imagination in that way. Paragraph after paragraph spoke of the drudgery of trench life, the damp, cold quagmire, the rats, and the inevitable tension arising from men stuffed together elbow to elbow without room to stretch, "condemned to sit like an animal in its burrow." The boredom of trench life was so suffocating that the men actually hoped for the dangers of night patrol or battle. Nighttime sentry duty allowed Seeger a measure of freedom from the cramped trenches and gave him time to reflect.

Alone under the stars, war in its cosmic rather than its moral aspect reveals itself . . . Regarded from this more abstract plane the question of right and wrong disappears. Peoples war because strife is the law of nature and force the ultimate arbitrament among humanity no less than in the rest of the universe. He is on the side he is fighting for, not in the last analysis from ethical motives at all, but because destiny has set him in such a constellation.

I wrote Kevin that I found this to be depressingly fatalistic. I felt none of the uplifting captivating energy that was motivating his fellows to seek war's glory.

Everyone said spring was two weeks late that year. It arrived with a serene splendor and a vibrant clarity that made one pause by the river to take a deep breath, allowing it to escape ever so slowly, as if to affirm the flow of life. Spring floods covered the river rapids, deceptively hiding the current and turbulence that lay beneath the surface. Looking downriver, I could count at least seven shades of green, ranging from the darkest symmetrical spruce, to the towering chaotic white pines, to the still pale elms and oaks, their leaves just now unraveling. The trunks of the white birch were dazzling; reflected in the still river pools and set against the darkened undergrowth, they served to draw the eye upward to the glory of the forest crown where the waves of green were underscored by the startling reds of the freshly sprouted maple leaves, appearing like red splotches dripped across the green canopy. White-flowered dogwoods, surviving in sheltered coves, played off of the birches. The fragrance of the lilac drifted easily among the trees, further sweetening the tranquility, and the lilac color predicted precisely the hue of the wild iris, which would blossom soon enough along the riverbank. Early spring wildflowers, the red and white trilliums, the yellow marsh marigolds, and the spotted trout lilies added sparkle to the foreground. In a few weeks I would be able to find my favorite, the timid yellow lady's slipper, hiding below the white pines. Beyond the river, the eastern pastures were marked with thousands upon thousands of dandelions, combining to form yellow migrating waves, rippling across the fields, to surround the vibrant greens of clover and grass. A few cows grazed tranquilly near the river while, further off, a pair of draft horses plowed the new earth, their drifting silhouette further accented by the backdrop of virginal white apple blossoms glittering in the sunlight. High pastures ringed with stone walls extended up into the eastern hills, their outline softened against the sky by supple new tree growth sprouting over the placid slopes. The stone walls of each pasture and the crest of each hill seductively beckoned, Come here, climb up to me, climb up to me. Never before had I experienced, or, perhaps it was simply that never before had I noticed, spring colors of such magnificence. This year they were equal to those of autumn.

Grandmother's lovingly cultivated gardens could not compete. The tulips and daffodils arranged among the lilacs and flowering crabapples, the interesting paths leading through the boxwoods, the inviting archways covered in fragrant wisteria, the carefully placed garden sculpture, and the central fountain, all drew well-earned praise, but I would not choose time in her yard above an afternoon picnic at the knoll, or a canoe ramble on the river.

This peaceful spring was still fresh when we gathered for graduation in June, wearing long pastel dresses and solemn suits of gray and black. The graduates donned long black gowns, which failed to cover their gay spirits. The class of 1915, the class of Jonathan and my cousin Anna, and many other of my friends, had no real fear of separation. Some were off to college, but mostly to Massachusetts schools, and they had plans to return to Birkett Ferry after their studies. That had always been the pattern. Many would stay to work locally, to marry, and to attend the graduation of their own children in twenty years' time. There was no threat to us in the death-strewn trenches of Europe.

The graduation speaker, a Roosevelt disciple, droned on about the lack of foresight, the lack of preparedness, and the lack of energy in our national leadership. "It is comforting to think that we might escape this war, but to not even prepare for the possibility of war, to not even prepare for our own defense, to bury our heads in the sand when we should be dominant on the world stage, this is the height of irresponsibility, and a betrayal of all of our citizens, but especially a betrayal of the generation represented by these fine graduates before us today. I urge each of you graduates to be ready for the glorious fight that surely awaits you." His words were of far greater interest to the adults in the audience. Some, like Grandfather, felt he was surely right; others, like Father, felt that Wilson's peaceful strategy would prove successful. Both of those generations felt the foreboding threat, but we were oblivious. The speaker's warning had the same impact on us as a parental admonition to begin our assigned summer English reading in July. And then, as he relentlessly continued, his words diffused outward beyond our hearing, borne away on the lightening breeze and the constant river currents, losing in competition with the pervading scent of narcissus that fed our daydreams. Our musings did not extend beyond our plans for evening celebration.

Jonathan had been hired by Mr. Bryden, who promised there would be enough farm work to carry him through the winter. He had reattached himself to my cousin, Anna, or perhaps it was the other way around. Anna took a job at the grocer's, so I supposed they would see a good bit of one another.

I went out with other boys occasionally, but I spent a good deal of time alone and with Matt. I read more, and wrote to Douglas and Kevin. I found Grandmother's salons more interesting. When they discussed literature and poetry, some of the ideas were useful in my correspondence with Kevin. But when the discourse veered to the political, and dissolved, as it usually did, into a debate on war preparedness, I would either lose interest or become embarrassed at the increasing vehemence of Father's antiwar position. He was spending more and more time with the writings of pacifists. He joined the struggle against war preparedness, opposing any plan that might increase the size of the army, or require military training for young men. I don't think his law practice suffered either from neglect (although he did devote significant time to his correspondence and reading) or from client anger at his political positions (his desire to avoid war was still a majority opinion in 1915). But it did put him at increasing odds with Grandfather. They both became incapable of rational political discussion.

"All young men would benefit from time spent training. Six months or a year would strengthen them, improve their minds, teach them respect and self-discipline."

"Yes, it would scrape away all individuality, leaving a compliant mind and body for the state to mold as it would. For sacrifice to the

European war, just as workers are sacrificed for the financial gains of the large trusts and corporations."

Neither would avoid the debate; they both became more entrenched, more resentful of the other's diatribe, and more irritated that their own opinions were not heard. Their arguments reflected the discord in the country, where pacifists and hawks each considered the other to be the essence of treason.

Matt remained oblivious to the turmoil as he read his books and walked the woods and hills through that fine spring. I didn't feel guilty in July, when I left him for my Cambridge summer. Mother was teary at my departure; Father was busy with work and politics.

I found Becky and Michael subdued in their opinions. They tended to agree with President Wilson and with Father that war avoidance was the best plan, but they also seemed to know that future events could easily change this course.

"What bothers me," Michael worried, "is the amount of arms we're sending to Britain and France. How can we claim neutrality while supplying the tools of war?"

"I'm sure we won't stop the shipments," Becky added, "not with the handsome profits our companies are making."

"And that may draw us into the fight. The Germans will continue to sink our ships—from their point of view it makes sense to stop the arms shipments—and that will soon wear out our patience."

"And does our government plan it that way?" Becky wondered.

"No, I don't think so, not Wilson . . ."

"Perhaps not Wilson, but what of those who are pushing for war preparation and a stronger military? What of Roosevelt, and what of the munitions makers?"

"Well yes, there are those who would have had us in the war a year ago. Wilson is holding fast for now, but he can't resist forever. It's far easier to be a war-maker than a peacemaker."

I had arrived in Cambridge late one afternoon, and the following morning, just after we opened the bookstore, Kevin walked in. I smiled to see his gray coat riding high at the wrists and his pants hanging loosely at the rear. And I was very glad to see him. He directed a wide grin at me while greeting Becky.

"Why Kevin, it is such a pleasure. It's strange though," Becky rubbed her chin, "I think we've seen you not at all this spring, and yet here you are, just as Gwen has arrived. What a pleasant coincidence."

Kevin blushed, "Well, actually, Gwen had written of her arrival . . ."

"Oh, did she now!"

I came from behind the counter wondering if he would embrace me, but he held out his hand. My first faithful correspondent. We had written of poets and authors, of school and teachers, of life and war. We had, of course, not written of love. I could have been easily in awe of him. He was four years my senior and had successfully negotiated three years of college to define a career direction. And to some extent I was in awe, but his shy social ineptitude brought us into more even balance.

Later that afternoon, we strolled along the Charles. Kevin's thoughts centered not so much on what the country should or should not do to prepare for war; his concerns lay with what he, as an individual, should do. It was important to him to define "right" and "wrong," but he was equally moved by motives of adventure and glory.

"I think this is our time, Gwen. We won't get another chance."

"Another chance?"

"Remember how we shared Alan Seeger's writing this spring. And if you read the classics of Rome and Greece, they also speak of the noble fight, the glorious battle."

"This isn't like knights on white steeds. This isn't a crusade."

"They say the experience of combat will stay with you through the rest of your life."

I suspected this was true, but not always in the positive fashion that Kevin imagined. While I knew that Father's war experience was not pleasant, he had not articulated the negative effects of his war. Perhaps, if he had, I could have argued this point with Kevin.

Kevin continued, "Imagine how the people of Belgium and France need our help." True, the atrocity stories had penetrated even to my level of attention. "Some of the seniors, just graduated, and even some of the undergraduates are going over to enlist with the British and French. Some to fight, and some to join the ambulance crews."

"Kevin, are you thinking of that?"

"Maybe, I don't know. It's all so glorious though." He pulled a folded paper from his pocket. "Here—something for you to read. It's Alan Seeger's latest article from *The Sun.*"

Written by Seeger at the end of April 1915, the piece was initially upbeat, describing the relative luxury of periodic rotation from the trenches to the rear. But then, in describing a night patrol, even as his prose soared, his imagery horrified.

> To escape from the eternal confinement of the trenches, to stalk out into the perilous zone between the lines and there where death may lurk in every thicket and uncertainty encompasses one close as the night, to court danger for several hours under a fine starlit sky, this is the one breath of true romance that we get in the monotonous routine of trench warfare . . . The night was warm and windless. There were fruit trees all about this part of the hillside. They were clouded with bloom . . . But another odor as we advanced mingled with that of the blossoms, an odor that, congealed all through the winter, is becoming more and more intense and pervasive as the warm weather increases. Among the breaths of April, fragrant of love and the rebirth of life, it intrudes, the sickening antithesis—pungent, penetrating, exciting to madness and ferocity, as the other to tenderness and desire—the odor of carrion and of death.

His patrol was crawling through contested fields among corpses left unburied for the past seven months. "Frenchmen and Germans alike, rigid bundles of soaked cloth, filling the thickets, sodden into the muddy beet fields, bare and exposed . . . The sight is one which may well be unnerving the first time, but one soon gets used to it . . ." Thus spoke the prose inspiring the college men to yearn for battle.

That's what surprised me. At my high school no one cared about the war one way or the other. Here at Harvard, it was the main topic of conversation, and many saw it in the same terms as Kevin.

Douglas had other concerns. He did not want the war to interfere with his life. We sat sipping tea and savoring chocolate cake at a shaded sidewalk café on one of the quieter Cambridge streets lined with giant elms.

"I hope Wilson holds his ground. It bothers me, these people who want to require military training for all of us. I don't want to spend a year marching around and setting up tents."

"My grandfather, the one in Birkett Ferry, worries that we're completely unprepared. He says our army is only one-tenth the size of Germany's."

"Your grandfather and Roosevelt too. If he had won the election, we'd already be at war. I'd be in the army along with all my friends."

"Not if you didn't want to be in the army."

"There's always the draft. Like in the Civil War."

"But why restart the draft? There would be a lot of volunteers."

"Don't fool yourself. There are some that talk boldly now, but I don't believe many would enlist voluntarily to sit in dreary trenches in France."

Douglas half raised his hand, but the waiter, hurrying off into the kitchen, missed the signal for more tea. Douglas scowled at his back, "Damn, it's a talent for them to turn about, just when you need something." Then, with an abrupt smile to me, "You should come to our parties. Those of us who are staying in Cambridge for the summer have vowed to get together every weekend. Sometimes a picnic, sometimes an evening party. It's great fun. Lots of college people. Lots of food. Lots of beer and liquor, too."

"I don't know. I'd need to ask my grandparents. They'll say I'm only seventeen."

"Oh, hell! What's the difference? A year from now you'll be in college anyway. There are people your age who are fighting and dying in Europe. And who knows? I may soon be among them. I say, enjoy life while you can."

Chapter 10
1915

Soon after I left Birkett Ferry, Mother wrote that she too would be spending the summer with Becky and Michael. I assumed she and Father had fought again. I chafed at her arrival, worried that others would imagine she felt I was in need of another chaperone. When I asked why Matt was not with her, she said he would travel to Cambridge in early August on his own. I never would have been permitted such a solo trip at age fourteen.

It wasn't difficult for Mother and Becky to guess that I was annoyed by their presence, so they would leave, arms linked, humming together or giggling over some shared remembrance, to shop and stroll on the Cambridge streets. One afternoon, they bustled into the bookstore with assorted paints, canvas, and easels. Mother was thrilled to have a willing companion, and from that day, Michael and I were assigned to staff the bookstore from opening until early afternoon to allow the painters the advantage of morning light. They would usually position themselves in the shade of an oak, by a bend in the Charles, with views both upstream and down. They painted river scenes: an elegant sailboat moving through dazzling sunlight, wind-whipped, blackened clouds in the distance; a pair of rowers sitting improbably high off the water, moving effortlessly backward, captured at the moment of emergence from the dark archway of a stone bridge, the slanting rays of the summer sun caressing their youthful faces.

They preferred to paint outdoors, but on dreary days they set their easels in the kitchen. Becky's compositions were those of a beginner. "She just has more Impressionistic tendencies," Michael joked. "She's simply ahead of her time." I had to admire the creative spunk shared by Becky and Mother. It made me wonder if Mother and I would ever attain that degree of ease. It would certainly not happen that summer as we argued over curfews and rules.

"These are mostly all people I met last year. I'm sure it's okay."

"Yes, I'm sure, but they are several years older than you."

"I'm seventeen. Next summer I'll be off to college anyway, and I'll be with whomever I please."

"Next summer, but not yet. I have just two requests: that you are back by ten, and that you not walk alone after dark."

"This brings back such memories!" Becky tried to control her smirk. "I can hear the echoes of the same discussion, the same words spoken right in this kitchen some twenty years ago. Some of the actors are the same, though the roles have shifted."

"Mother, please, I'm just trying to . . ."

"And," Becky continued, "if memory serves, the stubbornness of youth finally prevailed, but only after a protracted battle."

I loved my grandmother; how was it that she was so much more understanding than Mother?

"And if my memory serves," Mother turned to Becky, "there was no interference from your mother."

We compromised. I could stay out until eleven and I agreed to have an escort home. Later Mother went to buy groceries, leaving Becky and me in the store. "Thanks for your help, Grandma."

"Just don't let me down. Use your sense."

I suspected that Mother and Becky preferred Kevin, so it was always more fun to have Douglas call for me. He was unfailingly polite.

"Flowers for your table, Mrs. Sherwood. And, Mr. Sherwood, I brought the reading lists for some Harvard courses. I copied them from friends. I thought it would help you stock for the fall."

"Why, thank you, Douglas, that's very thoughtful." Michael didn't mention that they'd had the same lists since May. After all, they had run the bookstore for nearly forty years.

We walked hand in hand, passing through Harvard Square as it throbbed with Saturday night energy. Douglas waved and shouted to a surprising number of people. We stopped several times for introductions, and to compare notes about evening activities. His friends carried an air of social privilege that I found attractive. Their sophistication made me question the adequacy of my own background.

We entered a quiet street where a history professor, on sabbatical, had left his home in the care of two graduate students, friends of Douglas. The party spilled from the wood-paneled living room, where students mingled and gossiped, through the busy kitchen and into the backyard. Moonlight danced through two giant elms to speckle the lawn. Scattered groups talked and laughed while lounging on blankets or sitting at tables. They sipped beer drawn from a keg in the corner of the yard, or sampled gin and tonics prepared in the kitchen and brought round on a tray.

There was talk of the war, as there was at every gathering. The majority still expected a short war, which would not involve the United States. But one articulate young man suggested that he was "bothered by what sounds like a stalemate in the trenches. I'm afraid that this may not be so brief a war."

"The French and the British, they're just waiting to gather enough men for a decisive battle. They'll overrun the German lines soon," said the dark-haired woman with the tray of gin and tonic.

"If we think the Allies are in the right, we should be there fighting by their side," spoke a woman, a Radcliffe junior. "That would be the way to ensure a short war, and a victory."

"Oh, that's a lark for you to suggest war, isn't it, when it's us men that will fight and die." I think Douglas meant this to be humorous, but no one smiled.

"Sacrifice is always necessary," the Radcliffe student said. "We'll do our part too. Some of the ambulance drivers in France are women."

"That's who I admire most: those who have already volunteered, like Alan Seeger." The dark-haired woman looked dreamily to the stars; her tray was now empty.

"Did you see his most recent report in *The Sun*?" The girl from Radcliffe spoke. "I think he's making the most gallant sacrifice. To be there in the midst of it! And to find the time and will to write such poetic words! Imagine."

Douglas looked skeptical. "But would you give up all this—friends, comfort, college—to live in muddy cold trenches, knowing that any day could be your last, that you could die in some useless charge up some desolate hill?"

There was a quick rebuttal from the Radcliffe student. "Of course I would give up comfort. Once you decide the right course, there is no place for cowardice."

Apparently, in this group, one could still question the legitimacy of entering the war, but once the war was judged to be the proper moral course, there was no room to consider personal safety. Rather it was time to call forth heroic deeds and sacrifice for the good of the world. I had almost voiced my doubts about Alan Seeger (after my conversations with Kevin I felt somewhat qualified to comment on Seeger's judgment), but I had been intimidated at the thought of addressing a group of older students unknown to me, who likely had discussed all this in the recent past. Now I was glad I held back, for I saw that those not seduced by the splendor and adventure of the war were apt to be labeled selfish cowards.

My first taste of beer was not particularly agreeable, and Douglas had only a moderate amount. We left the party with sufficient time to meet my curfew. Douglas, his arm about my waist, was thoughtful as we walked along the Charles River. A light eastern breeze brought gentle waves lapping in to shore. The quarter moon had set, bringing forth a starry brilliance that drew my eyes upward.

War, death, and muddy trenches seemed impossible in this peaceful scene, yet his thoughts had not left the party conversations. "My friends speak bravely, but we'll see who volunteers to fight if the time comes." I didn't respond and we walked on. When we stopped under an ancient riverside oak, he turned to face me, bringing his hand up to my breast and bringing his lips to mine. I gave his lips a quick peck, and brushed his hand aside. "Douglas, it's time for me to be home."

The next Sunday afternoon I was back at the Charles under the same old oak, seated on a scratchy brown blanket with Kevin. I insisted that the war not enter our conversation. "Just for this one afternoon," I pleaded. This rule allowed no talk of Seeger, but it also implied no talk of future plans, for any discussion of the future was qualified by the now ubiquitous phrase, "unless the war intervenes." For a while we discussed poetry, but I thought our current selection too depressing.

I pointed to the nearby bridge with its series of three arches over the river. "That's the spot where we met Hezekiah when Matt and I were little." I related the story of the homeless boy and his family, thought by Mother to be too dangerous or too dirty to acknowledge. Michael had disagreed, bringing them food and allowing our friendship.

When I finished, Kevin paused to stare at the river, taking in the progress of an eight-oared shell emerging from the center archway of the bridge. "That's really it, isn't it? Helping others in need. Perhaps taking a bit of a risk, but helping them anyway. Offering food, and protection, and even a measure of freedom."

Likely, he itched to draw the parallel with the war but, honoring our agreement, he held back. While I admired his commitment to his principles and his willingness to sacrifice, I wasn't ready to abandon my concerns about the war. I found Father's arguments difficult to refute. Maybe I should listen more closely to his debates with Grandfather, especially now that I realized the dispute had engaged campuses throughout the country.

Father stayed in Birkett Ferry that summer, so it was just the five of us traveling to Hastings Beach. I offered to stay in Cambridge to keep the bookstore open, but Mother laughed and speculated that with me in charge, "the store would have unusual hours and unusual patrons." I didn't want to leave Cambridge and Kevin and Douglas, even for a week. After the beach, I would have only a couple of weeks left, and those weeks would be the busiest for the store.

But I was soon seduced by the lazy beach rhythm. Waking under the light sheets, stretching, ambling to the kitchen to collect fruit, bread, and tea, moving to the porch where I could smell the salty air, I would look out to the ocean where the glare of the sun silhouetted a lone beach umbrella. The haze blurred and twinkled the light, inviting a dreamlike journey out onto the beach, where the eastern breeze rustled my long white nightgown and rippled my hair, and the cool moist sand clung to my feet. I imagined myself Guinevere, sneaking off to meet Lancelot. There was no sound save for the rhythmic crashing of the waves, and the harsh cry of unseen gulls. And there was no sight save for the beach umbrella shimmering in the glare, and becoming more sharply defined at my approach.

Under the umbrella were two seated figures facing the ocean and reaching out to their easels. The spell was not entirely broken, even as Becky and Mother glanced up to smile a soft greeting when I sat on the damp sand beside them.

"Gwen, sit on this." Mother offered a beige blanket. "It would keep you dry. Aren't you cold in that nightgown?"

"Leave the poor girl alone," Becky smiled. "Can't you see she's still in a dream?"

I looked at Becky curiously. "I did feel like I was in a dream; like I was Guinevere."

Mother didn't try to contain her laughter. "A sleepwalking Guinevere all right, right here on our beach, carrying her mug of tea with her." I glanced down at the forgotten cup, and could not help joining the laughter.

They returned to their work and I looked back toward the house, its white clapboards gleaming. Matt was still likely abed, while Michael read on the porch. And the three of us on the beach, three generations, watching the waves crash through the glare to bring a fine mist around us, we felt a fleeting closeness that one does not speak of, one cannot speak of, where the meaning and purpose of life are clear. But the knowledge lasts for ever so brief a time. It is as if we are in a dream where the mystery is solved and we vow, even while asleep, not to forget and yet that is exactly what happens when we wake.

Chapter 11
1915

Matt and Mother returned to Birkett Ferry soon after our return to Cambridge. Two weeks later, as I rode west to join them, I had to consider the summer a success. I had established a degree of independence from my family, I had work experience and a small savings, and I was judged to be an interesting companion by two college men who, I suspected, also found me attractive. Kevin would continue to write to me, and Douglas, perhaps, would think of me from time to time.

Arriving in Springfield, I discovered there was to be a lengthy delay before the departure of the northbound train. "Derailment near Northampton . . . Got to clear the tracks . . . Five hours at least," the ticket agent explained. While I was not particularly anxious to be home, I was not interested in sitting around the dingy station for hours on end. I thought about phoning home, but calls were difficult to place, and I imagined Mother would be given the same information at the Birkett Ferry station. I brought out my book and tried to concentrate before deciding I needed a walk. Surely there would be a park or some place of interest to explore. I checked my luggage and paused at the station door, debating whether to turn left or right. I considered returning to the baggage counter, but would have felt silly asking, "Where does one go in Springfield?" The name "Springfield" reminded me that I did have one Springfield connection, albeit a rather tenuous one. My gradeschool teacher, Miss Robbins, lived here, or at least used to live here. I had her listed in my address book. Of course I had never written, and had not seen her since—I stopped to think—since December of my sixth-grade year. It had been more than five years! How many students had come and gone in her life since then? Would she remember me or have any interest in seeing me?

I pulled the address from my purse and asked directions. "You'll find that street five or six blocks down, Miss." A baggage carrier pointed south. "It's a short walk." I strolled up the elm-lined street seeking shade against the building August heat. The city streets were nearly empty; the stifling, windless day must have discouraged others from venturing out. As I turned onto Miss Robbins's street, well-landscaped homes with wide lawns and inviting porches gave way to townhouse-style buildings with tiny front yards and white picket fences, and the grand old elms were replaced by a smattering of younger maples and oaks. Two blocks along, I paused at her gate to double-check the number, and to plot what I might say to her. As I started to enter, a voice interceded.

"You won't find her at home, now." A man stood shaded under the maple at the corner of her lot, poking his pipe, eyeing me curiously.

"Oh," I stammered, "I didn't see you."

In spite of the heat, his dark jacket hung comfortably on his lanky frame. He held a topcoat over his arm and a light valise stood by his side. He was a few inches taller than me with clean-shaven cheeks that appeared thin or even gaunt. A smirk played across his lips as if he held a secret. His dark eyes reflected the sparkle of the sunlight, and his black hair was thick and unruly.

He seemed to be waiting for an explanation, so I continued to sputter, "I just stopped to see Miss Robbins. Is this her . . ."

"Yes," he interrupted with a smile, "she lives here." Again he paused, waiting for me to continue.

"Well, I've come round to see her . . ."

"Yes, you've just said that."

Why should I bear the burden of this conversation? "I'm a former student of hers. I didn't want to cause any inconvenience. I just thought it would be nice to chat."

"I'm sure she will love to see you."

Another silence. "Oh, I'm Gwen, Gwen Compston." Was that what he was waiting for? And shouldn't he have been the first to offer an introduction?

"And I am Marshall Robbins."

"You are married to her?" My awkward discomfort added to my confusion as I rushed in without thinking, then realized my error. "No, you couldn't have the same name . . ."

He laughed. "No, not likely . . . Though it would be theoretically possible I suppose . . . No, you see, I am her brother, hence the same name." I thought his manner a bit disarming. His eyes gazed directly into mine.

"Are you certain she's not at home?"

"Well, you don't suppose I'd just stand around in this heat if I had another option, do you?" I decided he was not rude, just direct. And he was quite attractive.

Again, I needed to fill in the gap, "And you've no key then?" I cringed at yet another useless question, but he allowed it to pass.

"No, I tried the door a moment before you arrived. I was just trying to decide a course of action when your approach captured my interest."

"Oh, well, you see, my train has been delayed and I thought it would be nice . . ."

"And I had just about decided to adjourn to a little café round the corner. I don't suppose you'd care to join me? I know they have excellent lemonade."

"That would be lovely." As we headed up the block I thought my quick acceptance of his invitation too bold, but probably not dangerous. He was, after all, the brother of Miss Robbins.

"Was my sister expecting you?"

"No, not at all. It was just that my train has been delayed, at least five hours, and I realized she lives close by."

"She didn't expect me either, or not until later in the week. I think she'll be back soon. Maybe she's gone round to be sure her classroom is set for opening next week. If she hasn't returned in a bit, we can check the school. Now where are you off to?"

At the mention of Birkett Ferry, he stopped in midstride to turn to me, but it was only a moment before he recovered. "Yes, of course . . . the train, where else? To Birkett Ferry . . . I should have put that together."

As we sipped our lemonade he asked about my schooling and my summer in Cambridge and my future plans. I learned that he was twenty-three, "ten years junior to your former teacher," and that he had just graduated from Amherst College where he "found the education to be quite adequate and the town to be quite provincial . . . I am ready to live in Boston or New York." He explained that he was returning from the Adirondacks, "from Plattsburgh in fact, on Lake Champlain. You know, perhaps, about the training camps there?"

I shrugged.

"Oh, well, they've gotten a bit of publicity, and I thought in Cambridge you might have heard something. They've organized these camps to train officers. Part of the Preparedness Movement. There is a strong feeling at Amherst that we've done nothing to prepare for war . . ."

"Yes, I do know about that."

"Well anyway, the camps have a great deal of support from people like Roosevelt, and the business sector, and the military. They feel we must do more to prepare, at least to have a group of trained officers ready. I think every male should be required to have some training, but the government won't endorse that, not yet anyway."

"Same debates we're having in Cambridge. I wasn't familiar with the camps though."

"Well, it certainly toughened me up; I lost a bit of weight too."

"Have you read Alan Seeger?" I wanted to show my knowledge.

"Sure, we passed around his articles at Plattsburgh. If the U.S. takes much longer to join the war, I—and a lot of others—may follow his example and enlist with the French."

I hesitated to share my opinion about the war. How had my judgment become so divergent from that of my peers? I just did not grasp the glory of sitting in cramped, rat-infested holes, waiting to get shot. There was some sense of mystical adventure infecting my generation which seemed to mask that reality. Finally I managed, "I don't really understand all the attraction. If you've read Seeger, you know about the horrors and the death."

"Sometimes that's what it takes."

The August heat continued to build as we walked back to the apartment. Miss Robbins must have seen our approach. She flew out the door into the arms of her brother. "Marshall, Marshall, it's so good . . . what a surprise . . . I didn't expect you yet. Oh, I'm so glad." She opened her embrace to hold him at arm's length, studying his face for a moment before turning to me, smiling. "Are you going to introduce us, Marshall?"

I realized that she thought me Marshall's girl, perhaps the latest in a string of girls. I thought him too hasty in correcting her misconception. "No, no, she is a former student of yours."

Miss Robbins studied my face.

"From Birkett Ferry," he added.

Her smile faded but there was no recognition.

"Miss Robbins, I am Gwen Compston. Remember?"

"Why Gwen, I didn't know . . ." I have never seen anyone pale so quickly. Her brother instinctively grabbed her arm as her knees buckled.

"Please Cindy, sit here." Marshall eased her down onto the front steps where she bent forward, her head almost at knee level. Marshall and I exchanged confused glances.

She whispered almost to herself, "He said he would tell you at some point, but I didn't know." Now she looked up with forced composure. "Gwen, I'm sorry I didn't know you were coming or I would have been better prepared. You've come to see Nick then."

"Nick?" I had no idea what was happening here.

"He didn't tell you his name? Gwen, Nick is your half brother."

"What?"

"Her half brother?"

Our combined exclamations further blanched Miss Robbins. Marshall stared at me with dawning recognition. "You are his daughter then . . . I think we'd all best go inside now." He helped his sister up the steps and through the door.

We were barely inside the door when a lively child of five came bounding down the stairs jumping from the third step directly at Marshall, completely trusting that his uncle would look up in time to snatch him from the air. "Uncle Marshall, Uncle Marshall!"

"Nick, it's wonderful to see you." He swung the boy twice around, holding his face at his own face level, their laughter twirling about the room with them.

"Nick, I would like you to meet Miss Gwen Compston. Your mother taught her a few years ago up in Birkett Ferry."

"She's too old for Mom to teach!"

"Ah, but she was younger then, and do you know what? Before that, she was exactly your age."

"Hello Nick, it is nice to meet you." I barely managed to speak although Nick's exuberance did serve to relax the tension. I had yet to comprehend that I was a closer blood relative to Nick than was Uncle Marshall.

Marshall was rummaging through his valise, "I tell you what, Nick; I believe there is something of interest here for you."

"What is it!" Nick crouched next to Marshall and started pawing through the suitcase.

"Ah, here it is." Marshall swiftly hid it behind his back. "I didn't have paper to wrap it."

Nick ran to his back. "A baseball!"

"Yes, and a very special one, too. You'll see it's a tad scuffed. This is one of the actual balls we used at camp, that is, when we weren't training and marching and all. Do you like it?"

"Thanks, Uncle Marshall."

My mind was whirring to such an extent that I had barely witnessed the scene. It must have been the same for Miss Robbins. But now she managed a smile to Nick. "What a lovely present. I think you and your Uncle Marshall should take that ball out back right now to try it out."

"I was just about to suggest the same thing." Marshall scrutinized us carefully. "Right, then. We'll be just outside if you need us. Let's go Nick."

"Gwen, I didn't want it to be like this. When I realized who you were, I just assumed your father had told you everything . . . although surely he would have let me know to expect a visit."

I still was not able, or perhaps not willing, to comprehend. I sat silently while she related the story from the time of her arrival in Birkett Ferry, the quartet, the "unfortunate mutual attraction" with my father. My mind refused to absorb much of what she said, but the outline was clear. I began to cry when I remembered how I had introduced them the night we met to ice-skate at the cove. She touched my shoulder and then continued. "I delivered Nick at a home for unwed mothers in New York. When I returned to Springfield my parents helped set me up in this townhouse. They told their friends that my husband had died in a shipping accident just after Nick was born. And your father helped too, of course. He has been quite the gentleman, all things considered. So here we have lived, Nick and I. Last year, when Nick started school, I was able to get a job at his school, fifth grade again. It all works quite nicely." She looked exhausted.

"Do you and my Father still see . . .?"

"Once in a while . . . once or twice a year he comes by to see Nick . . . and me . . . when he has legal work here. But," she hastened to add, "we no longer . . . are intimate." She went to the window to check on Marshall and Nick. "One more thing: Nick doesn't know Will is his father. He could never keep it secret. I plan to tell him at some point, just as your father planned to tell you and Matt—and your mother—at some point."

"My mother doesn't know either?"

"No . . . at least I think not."

Weariness hung in the air. But a moment later the screen door slammed.

"We need water!" Nick ran to the faucet.

"It is hot out there." Marshall eyed us both with concern.

Nick was already at the cupboard, his pure movement sweeping the stale air from the room.

"Nick, let me help. Bring me the crackers." Miss Robbins rose to slice cheese and apples.

I studied my half brother and saw Matt at the age of five. Possibly I was forcing the comparison, but there was the same lightly freckled nose and upper cheeks, the same green eyes, the same light brown hair with just a whisper of red. As he whirled around the kitchen I decided that his energy level surpassed Matt's, but maybe I had just forgotten the activity of a five-year-old. Even in my state, I had to acknowledge that he was a delight.

Later, as I prepared to leave, she posed the obvious question. "Will you tell your father or mother?"

"I just don't know, Miss Robbins. It's all a bit much right now."

"Please, I think you should call me Cindy. If you do decide to speak with them, it would be a kindness to let me know. I don't think it would jeopardize my job, but I would like to be prepared. I'm sorry, Gwen."

"Me too . . . Cindy."

Marshall insisted on walking me to the station. We were quiet while waiting for the train. At one point he ventured, "Are you okay?" I nodded and attempted a smile.

As I boarded the train, I managed to speak, "Listen, I'm sorry I haven't been much of a conversationalist. I appreciate your company. It's just that . . ."

"I understand."

On that late August day, I had none of my usual interest in the passing scenery. I stared blankly out the window, indifferent to the harvest scenes I generally found so entrancing: men, tired and content, climbing down from carriages laden with grain and vegetables, rinsing their arms, bare chests, and faces in the river, trudging back to their homes where children rushed out to jump in their arms, and wives waved from the stoop before returning inside to check on the roasts and potatoes and pies, their aromas surely passing through the train windows. It all seemed so futile. What was the purpose, really? I felt more akin to the occasional hobo camped alone under the willows by the river, his solitary form bent over a smoky flame, making do with some pilfered carrots and corn. But then I decided that even he was more content than me. As the train churned farther north along the river, the summer greenery was marked with the earliest autumn changes, especially in the marshy areas where the swamp vegetation and surrounding maples were now turning a vibrant crimson. This sight usually thrilled me. That day I would have welcomed the dull, dreary browns and grays of late November.

Mother met me at the station, all smiles and liveliness. As she wrapped me in her arms, I lay my head to her shoulder, suddenly shuddering with unexpected sobs.

"Why, what is it? What's wrong?" She tried to hold me at arm's length to see my face, but I resisted, keeping my face burrowed into her neck. She led me away from the bustling crowd to a side bench. My sobbing waned in a few minutes, but I did not lift my head until I could plan what to say.

Mother sighed deeply, perhaps enjoying, I now realize, the parent's need to be needed, and reliving all those traumatic childhood moments when I, or Matt, needed comfort. I was ready when she again murmured, "Gwen, what is the trouble?"

"Oh Mother," my voice still quivering, "nothing really. I'm happy to see you and be home, but I'll miss Cambridge so much."

She must have thought to herself, All this over that? Surely there is some other explanation—which of those boys is it? But she continued to speak soothingly, "Well then, that's it. Just one more year. Then you'll be off to college or Cambridge or something new."

Chapter 12
1915–16

The speech given by Teddy Roosevelt that autumn of 1915 did nothing to ease the tension between Father and Grandfather. The ex-president, very popular with my college friends, berated the Wilson administration. "Every young man just leaving college . . . ought to feel it incumbent on him at this time either to try to render some assistance to those who are battling for the right on behalf of Belgium, or else . . . to help his own country if in the future she is attacked as wantonly as Belgium has been attacked. The United States has played a most ignoble part for the last thirteen months. Our government . . . has declined to take action for justice and right . . . has refused to protect its own citizens; and . . . refused even to prepare for its own defense."

"Exactly the way I would have said it," Grandfather exulted.

"Most of the men I know at Harvard would agree, too." After my summer in Cambridge, I had more interest in the war. After my day in Springfield, I had more interest in opposing my father.

"I know the country will come around," continued Grandfather. "If we must be led by our youth, so be it!"

I mentioned the man who had trained at the Plattsburgh camps. When Grandfather eagerly asked for details, I repeated Marshall's brief descriptions, irritated with myself for not having obtained more information. I let them assume the meeting had been in Cambridge.

Father listened carefully but continued to insist that neutrality was best, that our entrance into the war would accomplish nothing more than to add to the misery of Europe, and that those who were advocating war had only financial interests at heart.

"I don't think college students have many financial interests," Grandfather countered.

"The students have been bamboozled, hypnotized by tales of glory.

And besides, many of them do come from families who would benefit financially . . ."

"It's more they feel the pulse of patriotism."

"Well, thank God that Wilson stands firm for neutrality."

But by November, Wilson had begun to shift gears. While still advocating neutrality, he announced his support for some aspects of war preparedness, including a buildup of the armed forces. Wilson's "abandonment of the cause" served to further radicalize Father and the pacifist groups with which he was spending more and more time.

I said nothing of my day in Springfield to Mother, Father, or Matt. What could I say? I could see no benefit to any of us. Nearly all of Father's time away from work (and perhaps quite a bit of his work time) was taken up by antiwar activity, and, if he thought of it at all, he would have attributed the increasing distance in our relationship to his absence.

Mother, assuming my aloofness a teenage phase, tried to make light. "It's a wonder you can get through the day without a word to us!" I'm sure she hoped for a smile or a laugh or a retort or any response, but she received only an irritated sigh, or a silent stare, followed by a slammed door. Did she share any blame for Father's affair? Perhaps if she had been more careful of her marital relationship, more loving, more attentive, and, yes, more suspicious, it could have been avoided. I knew this wasn't fair, but on some level I did think her culpable. And she did share a history—there was her liaison with André. But did Father know of her Paris romance? Had he seen the contents of the trunk? And, if so, did he see his own affair as justified—some sort of revenge for her behavior?

And I drove myself to distraction with other questions about the affair: questions of why it happened, how it happened, where it happened. The imagined scenes were disgusting and threatened to turn my stomach on the long, wakeful nights when I stared from my bed, through the unwashed window and past the windswept barren oaks to the dreary sky, all light of moon and star barred by cloud. Attempting at times to divert my mind, I forced my attention to Douglas and Kevin, but this took my thoughts to the war and the boys of my generation in Europe. Just how does one pass a night such as this, an agonized, sleepless night, in the frozen dark trenches? Each man was crammed so tightly between his comrades that there was not room to stretch out an arm or a leg for hours and nights on end, and yet each was terribly all alone, entombed with his agony. What hope was there, really?

There was no relief from worry in my usual outlets. I saw Jonathan occasionally when Mr. Bryden sent him to town for winter supplies or when he had a free afternoon. He had grown more attractive, his newly strengthened arm and chest muscles evident beneath his shirt, his skin darkened by the sun, and his hair and beard darkened by maturity. We spoke briefly, but he was always anxious to get to the store to see Anna, and there was speculation they would marry. School seemed tedious, providing more time for unwelcome daydreams. Even my relationship with Matt suffered as a result of the secret I was keeping from him. The secret and its ramifications were so vital and complex that I felt deceitful when with him.

I did receive some distraction from the rare notes from Douglas, and from the frequent letters from Kevin, correspondence to which I now found myself less faithful. But I did derive support, and even some joy, from Marshall's letters, perhaps because they were so unexpected, at least initially, and perhaps because he was one of the few people who shared the secret. I was mystified by the first letter, the return address showing origin from a Martin Roberts in Cambridge.

"I hope you do not mind the false name on the envelope. I thought it best to camouflage my name that would otherwise be so recognizable to your father, and perhaps also to your mother. Please advise if you wish me to correct this.

"I do hope all is well with you. I know you have been through a difficult ordeal. If there is anything I can do to help, I hope you will call upon me . . . The listed address is correct and, if you wish, you can write to me, using either name."

I quickly responded. I soon heard back from him.

"I am so grateful for your letter and I am gladdened that your spirits are in positive rebound. I admire your strength. I want you to know that I very much enjoyed your company that afternoon in Springfield. I feel badly that the day was subsequently so marred . . . I would like to stay in contact with you, if that is also your desire."

January brought repeated snows, covering fields, hills, and river in a luxuriously deep tapestry of the finest powder. The wind came from the north day after day, blowing snow onto the vulnerable sides of trees and homes so that when one stood looking to the south there were scant human landmarks to give perspective. There were only deceptive shades of white and gray, continuously changing in the dim winter light, blurred by the persistent flurries and the determined wind that piled drifts to the second-floor windows and buried the repeatedly shoveled walks. Travel was impossible save by sled or snowshoe. Automobiles were kept in barns with the horses, both useless in the face of these drifts. Trains stopped for two weeks or more. Even the river was not flat and predictable; rather its unstable topography of snow hills and valleys shifted hourly as the wind cleared the surface down to ice, before the next blast brought a new mountain of snow. The gusty frigid air prevented any thaw that might have marred the elegant snow surface with melting slush or rain. At night when the winds would calm, a snow-muffled quiet descended on our town, completing the isolation.

Father and Grandfather huffed at the inconvenience of not being able to travel, Grandfather to his business meetings, and Father to his political meetings. Mother savored our self-sufficiency. "We've got everything we need right here: jars of fruit and vegetables, dried meats, butter, eggs, and cheese. The store has months of provisions. Food and firewood, and," she glanced at me, "we have each other. What more do we need?"

Her warmth was not answered by Father. He grumbled into his breakfast, feeling marooned. And her warmth was not answered by Matt, still abed, stretching and rolling, then smiling to himself, before dozing off again, secure in the knowledge that school would not open that day, as it had not opened any day that week.

And her warmth was not answered by me as I laced on my boots. A pack stocked with bread, cheese, dried fruit, and writing paper rested by the door. I suppose she could not restrain herself. "Gwen, I'm not sure this is such a good idea."

"Mother!" I interrupted. My indignation roused Father.

"Marge, she'll be all right. She's been on the trails a thousand times. And the wind has let up today."

The wind had calmed. But low, brooding clouds defused the weak winter light to the same monotonous, dreary dimness, leaving only shadowless shades of gray, depriving the eye of depth and contrast, flattening together sky, hill, and field. There was no sound save the swish of my snowshoes through the powdery surface, followed by the lonely crunch of the cold, dry crystals compacting beneath my feet. I tested the depth with my pole: four feet, five feet in spots, and some drifts were, to my measure, bottomless. The landscape was devoid of all color save gray, or so I thought until gazing into the fissure left by my pole, I saw the palest icy blue, the very color of cold, floating up from the depths. Repeated probes made me wonder at the origin of this color sprouting from the desolate land; its presence gave faint hope, the promise of spring—of iris and lilac. When I stopped walking, the enveloping silence was stunning. No wind rustled the branches, no birds called out, no water dripped or flowed, no town noise penetrated the snow-muffled quiet.

Gradually my spirit lifted, aided by the exertion of the climb to the knoll. It was a strange sensation to be walking four feet above ground level, stooping under branches that were normally several feet above my head. The familiar trail became foreign. The massive erratic boulders were covered, leaving just a gentle mound of snow, and the huge trunks of oak and maple were hidden, emerging from the drifts as smaller trees, and the untracked trail was obscure, following a vague wandering space between the trees. The hardwood forest gave way to a grove of spruce; their sweeping green branches drooped to the ground with the weight of the snow, giving the appearance of symmetrical cones. Those spruce, so darkly muted in summer when surrounded by the lighter tinged hardwoods, now attained a vibrant green magnificence, in perfect contrast with the snow.

I noticed few tracks in the fresh snow. Squirrels had scampered about, and a lone raccoon had crisscrossed the trail. But after traversing the knoll I stopped to gaze back at my own passing. The line of snowshoe imprints, undulating down the slope to enter the cavern of spruce, offered an invitation to follow and explore. Each track, the interior crosshatch enclosed by a pleasing oval, skimmed the snow surface. The snow was so deep that the lake could have passed for meadow, only slightly more level than the surrounding area. The town and river were hidden by the cloudy haze that encompassed the knoll, insulating me from the rest of humanity. I used my snowshoes to fashion a seat on the stone foundation where I perched, mesmerized by the perfection of the spot. Only the wispy apple trees standing above the meadow, the barren oaks at the far end of the lake, and the lone maple at the near end stood out in this timeless realm, where earth and sky alike were cloaked in an ancient gray mist, punctured solely by my own meandering tracks.

I had envisioned myself resting on the knoll, composing heartfelt letters to Kevin and Marshall. I now readied pen and paper, certain of poetic inspiration, only to be distracted by this place of beauty. It was in this lake, now under a mass of snow and ice, where we rinsed the sweat and dirt from our summer bodies. It was on its banks that we regained the warmth of the sun. It was in that maple that Matt and I wove our stories. It was in those meadows that we found the spring flowers. It was from those untended trees that we harvested September apples. And it was from this foundation that we watched the dazzling autumn colors paint the entire landscape.

I lingered. The feeble January sunlight had not penetrated the thick cloud cover, making the passage of time difficult to mark. I preferred to walk while there was still light but I needed only to retrace my tracks. It was the numbing cold that eventually forced my departure. The dim light faded to complete darkness as I approached the edge of town. The glowing windows served only to make my homeward walk colder and blacker.

Mother's form disappeared from the window as I came up the steps. She tried to mask her relief at seeing me. "You must be ready for some hot tea!"

"Yes, but I can . . ."

"It's no bother. The water is hot on the stove; I've just had a cup myself." She was pouring steaming water before I had a chance to unlace my boots. "How was your walk?"

"Just fine." Did she want a complete description of my day?

"Oh, I nearly forgot: there are letters for you."

"Letters? But how did they get through?"

"I guess the tracks have been cleared to Greenfield, and the younger Phillips boy, well, he's not so young now—he's probably twenty-two— he had been in Greenfield and was headed home, so he packed in a mailbag." I hardly heard a word she said as I checked the return address-es, one from Kevin, and one from Martin Roberts.

"I've met Kevin, of course; he seems a fine boy. But who is this Martin?"

"He's the one who was at the army camps last summer." That's all I offered as I left the kitchen carrying the letters and my steaming mug. I knew she hoped I would plop down at the table, sip tea, tear open my letters, and even read aloud selected passages. We would then chatter, smirk, and gossip about these courting boys. No doubt she had been planning the scene for hours, ever since the letters arrived. I wasn't sorry to deprive her. I wasn't twelve anymore, and I needed separation from her cheery voice.

I removed my damp clothing, put on my favorite blue sweater, and snuggled into the bed, pulling the covers and quilt over my bare legs. I set the tea on the nightstand and opened Kevin's letter first. He answered my most recent letter, responding first to my poetry interpretations. And then he drew my breath away.

I have made up my mind to join the ambulance crews in France. I will leave next summer, soon after graduation. I cannot justify my absence from the war. It is the chance of a lifetime to stand for something true and glorious. Many of the seniors, and some underclassmen too, are similarly inclined. Some hope to travel to Britain or France to join their forces directly . . . many have been moved by Alan Seeger's words and have the illusion that they may serve with him . . . I have the fond hope of seeing you before I leave. I trust you will return to Cambridge this summer . . .

I put down my mug and tried to imagine Kevin, who was awkward walking down the street, driving an ambulance through the battlefields. What would it be like to tend to a man who had just been shot in the chest or the face? Or had an arm or leg blown off? Or had just witnessed half of his fellows slaughtered in some unsuccessful charge? And what of the voyage over to Europe with German U-boats circling, ready to attack at any moment? I shuddered, pulling the covers up to my chin.

I fortified with tea before opening the letter from Marshall, alias Martin.

I have been traveling much between Springfield, Boston, and New York. I spend my time meeting with friends from the Plattsburgh camps and with others who share the goal of preparing the country for our inevitable entry into the war. Various groups are forming to ensure that we are ready to meet our obligations, and to resist those of our citizens who lobby for peace. Several future opportunities may vie for my attention: there is rumor that Roosevelt will not wait for Wilson to enter the war, but will raise his own militia to travel to Europe to fight alongside the British and French. I suspect I could serve as one of his officers as he was a great supporter of the Plattsburgh camps. Or, if we do enter the war, I could serve as an officer in the regular army. I hope we can meet this summer, perhaps as you travel through Springfield or in Cambridge.

I passed that spring pulling away from my parents, speaking to them as little as possible, fearful perhaps that any entanglement would cause me to betray my knowledge of Father's affair. I spent more time next door at my grandparents' home, helping Grandmother prepare for her weekly literary or musical salons. I hoped that some of the cultured dialog would prepare me for college life. I listened more carefully to Grandfather's opinions on war preparation, and found his thoughts in tune with the views of my college friends. Father's vehement antiwar, anti-preparedness stance carried less influence. I was angry with him most of the time, reflexively dismissing much of what he said.

I barely remember my graduation. My thoughts already centered on Cambridge where I would enter Radcliffe in the fall, living with Becky and Michael.

Mother asked me to delay my departure until the second week in July, so that I would be home for my eighteenth birthday and our family July Fourth party. Just days before the party, a hastily written note arrived from Douglas. "I'll be passing through Springfield on my way to Chicago. I would love to make the detour north to see you. Let me know if this plan is ill-advised . . ."

I doubted there was time to mail a reply. Of course, I welcomed his attention.

Mother worried about where he would stay.

"In our guestroom, of course!" declared Grandmother.

"That should be a safe distance for the pair," winked Grandfather.

"We're hardly a pair!" I protested.

"The young man is going forty miles out of his way—eighty miles round trip—surely you are something to him."

Douglas had planned to stay in a hotel or rooming house, but Grandmother took him by the arm. "Nonsense, I won't hear of it! You will stay in our home—in fact you'll be in the very bed in which Mark Twain slept!" She could never resist a name drop.

"Grandmother, I'm sure Douglas doesn't care about . . ."

"But don't worry son, we've changed the sheets since then," Grandfather interrupted.

"Mark Twain? Really? I've always liked his writing. Amazing, isn't it, that he died with Halley's Comet. Just as he predicted." Douglas did have a way of making himself welcome. Grandmother was smitten.

I was afraid that Grandfather would prove intimidating when he cornered Douglas to ask his views on Roosevelt and the war. But Douglas handled it well, explaining his opinion that campus consensus was shifting into greater alignment with Grandfather's views.

"If I was, once again, twenty-two years old, I would be off to the fight right now. I wouldn't wait a moment longer for Wilson to figure out that we need to be in this war." He eyed Douglas carefully.

"I may yet take that course myself, sir. I am tempted by the nobility and adventure of it all. But, first, I have a commitment to interview in Chicago with the Northern Pacific Railroad."

"The Northern Pacific?"

"Yes sir."

The next day Grandfather handed Douglas an envelope. "Take this with you to your interview. It may help your chances. I know those people."

Douglas praised Mother's artwork. "If I am ever settled, I would like one of your landscapes on my wall." And he engaged Father, explaining that while he was, as yet, undecided, "Many of my friends stand firmly for peace."

To the July Fourth picnic he wore a white suit, nicely offsetting his dark hair, his brown eyes, and his tanned skin. When it was time for the ice cream, he stripped off his jacket, eager to churn the tub of strawberry.

The twilight lingered irresistibly as we reclined on the lawn, watching the reflected reds and oranges play off the water. The crowd had quieted as if to savor the best portion of the day. Children, having accomplished their day's duty of running and swimming, now rested by their parents, nibbling on cookies, listening to their mothers murmur stories, waiting for darkness and fireworks. A group of teens, Matt among them, gathered in the gardens just off the rear patio, watching the assemblage and giggling at who knows what.

Douglas and I walked through Grandmother's gardens toward the river. There was no discernable current under the drooping willow branches that arched out and down like the legs of a young ballerina, the branch tips caressing the water's surface as if to delicately test the warmth. Douglas pointed to the canoe and I nodded agreement, secretly admiring his bravery after our Cambridge fiasco. We paddled down to the island and paused at the southern tip. He asked if we should land. I declined. "It's almost dark, and we don't want to miss the fireworks."

It was nearly effortless passing around the island to head back upstream. To the east, a rising three-quarter moon, escorted by brilliant Jupiter, captured our eyes. We had nearly returned when murmuring voices drew my attention back to the west bank. I gasped at the beauty there. Across the river, completely stilled save for the faint ripples of our following wake, the willow stood guard over the gently rising lawn where our guests nestled comfortably into blankets and chairs, waiting for fireworks and watching the moon and Jupiter—and us. I imagined what they must see: the silhouette of the couple in a canoe, passing through the watery moon glow. Some guests were clearing and rearranging from the picnic, laughing lightly as they rustled up through the gardens, across the patio and into the house. The closing screen door delivered a muffled thump, inviting one into the warmly glowing home. My gaze was drawn up further where the house, set against the dark western hills, was encircled by the sky's deepening rustic burgundy.

The fireworks ended the spell, their brilliant light cascading into cheers and claps, and then yells gleefully directed to "the fools in the canoe" to watch out for the falling embers that sizzled into the river. We laughed from the water, bringing the boat in to shore after the display. There was only a brief hug and light kiss before Douglas went to his bed, and I to mine. I declined his offer of a midnight meeting, claiming too much risk under the watchful eyes of so many chaperones, both old and young. I was tempted though, finding him attractive and romantic. Perhaps I simply lacked the courage.

Several weeks were to pass before we heard that Alan Seeger died on the day of our picnic, July Fourth, 1916, as he charged into German lines on a French battlefield. (And several years were to pass before we learned that he had actually died on July 23; his reported death date had been manufactured as a more patriotic and romantic time to die.) Some said he was prescient of his death when his poem, *Rendezvous*, was published.

Robert Bissell

Rendezvous

I have a rendezvous with Death
At some disputed barricade,
I have a rendezvous with Death
At some disputed barricade,
When Spring comes back with rustling shade
And apple-blossoms fill the air—
I have a rendezvous with Death
When Spring brings back blue days and fair.

It may be he shall take my hand
And lead me into his dark land
And close my eyes and quench my breath—
It may be I shall pass him still.
I have a rendezvous with Death
On some scarred slope of battered hill,
When Spring comes round again this year
And the first meadow-flowers appear.

God knows 'twere better to be deep
Pillowed in silk and scented down,
Where love throbs out in blissful sleep,
Pulse nigh to pulse, and breath to breath,
Where hushed awakenings are dear . . .
But I've a rendezvous with Death
At midnight in some flaming town,
When Spring trips north again this year,
And I to my pledged word am true,
I shall not fail that rendezvous.

When his works were published in the following months, this poem received the greatest attention, with most readers focusing on the first stanza. But I was drawn to the last stanza. The contrast between contented love and dutiful death focused my thoughts back to my own July Fourth. While Seeger lay dying on the battlefield, I lay alone in bed, rather than in Douglas's arms, "Where love throbs out . . . Pulse nigh to pulse, and breath to breath."

Chapter 13
1916–17

Douglas left the day after the picnic, and within a week I was off to Cambridge—via Springfield. I had had ten months to digest the implications of Father's affair with Cynthia Robbins, not nearly enough time to accept it, but enough time to have made some decisions. The majority of the blame I placed with Father. I suppose I had difficulty finding fault with my grade-school teacher, the mother of my half brother. Besides, I wanted to continue to see Nick so I needed to be on good terms with his mother. And then there was the matter of her brother, Marshall. That winter, my desultory ruminations about the affair invariably led to a consideration of Marshall, and thoughts of Marshall never failed to lift my spirits.

I had carefully considered what to bring Nick, rejecting books (surely, based on his mother's occupation, he would already have a good supply), kites (required too much grown-up assistance), and marbles (too predictable a gift for a young boy). As I browsed through the Birkett Ferry general store, a set of toy Scottie dogs caught my eye. They were cleverly carved from soapstone, and small, only an inch long. One painted black, and the other white, they were attached to small magnetic pedestals.

Nick got it right away. Placing one dog above a sheet of paper and hiding the other below, he could use the magnets to make the top dog appear to move magically. He was occupied for much of my visit, drawing a miniature village and pathways through which the dogs would move. He had grown, I think, a couple of inches since the previous summer, but he retained the same Matt-like face and the same high energy level. Cindy and I needed to be circumspect in his presence, but we had time to talk candidly when he dashed to his room for more paper or bounded outside to demonstrate his dogs to a passing friend.

The young maple waved its branches in the wind, tossing light speckles chaotically about the small living room. The windows were barely cracked, limiting the breeze which sifted past the aged couch and the unmatched chair. The darkly stained tables supported volumes of books and sheaths of school papers.

"I've not said anything to my family," I told Cindy.

"That's probably best. I'm not ready to explain things to Nick. He recognizes your father only as an occasional visitor, nothing more. I've asked him not to bring Nick presents. I just don't want to formalize things or cause suspicion later on."

"If there's ever anything I can do to help . . ." I couldn't help glancing at the run-down furniture and the scuffed walls.

She laughed. "Oh, we are pretty much fine. I'm not much for housekeeping or maintenance, I suppose. But we are as content as one could expect. I should tell you your father continues to help us financially—on a regular basis. My parents do what they can. And Marshall wishes he could do more." His name brought a smile to us both. "You know, Marshall mentions you, asks about you. There is definite interest."

I met her gaze. "I suppose I suspected. We write often. His letters are," I searched for the right word, "uplifting."

"Sometimes I think he has as much energy as Nick. He's back in New York now, organizing and advocating with such determination. He's as committed to fighting this war as your father is opposed. I imagine them meeting at some point, facing off in opposing demonstrations."

"My friends in Birkett Ferry don't seem to think much about the war. But the people I've met in Cambridge mostly agree with Marshall. And I'm beginning to think that Father has it wrong . . ."

"I'm not sure where I stand. But don't be too quick to dismiss your father's opinions. Not many have the actual war experience he has had. Most people have no idea of the true horror."

So I was free in Cambridge, free to roam the city, free to come and go from the bookstore (save for my working hours) and mostly free from the supervision of Becky and Michael, who were moderately successful at masking the inevitable worries I must have caused. Perhaps they were actually relieved at abdicating responsibility, reasoning that freedom was to be expected since I was eighteen and about to enter college. Kevin, scheduled to leave in mid-August, became my daily companion for his few remaining weeks. Each day he had a list of items to accomplish which, mercifully, distracted him from his mounting apprehension.

"But, what does one say," I finally had the courage to ask Becky, "to a man about to go to war?"

She thought for a moment. "I suppose it's important to listen, to give him a chance to talk. Ask how he feels about it. Maybe he'd rather speak about other things."

Much of the time we did talk of other things. But, at times that August, Kevin and I were able to speak honestly: in an outdoor café sheltered by the shade of a massive white oak, people clattering by on horseback, bike, and automobile; or while strolling along the Charles, watching the rowing teams, sailboats, and canoes; or in the bookstore, at quiet moments when Michael and Becky went up for tea, leaving Kevin and me alone except for a patron browsing in the back.

When I said it was the U-boats that I would fear, he dismissed the danger. "Why worry about something I cannot see or control or predict?"

"That's exactly what would bother me the most, the not knowing."

"I'm worried more about my own performance. I know they will train us, but at night I dream that I am there on a battlefield surrounded by wounded men and I don't know how to treat them. Or the ambulance has stalled under a storm of shells and I can't start it. And in the light of day I simply worry about my own courage. What does it take to drag a stretcher into the midst of mutilation and death?"

His words tumbled out but I didn't know how to respond.

"You'll have some protection from the ambulance markings," I replied, the only encouragement I could muster.

For many, the death of Alan Seeger had intensified an abstract determination to join the glorious adventure. Some compared Seeger to a heroic knight sacrificing his life in a valiant quest. But for Kevin, and for others who had taken concrete steps to participate, the writer's death deflated confidence and increased foreboding.

I again turned to Becky and Michael for advice, but Becky only sighed, "I think you've done what you can." And Michael just shook his head, and turned his eyes away; I knew he thought Kevin a fine young man.

At night, I lay awake wondering if I should sleep with him before his departure. In the dark of my room, the thought raced my heart, and flushed my cheeks, making all rational consideration difficult. While I knew I was in control of our relationship, I had trouble imagining the series of words and acts that would lead to bed. My curiosity about sex was an inspiring motive, but there was also the sense of obligation, the debt owed to a man off to war. My assumption was that he had never had a sexual relationship. What if I was his one chance? The death of Alan Seeger haunted my decision. I thought of him dying after spending months and years sucked down into the muddy trenches, wet, cold, bored, exhausted, hungry, louse-infested, and rat-plagued. Somehow, with only hope or memory to sustain him, he had produced inspiring prose. And there were millions of boys still stranded. Perhaps I owed it to this one man, a memory to carry him through the bleak times ahead.

As the time of his departure approached I searched for a suitable gift in the Cambridge shops, something small and light but memorable. Finally, in the stationery shop, I found it: a nicely bound journal, its blank pages calling out for suitable inscription. I had the blue cover monogrammed with his initials, and then spent three hours composing a dedication for the first page: "Know that I will think of you each day. In that sense, I'll be with you. When you find time to write, write of the foreign things you see, hear, and taste. Write of the war. Write of the joy. Write of the burden. Write it all down—then write to me and then I can share it with you."

The night before he left, he took me to a stylish Cambridge restaurant. Becky clucked as she fastened my dark green gown. "Michael and I have never been there; it's way too rich for our blood."

When Kevin called for me, Becky dabbed her eyes and embraced him. "Godspeed," she murmured.

Michael gripped his hand tightly, "Best of luck to you, young man . . . and," he trailed off, "to all the others, too."

En route, I protested the cost. "Really, the café is fine with me."

"What else will I have to spend it on?" He was in a fine humor, excited about the voyage and the adventure.

As we lingered over cake and tea, I handed him the present. "We've written each other so much. I want to continue. Whenever there's a mail pickup, you can just tear out a page and send it to me."

He smiled after he opened the journal and read my dedication. "Wonderful, this will keep me on task. I can be just like Alan Seeger . . . well, not like him in every way . . . I hope!" I supposed it was good he could joke about it.

I had not known whether to expect a present from him, but he gave me a fine silver locket and chain inscribed with my initials and the date. He was pleased that I liked it. When I fumbled with the clasp, he came around the table to help, his hands lingering on my neck and shoulders after the closure snapped shut. I turned back to look at him, engaging his deep blue eyes. So this is how it starts, I thought.

We wandered along the Charles until I chose a bench facing east to watch the rising half-moon twinkle off the rippled water. The night was warm and quiet, with just enough northern breeze to rustle the leaves and drive off the summer heat. As he took my hand in his, I was lulled by the dinner and wine, and by his company, into a quiet contentment. It was as if I drifted serenely downriver drawn to the timeless moon where I thought to find his company.

But he was elsewhere. Although he seemed just as transfixed as I, he had taken a separate downstream journey. "It's not far, just around a couple of bends to the harbor. My ship must be ready by now."

And further east beyond the harbor—we both must have had this thought—is the vast dark ocean which cloaks the stealthy U-boats, and beyond that is the blood-drenched continent that cannot hide the countless bodies.

And in that moment I decided, so that when he turned to me and tentatively suggested a visit to his room, I could instead kiss him sweetly and then fix his gaze with mine. "I think it best that we not." I smiled and tried to make light, "Lip to lip, breath to breath, pulse to pulse, but not body to body—not yet anyway." I tried to tell myself that my rational mind had prevailed, that I would not have considered a sexual relationship if he were not off to war, and I supposed that was reason enough.

In acknowledgment of my maturity, Michael and Becky no longer waited up for me, but sometimes I sensed that they lay awake, especially that night. So I latched the door and creaked the stairs to let them know I was safely in. I paused outside their door. "Goodnight," I whispered.

I heard the rustle of sheets and then Becky's soft voice. "Goodnight, child."

I lay alone in bed, wondering for hours. But the next day, after a final embrace on the dock, as I stood below in the crowd, waving and cheering and shouting up to where he was stranded among all those others, silhouetted against the hazy morning sky, and about to embark onto that perilous ocean and battle upon that treacherous continent, I became certain of my decision. I needed to think of him but I needed to think of myself, too. And who could guess whether he would ever return?

Marshall came to Boston a few days after Kevin's ship left. It was only the second time I had seen him, but I had spent many hours thinking of him. I admired his writing, which flowed from witty and charming responses to my letters to stark and passionate commentaries on his cause.

I gasped as he walked by the front window of the shop. He paused to check the sign and then entered, smiling and confident, jaunty even, dressed in black slacks and a white shirt.

"I believe we have met," his lively eyes watched me and took in the whole shop at the same instant.

"Marshall! How grand. I didn't expect . . ." I smoothed my hair, then dropped my hand self-consciously to the counter where he intercepted it to bring it to his lips in extravagant welcome.

"Mademoiselle, it is indeed an honor!"

"Marshall! It is so good to see you!" I tried not to gush.

Michael appeared curious as he carried books from the back of the store.

"Oh, Grandpa, this is my friend, Mar . . ."

"Martin, Martin Roberts, sir, at your service." Marshall eyed me carefully.

"And I am Michael Sherwood, pleased to meet you, sir."

"I'm certainly pleased to meet the honorable grandfather of this fine young woman."

"Her beauty derives from my wife . . . and her obvious shyness from me, so our branch of the family can claim full credit for her many charms."

"Grandpa! Really!" I pretended shock.

Marshall studied me. "Shyness is not a word I would have chosen."

"Martin has been at the training camps at Plattsburgh; this is the second summer he's gone."

"Oh, yes. So he's the one you've spoken of. Listen, Gwen, I can watch the shop while you two catch up. Go for a stroll. Or maybe some tea at the café."

"We will take advantage of that offer, if Gwen is willing, but another time. I have a meeting on the campus. More talk of how to convince the country that we must be prepared for war . . . if it comes." He added the last phrase, I think, because he was unsure of Michael's opinion.

But Michael put him at ease. "The country may not need much more convincing if the submarine sinking resumes."

"But I fear that if Wilson is reelected we will remain mired in inaction." He smiled. "Enough of politics. Gwen, perhaps we can sip that lemonade this afternoon. Is four o'clock all right?"

That day, as I helped students find books for their fall courses, I contrasted Marshall, well traveled, worldly, and agreeably older, with my peers, the entering Harvard freshmen. There was no contest.

As August closed it was strange to remain in Cambridge when the rest of my family returned to Birkett Ferry. We had gathered again at the Hastings Beach house in the unspoken fear that this could be the last time. After all, Becky and Michael were aging, I was starting college, and the war was closing in.

Matt, about to enter eleventh grade, had preferred not to come, but acquiesced in the face of Mother's urging. "Who knows when you'll see Gwen again?" I was glad she had prevailed. He could have passed for a college student; his sharply defined chin and cheeks had lost their childhood curves, and stubble showed when he didn't shave. The two of us walked for hours on the beach, the soothing water lapping over our toes and the salty spray massaging our faces. Matt would run ahead a few steps, and gaze nonchalantly out to the sea waiting for my approach which he greeted with an onslaught of playful splashes. I would pretend anger, and chase him through the shallows kicking up water and foam, until both of us were drenched. Finally, collapsing in laughter, we'd fall backward into the sea.

I realized others, passing us on the beach and witnessing our frolic, might judge us a couple. The middle-aged man, walking his setter, the elderly couple forced to an agonizingly slow pace by the awkward stiffness in the man's right leg, and the couple in their late thirties not talking to each other or to the two sulky teens who shuffled behind, they all turned to us, or so I thought, with a wistful longing for youth and companionship.

Finally, the two of us would drop to the sand to watch the sea and sky and to laugh of our childhood past and talk of our adult future. I relished our closeness. But as we walked back to the house watching the afternoon sparkles play off the ruffled water, I realized my discomfort in keeping secrets from him. Over the years we had always been open with one another, and I knew it would have been good for me to be able to talk to him about Cindy Robbins and Nick and Father. But I could see no benefit for Matt, who had to spend two more years at home, to know of Father's escapade. Eventually, though, I would need to tell him, unless Father did first.

Marshall was the only other person privy to the entire tale, but I found the subject difficult to discuss with him. He had met my father once, years before, when they crossed paths at Cindy's Springfield apartment. It must have been a tension-filled moment for both. Marshall had not risked a visit to the beach, and Father had, as always, not come to Cambridge. Of course, my parents were curious when Michael teased me about "this Martin Roberts who's come round to the store—been there quite a bit recently," but they made no connection.

Late on our last night at Hastings, I walked alone to the ocean to stand in the shallows looking east. The full moon was overhead delivering only a scant shadow to my solitary form. The shuffling wind drove my hair back and forth and pulled at my frock. The whipped salty spray misted my eyes to blur the horizon. And I thought of Kevin, Kevin on the ship, Kevin landing in France, Kevin in battle. I looked from the eastern horizon up to the haze-distorted moon; if it was overhead here, it was just about to set in France.

In my morning exit ritual, I blew a kiss to Michael, gave an exaggerated wave to Becky, and hurried out the door. I inhaled deeply of the autumn air, taking the bracing chill down to the bottom of my lungs, carrying that vigor deep to my inner core. Striding confidently, nodding to the passing merchants, businessmen, and students, I entered the tree-lined Radcliffe campus. This was my new life, this was where I was meant to be, studying, debating, and socializing in this town at this college. I believe it was Kevin's influence that made me choose coursework in literature and writing. He had recommended several professors, and I was captivated by my classes.

Talk of the war dominated all other discussion, becoming the chief issue in the fall presidential campaign. The campus felt like the epicenter of the election, with each candidate's positions, tactics, and personality continually scrutinized. Charles Evans Hughes, the Republican candidate, seemed aloof; at times it was difficult to know where he stood on the issues. When he attacked Wilson for not protecting U.S. interests abroad, Wilson counterattacked, claiming Hughes was unpatriotic to question his presidential actions in this time of crisis.

When Marshall was with me, he dove right into the debates, his age and experience giving credence to his opinions. "Simply put, I am afraid if Wilson remains in office we will never recognize our obligation to participate with Britain and France to defeat a monstrous evil."

Marshall spent the bulk of his time educating and organizing. He continued to travel to meetings and speak at college forums in New York, Boston, and Philadelphia. There were persistent rumors that Roosevelt would organize a battalion, independent of government approval if necessary, to fight in Europe. In that case, Marshall was certain he would be appointed an officer, based on his Plattsburgh training.

My spirits rose when he was in town. I would attend his forums in awe when he spoke. I still had doubts that this war or any war could be a positive event. One only had to study history to appreciate the futility. And yet, since Marshall's words and personality were so forceful, and because I was now reluctant to accept the position advocated by Father, I was gradually persuaded that this war was different. In heated campus discussions I felt that those who attacked Marshall's views were actually attacking him. And I wondered how one could doubt his passionate sincerity.

When Wilson won the election, close in both popular and electoral vote (a four thousand vote switch in California would have given the election to Hughes), it was said that his campaign slogan, "He kept us out of war," secured the victory. That irony was not lost in the weeks after the election when it became increasingly clear that war would no longer be avoided. The excitement on campus was palpable that winter. There was not so much patriotic fervor as commitment to noble and heroic ideals, anticipation of adventure and travel, and for some, lust for the thrill of battle, a lust intensified by the writings of Seeger and others. As the Christmas holidays approached, I would have preferred to stay in Cambridge, but I knew I should return home.

Their political disagreement was so deep that Father and Grandfather were barely speaking to one another. Grandfather could have accepted Father's continued opposition to the war, but he could not fathom why he was taking so much time from his law practice, the practice that Grandfather had painstakingly built, to attend anti-war meetings and rallies in New York, Philadelphia, Springfield, and Boston. When he spoke at rallies, with Emma Goldman and others, his Rough Rider past added credence to his words. There were harassments from, and occasional skirmishes with, pro-war agitators, and these conflicts generated local publicity. And now the law practice did suffer, not only from Father's absences, but from his political activities that served to alienate clients and neighbors. Mother and Grandmother agreed with Wilson's patient course, which now seemed both to acknowledge the likelihood of entering the war and to offer the continued hope of avoidance.

Mother enjoyed hearing about "Martin." I'm sure she sensed my infatuation. We could laugh about the potential confrontation of Martin and Father, heckling one another at opposing rallies. "But Gwen, I think it best not to talk of Martin's politics with your father; he is so resolute in his opinions that he no longer tolerates other viewpoints."

"Martin is just as bad. He can't understand why everyone doesn't see the reality he sees."

Mother sighed, "And your grandfather, too. It's not worth tearing up a family over this."

"It's not that bad, surely . . ."

"I suppose not yet, but Grandfather hears complaints from his old clients. One urged him to reopen his practice, in opposition to your father."

I was irritated that Matt seemed oblivious to the war. He claimed no interest in the debate, refusing even to talk about it. While this stance did serve as an effective defense mechanism, allowing him to avoid the Father-Grandfather conflict, it frustrated me. "Here, at least read these." I handed him my file containing Seeger's articles and other pro-war compositions. He glanced at it and huffed away.

I was glad to retreat back to Cambridge for the January term. With a furrowed brow, Becky absorbed my reports from Birkett Ferry. She put her arm around my shoulder. "Poor child, you are certainly caught right in the middle between your father and Martin, aren't you?" She didn't know the half of it.

I hugged Marshall when he entered the bookstore the next day. I was so happy to see him. As we ambled through the Cambridge streets, he listened to my story before thoughtfully responding. "Your grandfather sounds like a wonderful man. He could give a lot of needed support to our cause. But I just don't see any way I could safely approach him." He frowned at the idea. "I'm sure my sister would not allow it. But maybe I could give his name to some of my associates."

"No, it would just add fuel."

"As you wish . . . but maybe he could give financial support . . ."

Chapter 14
1917

"It is, at once, more horrible and more magnificent than I had imagined." Kevin's first letter arrived in February.

We ambulance drivers have it easy by any comparison. Stationed well behind the front lines, and protected by the medical markings on our vehicles, we are at risk only to a random shell. Of course there are random shells. Just a few days ago a barn was obliterated—six men were bivouacked there. Three were killed in the rubble. I helped dig them out, tossing aside both wooden beams and mangled limbs to unbury the survivors. There was one chap, missing the end of his foot, who nonetheless was positively jubilant, exclaiming, 'It's worth a few toes to be out of this hell hole.'

A few months ago I could not have imagined myself dealing with this kind of thing, but, on the battlefield, the need for bandage and tourniquet is so great that there is not time to think. One simply acts in numbness. There is a premium on speed and efficiency. It's later, especially at night, when we try to sleep, that my mind replays the scenes of hopeless agony. There are some you can do nothing for; they've lost part of their skull, or have had their abdomen or chest blasted open, and yet have managed to cling to life; they cry out, pleading for help. But I cannot sit with them, not for a moment. I must tend to the men who may not be beyond help. It is those, who have had to die alone without any comforting companion, who visit me at night, first to keep me awake and then to haunt my dreams. But I have been at this now for only a brief time. My fellow ambulance drivers tell me that these agitated visitations will cease as I become more accustomed to it all. They are a committed bunch, but when not actively engaged with their tasks, they are liable to joke about their predicament, and to talk wistfully of filling meals, fine wine, and the girl back home.

But, it is also true that Seeger was right about the magnificence of this enterprise. In addition to horror and death, there is also great nobility and heroism. Everyday there are stories of men who risk their lives to help a comrade. And there are those who volunteer for the dangerous night patrols, or to lead the next harrowing charge from the trenches. There is the grandeur of hundreds of men marching toward the front, unified in patriotic song, and there is the majesty of the cavalry silhouetted on a distant hill at sunset. This is an adventure I would not have missed even if it is to mean the loss of my life.

All life is transient: that was the message from Kevin's letter. And what was I doing? Wasting my time in college. Maybe I should be driving ambulances in France or speaking at pro-war rallies or doing something useful. What is life for? Not for standing idly by. Life is about action and risk.

Marshall was one of the speakers that night at a Cambridge pro-war rally. He became anxious in anticipation, but his speech was always a success; the audience found him direct and intimate. He began with a humorous anecdote before launching into the main message.

The Germans are no longer secretive about their intent; they now openly sink our ships and kill our citizens. Many of our young men have grown tired of waiting; they have heard the call to arms from across the Atlantic, the call that France and Britain and Belgium need help, and they need it soon. They have enlisted with those armies to protect the freedom of Europe. In so doing, they are just as surely protecting our freedom. They are carrying the burden for us all, while our government refuses to act. How much longer can we wait? How much longer dare we wait?

Who among you has not read the words of that valiant young American hero, Alan Seeger, who has given his life to fight for the cause he knew to be noble and just? I have seen excerpts from his *Letters and Diary*, which will soon be published. I urge all of you to read it. Recorded in his diary are these words: 'I pity the poor civilians who shall never have seen or known the things that we have seen and known. Great as are the pleasures that they are continuing to enjoy and that we have renounced, the sense of being the instrument of Destiny is to me a source of greater satisfaction.' And his words, in this letter to his mother, are an inspiration to us all: 'Had I the choice I would be nowhere else in the world than where I am. Even had I the chance to be liberated, I would not take it. Do not be sorrowful then. It is the shirkers and the slackers alone in this war who are to be lamented. The tears for those who take part in it and who do not return should be sweetened by the sense that their death was the death which beyond all others they would have chosen for themselves, that they went to it smiling and without regret, feeling that whatever value their continued presence in the world might be to humanity, it could not be greater than the example and inspiration they were to it in so departing.'

Save for a few muffled sobs, there was complete silence at the end of Marshall's speech. Then thunderous applause and loud cheers erupted from the crowd as they rose to their feet. I proudly watched Marshall, a grim smile playing about his face, his wave turning into more of a salute. I studied the young couples near me. The men, standing straight with jaws thrust out and deeply determined looks in their eyes kept protective arms around their misty-eyed dates, who were cheering and stomping no less loudly than the males. The audience finally settled for the other speakers, none of whom, I thought, equaled Marshall's effectiveness.

I waited near the podium afterward while Marshall talked earnestly with a dozen lingering students. Finally, he turned to me. "Marshall, that was wonderful."

"Thanks." Now a euphoric smile replaced his stern expression and his shoulders dropped into relaxation. "I think it went pretty well."

I felt honored to be with him as we walked hand in hand from the auditorium into the biting February air. The crisp starlight danced on the darkened river, its surface roughened by a building icy wind. Thumping waves broke onto the riverbank. Marshall looked up to the leafless trees as a gust penetrated our winter coats. We kissed quickly once, and then our lips met again in long embrace. Soon I was shivering.

"You need some hot tea. Should we head to my apartment?"

I wasn't sure what was right. I paused a second, then nodded agreement.

His apartment was on the third floor of a townhouse, several blocks from the center of Cambridge. I had been there once before with a group of eight or ten students to plot strategy for an upcoming rally. We had filled his living room, spilling from the two worn couches onto the floor, sipping wine and scribbling notes, but we were easily diverted and frequently dissolved into gay laughter over some campus gossip. There was one wall of bookshelves half filled with books, the rest of the space taken up with a cluttered assortment of linens, newspapers, notebooks, and tottering stacks of books waiting placement. I doubted that Marshall did much food preparation in his kitchen, which seemed randomly stocked with plates, bowls, and glasses; tins of sugar, tea, and coffee sat on the kitchen table. The door into his bedroom was half closed, but still visible was a large, handsome quilt which had been draped over the bed.

A few photos were placed on living room tables and shelves. There was one, very nicely framed, of his sister seated on a dark couch with Nick standing beside her, his hand resting lightly on her shoulder. In the background was a white wall decorated with a painting of an elegant ship in full sail. Nick looked like he'd been forced into a jacket and tie, and as the photo was taken he seemed to be turning toward his mother as if he knew where to fix the blame. Cindy, unnaturally upright in a full-length white dress, gazed into the camera, a quizzical smile on her lips.

I was studying the photo when Marshall returned from the kitchen with two glasses of red wine.

"Where was it taken?"

"A studio in Springfield. This must be awkward for you to see."

"Why, no. It's lovely."

"Still, Nick is your half brother, and Cindy is my sister." He put down the wine to stand behind me. His arms encircled my waist and his chin rested on my shoulder.

At his touch, it was difficult to breathe. Perhaps I should leave.

"Well then, that makes you my sort of step-uncle," I managed to say.

"That makes 'us' a very awkward relationship." He buried his face into the base of my neck lightly kissing my shoulder. Shivers tingled down my back and around to my chest. His arms clasped my waist more tightly.

I relaxed his grip and turned to face him. I knew I should leave, but did I want to? Here was an opportunity to live—to live my life. "I'd like some of that wine now." I needed some time. We stood at the window, watching a man hurry down the street, escaping the cold. Then we moved to the couch. I bit my lower lip. What did I want?

Soon we'd put our wine back on the table and he leaned in to kiss me.

I was curious and excited, and I didn't want him to think me a silly college girl.

"Marshall, I can't stay the whole night. Becky and Michael will worry if I am too late."

We stumbled into the bedroom. He began to undress, but I

hesitated, feeling awkward and unsure. He reached into his bureau drawer and withdrew a condom. I knew I still had time to change my mind, to leave. I hesitated again as he watched me. "Here, let me help." He stood, reaching out to ease my blouse over my head before pausing to look at me. His hands slipped under my buttocks to lift me slightly and hold me next to him.

"Wait." I was having trouble talking and thinking and breathing as I hurriedly withdrew from his grasp to strip off the rest of my undergarments. We stood a few feet apart for the eternity of ten seconds before I took a deep, long breath. "Now," I said. And it was easy to fall back onto that welcoming bed.

I suspect that Becky heard me as I murmured my presence near her door at my three o'clock return, but the next day there was no mention, no questioning. It had been so hard to leave his apartment that night. Once at the bookstore, we had lingered on the doorstep for a final kiss and hug.

Initially, I wondered if our sexual experience was to be repeated, but we soon fell into a pattern. The next week I made my way to the Boston birth control clinic that Marshall had known about. While illegal, its presence had been tolerated by the authorities. I glanced through some waiting room pamphlets. My eyes stopped at the list of clinic sponsors where Emma Goldman's name was prominently displayed. Emma Goldman, the famous pacifist, anarchist, and activist, was also an unyielding advocate for women's rights, birth control, and free love. She was the same Emma Goldman with whom Father had corresponded for years; more recently he had joined her at peace rallies, introducing her to the crowds, or sometimes delivering a speech himself. I left with a diaphragm and with greater appreciation for Emma Goldman. But while I accepted her views on women's rights, I knew both she and Father were wrong about the war. Marshall had convinced me of that; my attachment to him had extinguished any lingering doubt.

We were together in his room once or twice a week in the evenings or, better yet, in the afternoons. We joked that the combination of rhythm, diaphragm, and condom had better work because we had no idea how to define the relationship of our issue to Nick. The introductions at a family gathering would be impossible.

Michael and Becky gave me great latitude, not forcing me into lies. Marshall continued his frequent trips to New York and Philadelphia, and his absences allowed me time to read and study.

Marshall's spirits rose as war became inevitable. In January, the Germans had decided to resume the indiscriminate torpedoing of all Allied shipping, and even Wilson could not tolerate the loss of more U.S. citizens. After the sinking of the Laconia and other ships, Congress met in March, and by early April there was a declaration of war. And this is when it started, when everything changed so rapidly, when international events and family events spiraled out beyond all control and reason. The political climate changed overnight. Many of those who had favored neutrality and many outright pacifists joined the war effort. Father was not among them. It became first unfashionable and then illegal to speak against the government's efforts to prepare for war.

Father was among those invited to speak in early April to a rally in Baltimore that featured the noted pacifist and retired president of Stanford, David Starr Jordan. Father was sitting on the stage listening to Jordan when word spread that pro-war vigilantes numbering over one thousand were assembling outside and preparing to enter the auditorium. As sweat beaded down his brow, Father rose to whisper in Jordan's ear. Instructions were given to the audience so that when the rabble entered, intending to rush the stage, the antiwar audience rose and began to sing "The Star-Spangled Banner." The mob was forced to stop halfway down the aisle, allowing Jordan and Father and the other speakers to escape through a side door. They were whisked away to a safe house where they listened through the night to the sounds of the vigilantes hunting them, "We'll hang Dave Jordan to a sour apple tree." The close call did not deter Father. Rather, Matt wrote me, he took great pleasure in relating every detail of the ingenious escape to all who would listen, further cementing his image as a fanatic pacifist in the eyes of his townsfolk and further widening the chasm with his father.

I wondered if Douglas, working for the railway in Chicago, would enlist. And what of Jonathan, only a year older than me, farming in Birkett Ferry, married to Anna, and soon, I had heard, to become a father? If the draft were enacted, how would it affect them? And I thought of Kevin, already in France. I worried about them but sometimes I thought it unfair that the same splendid adventures were not open to me.

Marshall applied to be a Four Minute Man. The Wilson administration, knowing there was still significant opposition to the war, initiated a propaganda campaign of surprising dimensions. The goal of the Committee on Public Information (CPI) was to educate the public to embrace the war and, as the CPI director said, "to win the fight for the minds of men, for the conquest of their convictions." As part of this effort, the government recruited seventy-five thousand Four Minute Men. They were trained to speak briefly (speeches longer than four minutes would bore the audience) of the justification for the war and of patriotism. They spoke in theaters, at rallies, in parks, and wherever people assembled. Marshall was a natural choice, with his obvious sympathy to the cause and his speaking experience.

During his exhortations, I watched the young men, and overheard their discussions. I knew that some left intending to enlist. Marshall was pleased to hear this; he felt he would get credit if they mentioned him as their motivation to enlist. And then he changed tactics to "strike while the iron is hot." He concluded his speeches with a challenge. "Who is now ready to be a patriot? Who is now ready to enlist in this grand patriotic cause, this adventure of a lifetime? Don't be a slacker. Join me now on stage." And men would march to the front, their chests thrust out, the audience applauding, and Marshall would escort them to the recruitment office. He became known as the most effective enlistment speaker in Boston, and soon the recruiters came to him, sitting through his rallies, ready to enlist the willing men.

Teddy Roosevelt still hoped to lead a troop of men to fight in France. Marshall was asked to help, by maintaining a list of officer prospects. He put himself at the top of the list. Ultimately Wilson refused Roosevelt's request, but Marshall had reinforced his connections in military and government circles.

Early one Sunday I surprised him. I left home just after dawn, stopped at the bakery for two sweet rolls, and arrived at his apartment before seven. I knocked lightly and listened to murmured rustlings and then his yawning hoarse voice, "Who's there?" In response I only knocked again. Feet shuffled across the floor. He opened the door clothed only in shorts. Pillow lines creased his cheeks and his eyes were blurry and red. He smoothed his ruffled hair and then glanced down self-consciously. I took his hand to lead him back to the bedroom where, standing by the bed, I slid his shorts down to his ankles and pushed him into a sitting position. I stopped for a moment to be sure he noticed me admiring his awakening body before undressing slowly as he watched.

Afterward, sheets kicked aside in luxurious disarray, the sunlight dappled across our limbs, we lay spooned together, savoring the closeness, our only movement to reverse the spooning, or to lie face to face, our legs intertwined and our eyes opening dreamily to check the other's contentment. The sweet rolls lay forgotten as we drifted in and out of a light sleep, our satisfied bodies touching, until the nerve endings were satiated, numbed to the touch of the other's skin, and I thought this, rather than sex itself, must be when two become one: our stilled closeness more intensely intimate than any physical act. And I was reminded again of Seeger's words.

Pillowed in silk and scented down,

Where love throbs out in blissful sleep,
Pulse nigh to pulse, and breath to breath,
Where hushed awakenings are dear . . .

Seeger's book was published that spring and widely read by my generation, buttressing our view that the war was a grand and noble adventure, an event not to be missed. I think these feelings, well articulated in Seeger's writing, and in Marshall's four-minute speeches, were best summarized by something I read years later. Historian William Langer, writing of the war in which he served, marveled at "the eagerness of the men to get to France and above all to reach the front . . . One would think that, after almost four years of war, after the most detailed and realistic accounts of murderous fighting on the Somme and around Verdun, to say nothing of the day-to-day agony of trench warfare, it would have been all but impossible to get anyone to serve without duress. But it was not so. We and many thousands of others volunteered . . . We men, most of us young, were simply fascinated by the prospect of adventure and heroism. Most of us, I think, had the feeling that life, if we survived, would run in the familiar, routine channel. Here was our one great chance for excitement and risk. We could not afford to pass it up."

I wrote to Douglas and Kevin and Matt, describing the stirring Cambridge rallies at which Marshall spoke. I asked Douglas if he had seen Seeger's book yet, and I wondered about the war effort in Chicago. And soon I had a rare letter back from him.

Here, there is the same enthusiasm that you describe. There are the daily rounds of war rallies and Four Minute speeches. We see proud women accompany their men to enlistment centers, and just days later, the tearful good-byes as they leave for training camps. But we also have our share of slackers and disloyal citizens who seek to disrupt the war effort.

That's why Mr. Alfred Briggs (he's an advertising executive who I've met through work) has organized the American Protective League to check up on socialists, anarchists, pacifists, and anyone else who tries to interfere with the war. He has permission and financial support from Wilson's Attorney General to monitor any suspicious activity. I've become a member. I feel I can help the war effort right here in Chicago, and maybe I can be more useful than if I was fighting at the front. It's all very exciting: I've helped with several cases already. One man, a history professor at the University of Chicago, was speaking at rallies of student pacifists, encouraging everyone to resist the war and the draft. So we began to follow him, to keep track of those he met and to open his mail. We searched his apartment when he was off at some lecture. And, sure enough, there was all manner of incriminating material: he gets socialist newspapers and corresponds with pacifists across the country; they're all plotting against the war. So four of us went back and confronted him. He resisted so we had to subdue him which wasn't all that hard. We hauled him off to the police and he's in jail now. The university has announced he won't be rehired if he's released.

Now I'm monitoring a man from my office who has been seen at pacifist rallies and I've been asked to spy on one of my neighbors, a man with a German accent who gets quite a bit of mail from Berlin. I think the next step will be to open (and translate) his letters.

I think it's very exciting what your friend Marshall is doing in Boston and New York. Please keep me posted. It's important for all patriots to stay in touch!

Later, when I asked Marshall about the American Protective

League, he said they were making a fine beginning in Boston. They were monitoring quite a few people and had made several arrests.

I wrote Kevin that everyone admired his sacrifice, that some were jealous, and that I supposed it would be grand for him to soon welcome American soldiers to France. To Matt I sent a copy of Seeger's book. I advised that he keep it out of Father's sight as there was no need to increase family tension. But I needn't have worried about that. Father had enough troubles of his own.

Chapter 15
1917

With the declaration of war came the draft—just as Douglas predicted. Despite the patriotic passions sweeping New England, there was a lot of doubt about the war in the rest of the country, and the Wilson administration feared that volunteerism alone would not supply the one million men needed to fight in France. Congress agreed, passing the Selective Service Act in May 1917. Several days before the mandatory draft registration in early June, Wilson declared that anyone speaking against the draft or encouraging others not to register would be subject to arrest. So when Father joined Emma Goldman and several others on a stage in New York and spoke to encourage young men to resist draft registration, they were arrested and jailed. Marshall heard the news reports first and hurried to the bookstore. I left for home that afternoon.

Mother was surprisingly calm. "They cannot hold him long for this. All he has done is to give his opinion at a public meeting."

Grandfather was not so sure. "But his opinion was to object to the draft and to encourage others to object."

Matt was quiet; I think he was angry at Father and at all of us for disrupting his life. What did he care about the war and the draft? But I was worried about Father after witnessing those Boston rallies where war passions could be inflamed by just a few words. When he was not immediately released, Grandfather took the train to New York to see what could be done.

And then they came to the door, five of them: Mr. Warren, the town sheriff, Mr. Browning, the owner of the store where Anna worked, Mr. Hayward, the president of the Ferry Street Bank, and two burly farmers. They all knew Father well, had known him for years, and for generations their families had commingled with ours in this small

152

town. They wore badges reading American Protective League—Secret Service. Their faces were serious as the police chief spoke. "I'm sorry, Marjorie." I'm sure Mother thought this was a sympathy call, but I was petrified when I connected their badges to Douglas's American Protective League in Chicago.

Later, Grandfather wondered why we hadn't asked if they had a search warrant. But we were numbed, incapable of challenging men we had known forever as they searched our home with self-assured briskness. Oh, they were polite to us, and sympathetic. But they asked us to stay in the kitchen while they sorted through Father's papers, books, and financial records.

As they carted off several boxes of material, Sheriff Warren, the very man who had rescued me at the age of four when I had wandered to the river and stood watching the currents, had taken my hand and bought me a peppermint stick and walked me home, this man turned to Mother. "Now Marjorie, I know this is difficult for you but there is no suspicion of the rest of the family. We must search the office, too. It would be easiest if you gave us the key."

They could not have found much of surprise: correspondence with Emma Goldman and other pacifists, small contributions to their organizations, subscriptions to their publications, news clippings about peace rallies and speeches. It all added up to Father's devotion to peace, nothing more.

Grandfather was back from New York a few days later, unsuccessful in his attempt to have Father released. "There will be a hearing in a few days, but they will not set bail yet."

As Mother prepared to travel to the New York prison, Sheriff Warren and Banker Hayward reappeared, wearing their American Protective League badges, to ask "just a few routine questions." Mother had the presence of mind to send Matt next door for Grandfather, who appeared in the doorway with a red face and determined eyes.

"Sheriff Warren, you had no right to search my son's home or office. No search warrant, no legal right. You're acting like a bunch of vigilantes."

"We've been authorized by the United States Attorney General and the President. The American Protective League, as you well know, is committed to root out those guilty of sedition and treason. Your son was arrested for encouraging draft resistance at an illegal rally." Then, more quietly, "In any case, we have all the evidence we need. I just have a few more questions for Marjorie."

He turned to Mother. He asked her about Emma Goldman and other pacifists whose letters Father had meticulously saved. Mother had only a sketchy idea of these people. They asked about the newspapers and books found in his study: what was Father's association with the publishers and the authors? Some books had been signed by the authors; surely, Father knew these people well. Again Mother was uncertain of any details. And there were names not recognized by the investigating team, names appearing on canceled checks or in Father's address book. Could Mother identify these people? She recognized a few names as clients or old college friends, but for many she could supply no useful information.

"I think this has gone far enough," Grandfather stepped forward.

The sheriff checked his notes. "I have just one more question at present."

Grandfather sighed and nodded.

"A check made out to Cynthia Robbins. Who might she be?"

A wave of nausea flipped my stomach and pulled the blood from my face. I'm sure I would have fainted had I not been seated. I gripped the sides of my chair for support and watched the others for reaction. Matt simply looked vacant, and the name did not register with Grandfather. Eight years had passed since Cynthia Robbins left town. Mother's brow wrinkled and her eyes searched the corners of the room as if trying to attach a face to this name. So she did not know of the affair; that was clear. I prayed she wouldn't notice my terror, but she turned away gazing out to the river. I wondered if I should identify Cindy and hope to quickly dispose of her name but my throat was so tight I might have gasped or choked trying to speak.

And then a warm look came to Mother's face. "Oh yes, I remember now. She taught school here quite a few years ago. And she played the viola. She played with Will in the chamber group." She turned away from the window, her hands clasped together at her waist. "I believe you must have come to one of the concerts, Sheriff. Will hasn't played the cello much since. Too busy, I guess." She glanced at me as her memories connected. My face must have recovered for she continued blandly, "And she was your teacher, too. What grade was that?"

"Fifth grade . . . and part of sixth." I managed to speak in a voice just above a whisper.

"Well now, I do remember her." Banker Hayward spoke in a sure voice that made me wonder if he had known who she was all along. "A young woman . . . from Springfield wasn't it?"

"But why," Sheriff Warren paused, looking at his notes, "why did he send her a check?" They found no help in Mother's complacent face. Grandfather still appeared confused by this line of questioning but bit his lower lip as he watched the sheriff and banker. My face must have blanched and I was again thankful that no one noticed.

"I'm sure there was something still due her from teaching, or perhaps some legal matter he helped her with." Mother would not be rattled.

"But why would he send money from his personal account?" When there was no answer, Banker Hayward continued. "And Marge, I'm surprised you don't know this, but there was not just one check to Cynthia Robbins. There were many checks. And significant amounts."

Although Mother remained oblivious, Grandfather sensed a problem as he stepped toward the men. "And your conclusion, gentlemen?"

"We think he was funneling money through Miss Robbins to his pacifist organizations—illegal organizations."

Yes, I thought. Yes, there's still some hope. Let them think that. Let them believe that.

But then Cindy was interviewed by the authorities in Springfield, by men who were also members of the American Protective League. Under threat of arrest for sedition, she had to explain the reason for her financial support from Father. And there was Nick; he was all the evidence anyone needed.

I suppose there was official disappointment that the trail did not lead from Father to bigger fish. But in the publicity case against him, the illicit affair was very useful information indeed, especially in our town. If the man was guilty of fathering a child out of wedlock with his daughter's grade-school teacher and hiding it from his wife for eight years, if he was that morally bankrupt, then he must also be guilty of those government charges, charges which seemed vague and uncertain to many people who were not exactly sure why it was a crime to oppose the war and the draft.

And we had to face this in our small town. We all suffered, but none more than Matt. Still in school that spring, finishing his junior year, how was he to deal with such convoluted issues? He could not really understand it all, and did not want to understand. Because he was six feet tall, and physically mature, he didn't face direct taunting from his peers. But the humiliation was difficult to take. His father was dishonored, guilty of philandering and treason and God knows what else. And it was impossible to defend him. We all suffered the overly polite greetings, the condescension, the false sympathy, and, worst of all, the conversations with lifelong friends who chose not to mention Father's imprisonment.

Grandfather busied himself with repeated trips to New York, sliding down the tracks through western Massachusetts and Connecticut, hatching new legal arguments to win the release of his son. A few days later he would reappear, tired from the fruitless courtroom wrangling. Mother made repeated plans to visit Father and, although she must have been eager to escape the polite scorn of Birkett Ferry, regularly cancelled these plans, finding excuse in the needs of Matt. How could she see Father? What would she say to him? And yet he must have hungered for her face and eyes.

I had an easier time of it, returning to Cambridge after one week in Birkett Ferry. I told Mother and Matt I could not afford to miss more classes. Marshall met me at the station and I fell into his arms. He was still here, still on my side. I wept quietly into his shoulder as he stroked my hair. He had been in Springfield that week to soothe Cindy's frayed nerves after her interrogation and now he had to contend with me.

"Marshall, can we walk back?"

"But it's several miles . . ." He stopped himself as he took another look at my tear-stained cheeks. He put his arm around my waist and took my small suitcase in his other hand. "Of course we can walk."

That late spring day was lovely along the Charles. A light breeze from the sea sporadically grew to a bluster, enough to lift the flags and fill the sails of the occasional boat tacking on the water. And enough to press my skirt into the back of my legs, billowing both skirt and blouse outward, pushing us along. The scents from the sea traveled far inland, diluting the wharf-side aroma of fish and bait with fresh, salty moisture. I inhaled deeply and repeatedly, holding it in as long as possible, as if the timeless ocean scent could convince me that all these troubles would pass. The wind blew my hair about my face, and we stopped at a bench so I could fix it back. I took my time sitting there, Marshall's arm around my shoulder, the sweet breeze singing by us, the waves lapping at our feet. I thought I could stay there for hours or days. No words were needed.

But Marshall must have missed the cue. "Your father," he began.

Did we have to talk of that? Hadn't I had quite enough for one week?

"He and the others have been the focus of a lot of discussion this week on campus."

That's just wonderful, I thought. I had hoped the arrest would be a small news item in Boston.

"He's even a bit of a hero among our friends opposed to the war."

A hero? This was difficult to believe after our Birkett Ferry treatment.

"And among our pro-war friends, how does he fare? How does he fare with you, Marshall?"

"They don't agree with him, of course. But he is uniformly respected. People realize he has taken a stand based on conscience. He's been arrested for his beliefs and that's uncomfortable, even in our camp. And everyone knows he is a veteran. That really helps."

"And the affair?"

"That hasn't attracted much notice here. I think people see it as irrelevant, or they just don't care. Our friends don't connect it to his stand on the war."

"And you, Marshall," I asked again. "How does this affect you?" He must have known that I was really asking about us, our life, and our future.

"I respect your father. I think he's wrong about the war, but that's an honest disagreement. He shouldn't be in jail over it. That's for sure."

"And how does the affair affect us, Marshall?" I held my breath.

"The affair is old news for me. At one point he brought some happiness to my sister and he has helped to support her since. And without the affair there would be no Nick, and he has brought happiness to us all, especially to my sister."

"But without Nick, there might have been a different man, a marriage, perhaps more happiness."

"Water over the dam. Don't torture yourself. For us, I hope we can go on. In some ways it will be easier to be more open."

"In some ways, maybe. Until people make sense of the tangled family connections."

"I suppose it might provide some brief, gossipy entertainment, but I don't think most people care. It will be more difficult for our families."

Like Mother and Matt and Becky and Michael, I thought.

I removed my shoes and walked to the river's edge. I sat on the grassy bank to dip my feet in the icy water. I could stand the numbing cold for only a few seconds. The wind had whipped up the waves; whitecaps broke out in the middle. An invigorating day to be out sailing, I thought. It would have been a difficult day to canoe, but one could have done it; one could have done it.

After Mother, I suppose the people who should have been most angry at Father were Becky and Michael. But they were accepting and supportive.

"I've been around long enough to know it's not the end of the world," Becky said, "but I'm not sure how your mother will manage. I suppose we'll know soon enough." Mother was on the way to Boston; Becky and I were to meet her at the station. She had finally managed to see Father in prison, but I could not fathom how that meeting might have gone. She had left Matt with his Compston grandparents to finish the last weeks of school. I wrote to him, urging him to come to Cambridge for the summer.

Mother permitted only a lukewarm hug at the station; her gaze was directed downward, her affect flat. Becky's cheery voice did not provide much of a counterbalance. Later Becky attempted serious talk in the kitchen while Michael and I remained in the bookstore. Becky emerged shaking her head in failure; the barriers would not break down. A week later Mother took me for a walk by the Charles.

"You are old enough to be part of this. I'm not sure I can be together again with your father."

I couldn't say anything at first, but my stomach rolled in nausea and my legs felt fatigued beyond measure. "Can we sit?" The path and the river had blurred.

"I was allowed to see him for an hour. He said he was sorry about it all . . . You know, I can almost forgive him the affair. But he kept it secret for eight years. The secret of the child and the money he sent. And all along he was seeing them in Springfield. And why did he get himself arrested? To make a useless gesture and become imprisoned. It hurts that he deserted us without a thought, left us without income, dependent on his parents and mine. It's hard to make sense of it. It's hard to forgive."

I had my classes and my life with Marshall to distract me. Mother had nothing. And she would not allow Becky to penetrate her icy gloom. Soon, she left for the shore, to be alone, to paint her canvases, and to walk on the beach.

Marshall's relationship to Cindy remained our secret. I felt I could safely confide in Becky and Michael but to what end? I knew it was too much for Mother and Matt just now. And I could only speculate on how Birkett Ferry would use this juicy tidbit to further destroy Father.

Matt was soon with us in Cambridge, arriving the day after his last exam, not waiting for the graduation of his senior friends, not staying in Birkett Ferry a day longer than necessary. We both lived with Becky and Michael and, more than ever, I was thankful for their permissiveness, for, that summer, rules would not have worked with Matt. My brother, my shy, sensitive, secretive brother, became wild. Angry at Father for disrupting his life, angry at both parents and me, for desertion, angry at the humiliating small-town gossip, it was his time to rebel. It seemed, at first, healthy and normal. What did he have to lose? No one knew him here; it was natural to try on a new persona. He came to hear Marshall speak at the pro-war rallies. (We told him that Marshall used both names. Martin Roberts, his real name, was used only by family and close friends. Marshall Robbins was his stage name). My brother joined right in, stomping, clapping, cheering, and singing patriotic songs with the rest of us. He was now in favor of the war, since Father was opposed.

At first, worried about his shyness, I went out of my way to make him comfortable, introducing him to my friends and fellow students at planning meetings and social gatherings. I needn't have worried. I had just introduced him to three Radcliffe women, all involved in planning a rally for the following week, when I was pulled away to greet others at the door. A few minutes later I looked across the room to see Matt still in comfortable conversation with the trio. His tall, solid frame stood out and I could see how handsome he was with his sandy red hair whisked back over his forehead. His light tan freckles adorned his nose and upper cheeks as if to accent the green eyes. An hour later he was still talking with Deborah, the two of them sitting at the table each with a glass of red wine. As the meeting ended, I was relieved to see that they did not leave together. But as we were cleaning up, Matt asked me not to give him away.

"What?"

"I've been telling people that I'm nineteen and I'll be a sophomore at Amherst College."

"Matt!"

"But that I'm thinking of transferring to Harvard because there's more political activity here."

"Oh Matt! You're not even seventeen!"

"Really, what's the harm?"

And I told myself he was right. What was the harm? He needed this outlet. It was healthy and normal. Matt and Deborah began to date. Sometimes he'd be out quite late; I'd hear him come up the stairs at two in the morning, and I'd wonder if Becky and Michael were sleeping or if they, like me, were restless until he was in. Sometimes we were at the same events and I watched him with a sister's pride. But other nights I wondered where he was and whom he was with and what he was doing until the early morning hours. Deborah had an apartment that she shared with two other coeds, but surely they were not sleeping together. Surely, it was not my role to counsel my younger brother about sex.

It was enough for Michael to notice. "I guess he inherited a few things from me." At this, Becky rolled her eyes and pretended to be shocked and they both laughed. I thought they should take this more seriously but in the end I said nothing.

At times Matt drank too much. I could smell it in the bathroom after his late-night forays or on his clothing the next day. Occasionally, the sweet odor of stale alcohol mixed with the sickly fermentation of vomit.

More than eight thousand marchers appeared at a peace parade in Boston on July 1, 1917, my nineteenth birthday. Primarily organized by labor unions and socialist groups, the rally also attracted some of our friends, students with whom we remained on good terms despite our divergent political views. I watched from a corner with Marshall as marchers and banners streamed by. Quite suddenly they were attacked from a side street by a mob of uniformed soldiers and sailors. We watched in horror as our friends were bloodied with clubs and fists. We helped a battered young man to the curb; he had a nasty forehead gash and was holding on to his left knee. We stayed with him until he was able to limp home. Later we learned that the enlisted men had attacked on orders from their officers.

I knew that Father, had he not been in prison, could have been among those wounded at the rally. But there was little conversation of Father. Matt was sure he was wrong about the war and that was that. No further discussion needed. We'd get letters from Grandfather about the progress of Father's case. It did not look good for him as the country's mood veered to patriotic fervor. Matt did go, for five days, to visit Mother at the beach, but he came back angrier and more detached than ever. All he would say is that some of her canvases were "looking pretty good."

Soon I had another letter from Kevin.

I'd like to be able to write the type of noble report you are used to reading—the type I fully expected to write—like those written by Alan Seeger and, it turns out, by many of my friends who talk of the glorious righteous splendor of war. It isn't so. Where is the glory for the boy I drove back from the front so badly wounded by machine gun fire that he would loose both legs? Where is the splendor for the lad whose head, German helmet in place, was grotesquely staked by the side of the road, no evidence of a torso nearby? And the young man who could not tolerate another hour in his cramped muddy foxhole—he stood to stretch, just for a moment—he thought it would be safe in the darkness but he was mistaken for the enemy and riddled with bullets by his comrades. And the couple secreted in the sheep barn a mile back from the front. He had been sent back to fetch supplies and stole an hour for love with his French lady when a misdirected shell blew them apart.

Now that the U.S. has finally entered the war, my only hope is that there will be a rapid and overwhelming influx of American troops so that this daily carnage, benignly called a stalemate, may be ended . . .

I briefly thought of sending this letter for publication, but where would I send it? And for what purpose? Who would print it? Speaking against the war was now treasonous.

Just a week later, in late July, Matt came to breakfast limping. His right cheek was puffed out, the bruise extending over his swollen eye, and there were cuts on his right ear and chin. The wounds appeared clean, but Becky hurried to get cloths and bandages and an ice pack. Matt sat up straight, his one good eye looking proud.

"Who were the bastards?" Michael was more disturbed than Matt.

"They asked why I wasn't in uniform yet. They didn't believe I wasn't twenty-one, and they started pushing me around." Gangs of young men, most of them already enlisted or pledged to enlist, had begun to patrol the streets of Boston in a self-appointed patriotic effort to root out those avoiding military service. They'd demand to see evidence of draft registration or enlistment and, if such evidence was not forthcoming, there would be physical intimidation.

"Matt, start from the beginning."

"Deborah and I were down on Boylston Street. We'd been to Fenway Park, to the Red Sox game, and stopped in at one of the bars afterward. We drank a beer and left, but this group of men followed us out. A couple of them had on uniforms. They wanted to know why I had time to lie around in the bar when I should have been off training. And they wanted to see my draft registration. I told them I was only nineteen, but . . ."

"Nineteen! Matt, you're not even seventeen yet!" I yelled.

He looked down sheepishly. "Yes, well, I was with Deborah, and she thinks I'm nineteen."

This lie was news to Michael. "If they thought you looked older than nineteen, they certainly wouldn't have believed you were sixteen." Then he paused. "But it might have forced them to think a minute."

"Well they didn't believe it. They started calling me 'slacker' and . . ." He looked at Becky. "And they called me worse. And then they started criticizing Deborah for dating the likes of me. So I pushed the one nearest me, but there were five of them. I think Deborah's shrieking made them stop. She took me back to her apartment and cleaned up my cuts and here I am."

Michael was grim-faced. Becky bit her lower lip as she held the ice to Matt's cheek.

"It's not the first time, either."

"What! You haven't said anything." Why had I encouraged him to come to Cambridge?

"There wasn't a fight the other times. Just groups of toughs. They want to know what you think of the war. Did you register? Where is your registration card? Are you enlisting soon? You're not a slacker, are you? And they draw out the word so it's 'slaaaacker.' If your answers aren't right, they give you a little shove and say that next time they see you, they hope you'll have a uniform on. It's happened to me four or five times now."

"Oh, Matt."

It hadn't occurred to me that Matt would be subjected to this type of intimidation. And it got worse; the actions of the unofficial, self-appointed bullies were soon legitimized by the government, resulting in arrests and detainments of those over age twenty-one who could not document draft registration. I wondered if I should write to Grandfather Compston for evidence of Matt's birth date. Surely, before the summer was over, I would need to produce it at some Boston police station.

Chapter 16
1917

Marshall was spectacular in his speeches. His pro-war stance was now more popular and his audience more receptive. Soon it seemed that everyone wanted to be part of the effort; the patriotic currents swept the country to the vortex of war, leaving no time for calm reflection, no eddy for refuge. People were exhorted in theaters, restaurants, and parks by Four Minute Men and by other speakers. Sometimes they were accompanied by the type of thugs Matt encountered in Boston.

But Marshall was the most eloquent and persuasive of them all. He gave plenty of Four Minute speeches, but he was at his best in more formal rallies where he talked for fifteen or twenty minutes. He started by listing the causes of the war. Then he talked of the inhumane submarine attacks and built to the humiliation and atrocities visited on France and Belgium. His natural cadence slowed and accelerated while he gestured and pointed to the crowd and swept his dark hair from his forehead. He strode from one end of the platform to the other, never breaking the eye contact that seemed to penetrate to the back of the auditorium to engage every member of the audience. He spoke of the nobility and valor of the French soldier and the heroism of the Americans who had volunteered. Often, he included a passage from the writings of Alan Seeger, whose words and self sacrifice motivated so many.

By this point, there was no sound save for a muffled weeping, a softly hushed sob that seemed to accept the inevitable. There was no movement except for the quietly dabbed handkerchiefs. The men, Matt among them, sat straight and grim, determination in their eyes. And then Marshall reminded all that the chance to fight for this just cause was also a chance for splendid adventure, a chance to escape the humdrum jobs of farm and city. Who could resist the call to a gallant and noble journey? Who could ignore the call to serve the country and the world? The opportunity would not come again in our lifetime. And now it all became quite evangelical. Marshall asked those ready to enlist to come forward. They always did, a few at first, and Marshall grasped each one at the shoulders, bowed his head as if in blessing, and then led him to the side where the recruiters were ready. And then more came forward and the audience applauded each one; sometimes the whole audience rose and clapped and cheered and the women waved scarves and someone would start to sing "The Battle Hymn of the Republic" or "America the Beautiful" as more men marched to the platform.

Marshall would get fifteen men and sometimes thirty enlisted. The recruiters gave him the list of names, which he forwarded to Washington so as to be certain that his superiors were aware of his effectiveness. He was one of the top recruiters in the country, the best in the Northeast. He had signed up over nine hundred men in the four months since the war began. I hoped that his talents would keep him here with me and away from the European battlefields, and I suspect he had the same wish.

One summer night I sat with friends near the front of the auditorium. When the rally ended they hugged me, laughed, and suggested we meet later in a Cambridge café, an offer I declined. The recruiters gathered up their papers and Marshall finished talking to his last admirer, and finally looked to me and smiled. The foot stomping excitement had left with the audience but Marshall's face was still flushed and his forehead damp with sweat. I basked in the confident charm of his eyes as I approached and hugged him. I felt the tension of his arm and back muscles through his damp, clinging shirt. His pulse was still bounding, even in the vessels of his hand. As we walked out into the darkness, we felt the soothing salty breeze come from the east to cool our overheated bodies. We spoke of Europe, and I wondered what wind might stir the battlefields there, the differences of time and place difficult to comprehend.

I suppose I should have felt guilty commandeering his time, time when he could have been plotting further strategy with friends in smoky coffeehouses, but the next ten hours were mine. I wanted to walk back through the night along the lapping river, arm in arm, as his pulse slowed and his muscles relaxed. I wanted to stop to watch the moon sparkle on the river, to sit next to him as the sounds of car and buggy mixed with the croaking of frogs, and the smells of ocean, fish, and salt mixed with his sweaty scent and my own. I wanted to stand waiting as he unlocked the door to his apartment not quite anxious and worried like the first time but still with a shudder running down my spine, trying to calm my breathing and wondering what this time would be like, not because each time was different, I suppose, but because I could never really remember afterward; I could never recapture those longing sensations in my mind. I wanted to begin to remove my clothes the instant his door shut, simply shaking my head, almost unable to speak when he asked if I wanted a drink, so that I could lie naked on the bed and watch in the softly filtered moonlight, as he poured water and drank, all the while watching me, and then as he undressed, more slowly than me, unbuttoning his shirt and then removing his trousers. And then I wanted him to come to me slowly so I could have time to gaze at him. And then I would have him pause by the window in the moonlight until we could no longer stand the tension and he would fall beside me. And I wanted the kissing and touching to last forever because the climax was over quickly and then I would sleep and, when I woke, I would not really remember the intensity and joy of that brief moment. But I wanted him there when I woke, to stare again at his sleeping body and then to spoon against him, his front to my back, to be enveloped by his arms and feel his breath on my neck.

Matt and I were left in charge of the bookstore when Becky and Michael traveled to the beach. It would hardly be a relaxing time for them as they tried to restore Mother's shattered life. That same week Marshall was in Washington for conferences, but I would have had little energy for him anyway. All of my time was taken up by the bookstore and household chores and by worry about Matt. He couldn't help much with the store after being up so late each night. Becky and Michael didn't have many rules, but their presence must have held Matt somewhat in check. Now he reveled in his first chance at life without adult supervision. After an evening in the bars, I'd hear him stumble in at two or three o'clock and clank about in the kitchen. Then I wouldn't see him until noon.

It was too much for me to handle. I knew he was a teenager in the process of breaking free. Father's arrest, and the exposure of the affair, came at the wrong time in his life. But he wouldn't talk about any of it.

"Look, I just need to relax this summer, before I face that town and school again," he said when I complained I needed more help with the bookstore.

"Matt, I'm worried about you. You're drinking a lot and not sleeping enough, and you've gotten in fights." I paused. "And what about Deborah?" I didn't mean this to sound so awkward.

"Don't worry about me."

And that was the end of the conversation. But I was worried. I realized how difficult it would be for him to return to Birkett Ferry and high school. The publicity about Father's case would only intensify over the coming year, and it would be magnified by the patriotism sweeping the country, and by the gossip surrounding the affair.

Michael and Becky returned from the beach subdued and defeated. "She's just shut your father out completely; won't even talk about him," Becky confided to me. "She sits in the dunes or on the porch and just paints and paints for hours."

I was surprised when Matt told me he wanted to meet Cindy and Nick.

"Okay, Matt." Anything was better than his behavior of the past few weeks.

"He's my half brother; I should be able to see him." Matt didn't need to defend his request as far as I was concerned.

I warned Cindy to expect an afternoon visit and then spent several days and nights considering my options. I finally decided I needed to tell Matt that Marshall was Cindy's brother. Marshall concurred, but was relieved when I suggested that he not be present for the revelation. I told Matt during our train ride to Springfield.

He was shocked, unable to speak for a time. The rural Massachusetts landscape swept by the window. Men in horse-drawn carts roamed the fields checking the late August grain. The apples, large and red, tugged the branches to the ground. An occasional auto stopped at a crossing, waiting for us to pass. A group of boys, maybe thirteen or fourteen years old, frolicked in a lake and waved to the train, their big grins flashing. And younger children, two of them, sitting on a swing suspended from a huge old elm, pointed to the train while their three friends ran up the path beside the tracks, racing us along.

"And you think I've been acting strangely," he finally said.

"Matt, I didn't want to tell you. I know it's hard. Mother and Father don't know; no one else knows." How could I explain to him about Marshall and me? I wanted to say that Father's affair was just an unfortunate coincidence, that it had no bearing on our relationship.

Nick charged down the stairs to hug me. He must have been pleased that my brother was such a manly type; he'd be good for all kinds of play. It was a joy to see them together, and I almost wished Father could see it. Nick's skin tone was a shade darker, but they both had the same sandy red hair, the same freckles about the nose and cheeks, the same straight jaw, the same smile. Soon they were tossing a baseball out back. Matt tossed easy pop-ups and gentle grounders and Nick fired the ball back. Cindy and I watched from the kitchen window and then brought out lemonade.

While they sat on the steps sipping their drinks, Matt sealed his hero status as he told Nick about some of the games he'd been to at Fenway Park.

"It's such a big ball field, Nick, thousands of seats all new and shiny, just six years old.

"Hey, Mom! I'm older than Fenway Park!" His attention quickly returned to Matt. "Have you seen Carl Mays and Babe Ruth and Ernie Shore?"

"Yes, I was there in June when Ernie Shore pitched his perfect game—in relief and . . ."

"And Babe Ruth hit the umpire!" Nick interrupted.

"Well, yes." Matt looked to Cindy to see if this discussion was permitted.

"Wow. Mom, can we go someday?" He didn't wait for an answer. "There's one thing I don't get. How come Uncle Marshall has never been to a game?"

His name hung in the air, stopping the conversation, but it was only an instant until Matt rescued the moment. "He's a busy man, Nick. And he's doing important work."

Before we left, Matt opened his satchel to reveal a package, hastily wrapped with tissue paper and string.

"It's for you, Nick."

Nick's eyes doubled in size.

"But Nick, I want you to know I've always treasured this and I hope it's special to you, too."

Cindy and I were just as curious as Nick, who swiftly tore off the paper and pulled out the gray trainman's cap. It had been years since Matt had worn that cap, but until the age of twelve he practically slept in it. I was touched, watching as Nick proudly placed it on his head.

On the evening train back to Boston, the western sky's reflected light danced forward to color the eastern clouds orange and red. The slanting rays colored golden the grain and corn fields and pulled my gaze to the bordering stone walls that ran straight across the land, ignoring the hills and valleys and going on forever. A young woman, not much older than me, stood on one of the farmhouse porches ringing a triangular chime, summoning her man in from the barn and their children in from the yard, all to sit easily round their dinner table, joking about the follies of the animals and the neighbors, and the school friends, and each other. It seemed as if I could travel on this train in this light forever without seeing any change.

The train was nearly full. Across the aisle from us was a businessman dressed in a brown suit, coat folded across his lap, tie askew, absently studying a sales list, and later pretending to sleep to avoid conversation with his seatmate, an elderly grandmother. She was traveling, I imagined, for the first time by train, sitting upright and tense, purse grasped tightly, eyes held straight ahead yet nervously studying all the other passengers, almost afraid to breathe.

And, in front of us, sat a young woman. I supposed she was on her way to Boston, but for what purpose? A student? Maybe, but her single worn suitcase, her shawl pulled about sunburned arms, and her bonnet enclosing wispy, straw-colored hair, all gave the air of a farm girl escaping to the city to work, perhaps as a seamstress or a sales clerk in her uncle's clothing shop. I had watched at the station as a soldier, about her age, surveyed the occupants of the car before sitting next to her. The car had quite a number of traveling servicemen and, as he looked about, I'm sure this fellow thought he had chosen the best seat. He smiled and made repeated attempts at conversation. She replied with shy nods and single words. He seemed to accept this as a challenge and turned in his seat to face her more directly, surely hoping she would notice his sparkling, interested eyes. He began to tell her of his life and why he chose to enlist and how he hoped to fight in Europe. The train swayed from side to side, moving them in synchrony, as in a rhythmic dance.

Matt had receded into his seat and appeared to be studying the passing countryside even though it was now too dark to see anything but his own reflection in the window. He avoided eye contact with the other passengers, and I realized what it must be like for a young male to be unadorned by a uniform. He had experienced fights and challenges on the Boston streets, but even here I could detect it: condescension from the servicemen in the way they looked quickly away from us while holding their bodies erect, a subtle contempt from the conductor whose son, no doubt, was already in the service, and disinterest from the young female passengers.

And I had added to Matt's burdens. I imagined the disclosure of Marshall's identity to be the last straw in the list of family abominations. As complete darkness settled over the countryside and clatter from the train obscured the murmuring of other passengers, he turned to me, tears threatening to spill down his cheeks.

"How can I go back to school in Birkett Ferry? How can I ever live there again?"

"It's only one more year." I just wanted to keep him talking.

"One more year. Last spring, I couldn't have stayed one more week."

"What other choice do you have?"

He looked at me, his green eyes searching for release, his lips quivering in defeat. "None, I guess."

He turned back to the window and stared out, surely only seeing himself—and me. I waited but he made no move to continue. I couldn't let the conversation end here.

"Matt, I think you have three choices." He turned to me, eyes dull and sad. "First, you could return to Birkett Ferry. It is only one more year, and how bad could that be? You'd have to live with the grandparents; we can't count on Father being out of prison, and now I don't think we can count on Mother, either. Second, you could do your senior year in Cambridge. We could both live with Becky and Michael. That's fine with me, but," I needed to rush through this part, "but you need to cut out the drinking and the late nights. And you need to date someone your own age." I paused to watch him. "I mean it, Matt." And I did mean it; sometimes I wondered where the old Matt, the Matt of our childhood, had gone. It seemed like a tremendous burden on me, to play the part of a parent; I wasn't sure I was up to it.

"And my third choice?"

"Your third choice, Matt," I paused because I wasn't sure I had considered this carefully enough but then I plunged ahead, "Your third choice is to enlist."

He didn't look surprised, so I suspected this was not a new idea for him. Instead, he studied me carefully as he calmly stated, "But I'm not eighteen."

"You know as well as anyone that you look like you're twenty-two; I don't think you'd have a problem."

He turned back to the window. "Do you think that's the best plan then?"

"Oh, I don't know, Matt. It's just an idea; I'm not sure what is best. I do know that if I were male and eighteen or twenty-two, I'd enlist. Marshall has convinced me of that. But I'm not male and I'm not seventeen, and I don't know if it's best for you."

He was quiet for the remainder of the trip. When we arrived in Boston I wasn't surprised to see the soldier holding the farm girl's bag and helping her down to the platform. I doubted that her life had changed for the better.

A letter from Father waited for us at the bookstore.

My dearest Gwen and Matt, I've received and appreciated your letters and I know you've received mine, shallow as they've been. I've avoided the sensitive issues because I wanted to have this conversation in person. I keep expecting to be released the next day and the next week. In spite of the zealots who now run our government, I cannot understand how I can be held simply for speaking my mind in this democratic land so dedicated to the freedom of speech. But now I've been here four months and I just don't know how much longer they will keep me. There are things I need you both to know. Though I'm sure it has been hard for you, I do not regret my stand against the war. I think that, someday, you may better understand my position but even if you never agree with me, I'm sure you respect my right to disagree with the government.

"I will regret to my death, the pain I have caused you, and Mother, and others who have suffered so severely from the exposure of my liaison with Cynthia Robbins. There is nothing I can say or do to excuse my behavior. I can only hope that time will ease the wounds. Please accept that I meant to act honorably in offering some financial support to her and Nick. Please don't direct your blame at Cynthia. In fact, I hope that you might see fit to meet them.

Matt had nothing to say but I was pleased, and I suspect he was too, to have already acted on Father's request.

Chapter 17
1917

By the last week in August there wasn't much time for Matt to choose his future. I suspected he would return to Birkett Ferry for his senior year, and I suppose I was relieved that I would not have to tolerate another ten months of his antics in Cambridge.

So when he sat beside me in that stuffy old auditorium with his shirt torn, his eye swollen, and his breath reeking, I hoped this was his last fling. I wasn't prepared when he rose to stand in line with the rest, to be welcomed by Marshall, to be led to the enlistment table. Why did I let them do it—Matt and Marshall? Why did I not stop it? But over the following days, when there was still time, I wondered about his response if I undermined his plans. Would he even return to school? Or would he simply go south or west and enlist elsewhere? Or would he go on some drunken binge? How much longer would I have any control over him? And he was taking such a toll on my time and energy. Marshall didn't offer much help with the decision, but he did point out that Matt was not the only underage recruit.

It was Matt's idea that we not tell Becky or Michael or Mother or anyone else. The plan was simple enough. Becky and Michael assumed he was going back to Birkett Ferry that week. Mother and Father thought the same. Mother told Matt that she had spoken with our Compston grandparents and they were looking forward to having Matt live with them. But Matt wrote to them, apologizing for the late notice and explaining that he had decided, only at the last moment, to stay with us and attend school in Cambridge. He hoped he hadn't caused them much inconvenience.

It was sad to think of our home, now vacant, after all the years of bustle, energy, work, and love. How welcome a sight was that home on a January afternoon, the fading light scarcely reflecting off the shadowy blue snow as the chill penetrated my clothing. How welcome a sight to see the warm glow across the snowy green as the stark trees waved their dark branches against the dimming sky. I would stand on the green, defying the icy cold and wind, waiting for inactivity to further deaden my tired, chilled limbs. I could see a dozen houses around the green and I found our home the most inviting. The interior light roiling about on the frosted windows could have stirred a sense of mystery but there was no mystery to me. The path, freshly shoveled by Matt, guided me to our door. And when I entered, the heat embraced me even in the outer room where I left my boots and layers of wool clothing before finding the sweetness of the kitchen. Mother, I knew, would be smiling to me as she pulled a pan of gingerbread from the oven, and the fragrance of that gingerbread with cloves and nutmeg and cinnamon would so arrest me that I really wanted just to sit at the table and breathe it all in.

"Your cheeks are so red," she'd say while touching them quickly, "and so cold," and she'd recoil in mock surprise. "We were just beginning to wonder where you were. Your brother checked the green a while ago. He's got a wonderful fire going now. Why, if your father is late, we'll just eat this gingerbread before dinner. Let's go sit by your brother."

And Matt would be stretched out prone, reading by the crackling fire, and he'd smile at me too but just briefly before returning to his book. And Mother would stay only a moment before returning to the kitchen but then she'd be back and forth, standing in the doorway only long enough to ask about our day, looking, I think, for an excuse to gaze on her children. And I'd pull my chair a bit closer until the fire had driven the last chill from my muscles, and then I'd curl knees to chin and watch as a log collapsed onto the coals in a glorious cascade of sparks. Then Matt would look up and poke the fire and add another log. And soon I'd hear Father enter the kitchen, and I imagined the warmth and the glow and the gingerbread and the family love would affect him in the same way. And I'd listen to their quiet murmurings, not able to hear the words, but knowing they spoke of their day and their children. And in the pause that followed I'd picture them, as he came up next to her by the stove and turned her toward him to kiss her lightly on the lips before pulling back at arm's length still holding her at the waist to gaze into her merry eyes, and then he'd return for a drawn-out kiss that finally made her pull away in mock fluster. "Will, I've got to finish this dinner." And then he'd come in to us to exchange quiet greetings and to sit for a time as I had done to absorb the warmth into his soul.

In spite of my family's troubles, I like to believe that there were times, at least a few, that were like this. But now this scene could never be repeated. Was it any wonder Matt couldn't go home? There was no home.

So, after good-byes to Becky and Michael, I took him to Marshall's apartment, where we left most of his possessions, keeping only what he needed for training camp. At the station he was as resolute and determined as any of the young men who boarded the chartered train taking them through New York to the camp in New Jersey. And I was as teary eyed as the other women, the mothers, wives, and sisters who were seeing their men off amid the jumble of luggage and the bittersweet talk of lovers and families trying to meaningfully fill the time before departure, anxious for the train to leave yet dreading the moment, proud of their men yet enormously fearful for them. Matt and I shared a final hug and he was up the steps. And then, waving through the window, he was gone.

Once again I wondered what we were doing. I supposed there was still time to change things round. All I needed to do was notify the proper people of his age.

It was only six days before I had the first letter from him, mailed to Marshall's address.

You really will not believe who I met on the train; I sat right next to him. You must remember Hezekiah, the Charles River boy we befriended that one summer. I must have been about seven and we would see his family camped under the bridge. Michael began taking them food and once we took him out in the canoe. I told him how, for years, he was our imaginary playmate; we'd rescue him from blizzards and shipwrecks or maybe he would rescue us. Well of course I didn't recognize him. But how many people are named Hezekiah? Of course, he remembers that summer too. He just turned eighteen, so he's barely of legal enlistment age himself. He kept asking about my age, remembering me as younger, so finally I told him the truth and swore him to secrecy. He still lives in Boston but, believe it or not, he's married with a baby daughter. He thought he should enlist; they've not had much money and, without prospect of a decent job, the army pay seemed pretty good. Miraculously, we've been assigned to the same unit and have pledged to help each other through training. I wish you could tell Michael about Hezekiah but that wouldn't do, would it? Not yet anyway . . .

No, not yet. Although it would be fun to tell Michael. I knew he would enjoy the memories of that summer. I wondered how long it would be before it was discovered that Matt was not with either set of grandparents. The grandparents generally did not communicate with each other; their news was filtered through Mother or Father. Mother assumed Matt was in Birkett Ferry, but she wasn't interacting much with any family member. Father now thought him to be in Cambridge; that's what his father told him during their frequent meetings in prison. I set up an elaborate scheme whereby mail from Matt would have the desired postmark. He mailed letters to Marshall, several at a time, all in a large envelope. Those needing a Birkett Ferry postmark, I forwarded on to Cousin Anna. I had reluctantly recruited her, telling her only that Matt was having a difficult time because of Father's imprisonment and the subsequent separation of our parents—all true enough—and that Matt needed Mother to believe he was in Birkett Ferry, while, I told her, he was really in Cambridge. And I had arranged for Matt's mail, arriving in either Birkett Ferry or Cambridge, to be forwarded to Marshall's apartment, where I could send it on to him.

This whole contrivance sapped a lot of my energy. I suppose I worried and schemed more than needed. The world was in such chaos; no one would notice that one boy was missing. The starry-eyed young men were off to glorious war. Among them was Jonathan, Anna's husband, my first boyfriend. He had been drafted only a month after becoming eligible when he turned twenty-one. He was training in Connecticut, and it was expected that his unit would ship to Europe before year's end. All those young men—they were thrilled to be a part of the spirited adventure, certain their cause was righteous, certain of victory. And it would be wrong of us to deny Matt the opportunity to participate, wouldn't it?

Women took jobs vacated by men in factories, farming, universities, and government. Everyone volunteered in hospitals or by planting fallow ground to increase food production or by making up packages of clothing and food for servicemen. I often felt my class time wasted. I should be sewing uniforms or caring for children whose mothers were working an extra factory shift. Free time was suspect. One needed to constantly contribute, to be worthy.

Marshall was continually planning more rallies and speeches and, because of his success, he was now training other recruiters. Many of his friends, having also attended the Plattsburgh camps, agreed to serve as officers in some of New England's best units. He was approached several times but declined and soon received a draft deferment based on his current service. We had less time for one another and, when we lingered in bed on a Sunday morning in October, I felt the war effort might suffer due to our indolence. We should have more enjoyed that crisp autumn Sunday with the rusty red maple leaves waving gently about our open window, seeming to fan in the cool, night-freshened air. We could have pulled the quilt up to our chins, snuggled our bodies together, and rested a moment longer. We could have waited for the sun to burn through the misty vapor that hung low over the river. The air eventually would have warmed enough for me to stir from bed. Then I would have donned my bathrobe and stood in the sunlight that streamed through the window. He would have watched as I brewed the tea and scrambled the eggs. And I could have brought the food back to bed for him and, when we finished eating, he would reach without a word to loosen the tie on my robe and pull me toward him and we'd delight in each other as we lay in the sunlight which covered the bed.

But no. Now a sense of duty drove us out of bed to dress and eat quickly, not a moment to lose in our patriotic devotions.

Chapter 18
1917–18

As I returned from class one December afternoon, Michael stood at the bookstore counter and nodded toward the kitchen. "You'd best go in there."

At the table with Becky was a plump woman in her late thirties. Crease lines about her cheeks hinted at frequent merriment though now her eyes looked at me with a somber gaze as she slumped in her chair. Sitting next to her was a young woman about my age, petite with a sharp chin, prominent nose and dark features, holding a child perhaps nine or ten months old who bore a strong resemblance to her mother.

Becky gestured to the center of the table where a pecan pie, half consumed, was surrounded by tea cups and small plates with crust remnants. "Mrs. Chalmers has brought us a lovely pie." Becky was watching for my reaction but I was at a loss to place these people. The older woman brightened as she studied my face.

The child squirmed in her mother's lap, reaching toward the floor and, when her mother put her down, she crawled briskly, confidently crossing to the chair of the older woman whom I supposed to be her grandmother. The child looked back to her mother with a confident grin and then, turning to the business at hand, she placed first one hand on the lower dowel of the chair, before reaching with the second hand to grasp the seat and thereby pull herself to a stand with such a practiced movement that I wondered if she had been doing this for hours.

"I'd have known you," said the older woman. "Even after all these years I would have recognized your face and your eyes. But I've a mind you don't know us."

"Well, I'm not quite sure . . ." I stammered.

The toddler squirmed about in her lap, aiming toward the floor, and the grandmother bent to put her down to return to her mother.

"I'm Hezekiah's mother, and this is my daughter-in-law and my granddaughter. We met you all those years ago, it must have been 1908. We saw you on your walks when we were staying under the bridge without a home that summer. Your grandfather was so kind to us . . . and you kids too, so nice to Hezekiah. I'll never forget it . . ."

I was thankful for the respite as she chattered on but there was no hope of composure. I grabbed a chair to steady myself but I must have looked frightened and pale. After Matt left I worried each day that our fraud would be unmasked. But then, as time went by, I began to fret that he would escape detection. "Surely," I wrote to Matt, "surely, you cannot finish training and ship to Europe and fight in a war without telling Mother and Father."

" . . . So when Hezekiah wrote to us about teaming up with Matt, I remembered you all so well from that summer when your grandfather had told us about his bookstore, and I knew right where it was and I thought I'd take you a pie. And show off my granddaughter, too." She beamed down at the child who was again making her way back across the floor. But then she frowned. "I had no idea really; Hezekiah never wrote a word, that you didn't know where Matt was."

"I think it's apparent that you did know," Becky sighed. "Am I right, Gwen?"

The upshot was far less than I'd feared. There was a great deal of talk, and to some extent, I was blamed. Even in self-defense I couldn't bring myself to tell them of Matt's drinking or the worry he had caused me that summer. And surely Mother and Father must have recognized that their own behavior, resulting in the breakup of our family, was responsible for Matt's rudderless summer and his undetected enlistment.

There was not much Father could do about it, not from his jail cell. Mother and Becky wanted, at first, to go to New Jersey to haul him back home—as if there was a home to haul him to. I had always thought this would be the end result. But, as Grandfather Compston reasoned with Mother and Becky and Michael, he would be eighteen in less than a year, and Congress was ready to lower the draft age from twenty-one to eighteen. By the time they got him released, he would be drafted. At least now he was serving with people he knew and liked.

And they all tried to imagine the publicity that would result when the family of a man jailed for pacifism appealed for the military discharge of his son. So many boys were going now, enlisted, drafted, trained, and starting to sail for Europe, and how many of them were underage? And, truth be told, we were all caught up in the war frenzy now, all of us except Father. His lonely voice rang hollow, echoing about ineffectively against those prison walls.

In reality, we were all quite proud of Matt. Grandfather Compston boasted that his grandson was grabbing the opportunity that he had missed.

They were scheduled to sail in mid-January. General Pershing wanted one million American men to join him in France by spring; some experts estimated that three to four million Americans would eventually be needed. There was such a shortage of ships that the men could not be transported as quickly as they were ready, so some units had a ten-day leave before boarding.

When I found Matt at the Boston train station, he stood artificially straight in that poised military stance, grinning widely in a self-confident way. His chest seemed broader and there was a healthy red glow brightening his lean cheeks. It was wonderful to feel his embrace. Hezekiah was six inches shorter than Matt and broader at the shoulders with a well-tanned face and dark hair. He hugged his wife, daughter, and mother and then vigorously shook my hand.

We all looked proudly at our boys and so did strangers. College girls blew flirtatious kisses from sixty feet away. The gesture was innocent, I knew, but still it surprised me and made me wonder what other benefits were available to these boys in uniform. A middle-aged man clapped Matt on the back and pumped Hezekiah's hand, "Well done, boys," and then he was off to his train. And for men of the proper age not in uniform, there were disapproving stares and scowls, and this pattern was now socially accepted, even contagious. How often had I directed a special smile to a man in uniform or hurried to help him in the bookstore? How often had I stared at a young civilian, not exactly frowning at him but wondering if there was any good reason why he had not yet signed up?

There were hugs all around of course. Mother came in from the beach and the Compston grandparents came from Birkett Ferry, and somehow we all squeezed into Becky and Michael's small home. I slept on the living room couch, and Matt spread his bedroll right in the bookstore, back in the corner, just by the empty bottom shelf where he used to hide and read for hours in his secret den.

It was all quite gay, and on the last night Grandfather Compston took everyone out to a grand dinner. He offered a toast to Matt that recalled the regret he had "always felt, really just a tinge of regret now, after all these years, but still regret nonetheless, at missing my chance to serve the country in the Civil War when I could have fought alongside the best of men. And your father, Matt, who has certainly made some mistakes and who, I think, is wrong now about this war, fought so proudly in Cuba in 1898 and I salute him for that, and even though he isn't here, I know how proud he is of you. And now it's your turn Matt. Our love goes with you."

Mother caught a sob in her throat and dabbed her eyes, but I just let the tear slide down my cheek as we raised our glasses to Matt and brought the red wine to our lips.

There was one more visit to make, and the next morning Matt and I left Cambridge for New York. Matt was still too young to visit the prison, but Grandfather suspected that his uniform would gain him unchallenged entrance. We passed through several locked gates to a small, dank visiting room open to the corridor on one side. There were no windows, no sunlight, no relief form the stale, musty air. As echoing footsteps approached, my heart raced and I squeezed Matt's hand. We had not seen Father in nine months. Then he was in the room, face thinned, full beard scraggly, and hair poorly kept. But his strong eyes peered forth, undefeated. He strode forward to embrace us each in turn and then both together before pulling back to gaze at us.

"You know," he smiled at Matt, "I think this will improve my standing among the guards—to have my son visit in uniform. You both look great."

Matt told him of the training camp and they compared it to the training Father had in 1898. He stared beyond us for a moment. "It was just twenty years ago . . . how could that be?" he asked. "It seems so long ago, several worlds away. How could it be that my grown son is now set to fight another war?" We were still while he reflected, and then he turned to me. "You were born while I was in Cuba, just about the time we charged up San Juan Hill."

Matt asked about the progress of his case, which seemed to be proceeding at such a dreary pace. "Your grandfather has been an immense help, but I think the war will be ended before I have my trial." And he told us of his tedious life in prison. There was not enough to read, his letters, incoming and outgoing, were censored, the food was atrocious, there was not much exercise, and he saw far too little sunlight. It was difficult, he said, to maintain any optimism.

When he asked about Mother, I said I thought she'd had more difficulty than anyone else. But Matt quickly added that she had seemed livelier that past week during his visit. "She's brought some canvases into Cambridge and there's a dealer interested in a show."

"Painting is probably the best thing for her right now. She hasn't answered my letters, you know." We had no response to this.

"And thank you for visiting Cynthia and Nick. I know it meant a lot to Cynthia, and I hear that Nick thought the world of you, Matt."

Matt glanced at me and I'm sure my face flushed, but I couldn't bring myself to tell Father about Marshall and his relationship to Cindy.

Our visit was limited to one hour, but the guard gave us a few extra minutes for parting words. As the gates clanged shut behind us, I was grateful he had not criticized Matt for his enlistment, nor me for allowing it.

Two days later I stood on the docks of Hoboken, New Jersey, watching the loading of the decrepit freighter that had been hastily converted to transport troops. I was waving my blue hat back and forth above my head, hoping that Matt and Hezekiah could see me among the thousand others who were yelling and cheering. Then Matt, standing on the deck next to Hezekiah, pointed in my direction and waved his cap in return.

From that day forward there was not a day without worry. The German U-boats were active just a few miles off the East Coast and I couldn't help imagining the torpedo penetrating the hull and the old freighter quickly listing as the tiny lifeboats were lowered into the giant swells of the North Atlantic, the January winds buffeting the men and freezing their wet clothing to their bodies. Another ship in the convoy would attempt rescue, but they had dismal prospects in those conditions.

Matt's letters were upbeat and offered transient relief from worry, and I was supremely thankful for each one. But they arrived weeks after being written and there was no way to guess what might have happened in the meantime.

> You must make the voyage to Europe some day, though
> I would suggest a time of peace. Then you could better enjoy
> the magnificent expanse of ocean and sky. There is nothing

else to be seen save the fleet of clouds racing across the heavens from west to east, as if to mimic the ship's progress across the water. You could lie on deck at night as we did (although I would suggest July instead of January as a time more conducive to this activity) and admire the brilliance of the starry heavens and later the half-moon would slide up in the east to sparkle over the water. And you could be lulled to sleep by the gently rocking waves. I'm sure you would have your own cabin and not be crammed below decks in hammocks and berths stacked four on top of each other, every foot of space taken up by gear and men, the air trapped below and fouled by the stench of sweat, vomit, and toilet. And I'm sure you would not suffer from seasickness as Hezekiah did when, unable to eat a thing for the first three days, he must have lost ten pounds. You would stroll pleasantly about the deck until it was time for an elegant dinner served while you gazed out over the ocean. There'd be no need to stand in line for an hour to receive a bowl of poorly defined gruel that would soon be retched overboard.

"But we have made it to solid ground in France; the sight of the harbor and the rolling hills beyond were welcome. And we expect the food rations will now be better and more inclined to remain in our stomachs. I'll write again in a few days. My love to all, Matt.

Even though he was faithful to his promise to write soon, it was weeks before his next letter arrived and then there were several, all within a few days.

We were happy to leave the ship; we hoped for a chance to stretch our legs past the foreign shops and cafés, eager to hear the language and see the people. We imagined even a day of leave to stroll past farmyards and gray stone cottages to the distant hills colored white under a layer of snow. But we scarcely had time to walk through the port before we were herded (most literally) into railroad freight cars, which surely traveled right past all the picturesque scenes I imagined. There were no windows to verify this suspicion, and even if there had been they would have been blocked by stacks of gear. A few men perched uncomfortably atop the mounds of supplies and packs, but most of us had to stand as the train lurched and shuddered along at the slowest possible speed often stopping completely for an hour. We lacked sufficient food and water and soon I wondered if the current stench and discomfort exceeded that of the ship. Twice, we were allowed off to fertilize the trackside brush and then we could look out over the countryside of France. Back in the west the port and the ocean were lost to view, replaced by the valleys and hills which stretched in all directions. I'm sure it must be a magnificent sight in May, when the hills are covered with wildflowers and the fresh green of spring sparkles from one hilltop to the next, or in August when the grain is waving golden in the sun and the fruit trees are burdened.

But now, wearied and sickened by our travels, we are as tired and pale as the stark land. There is hardly a tree to be seen aside from the occasional orchard that stands empty and barren with gnarled trunks and spidery branches appearing black against the bleak frosty ground. At the horizon, the sky is of the same hue, covered with such heavy clouds that the sun's location is not discernible. There are, to be sure, a few scattered farmhouses that should appear welcoming, but the stagnant wisps of chimney smoke only accent their isolation and make me wonder who is left inside. It is said that the younger men are all gone to war or dead or disabled. It is the women and children and perhaps the old grandparents who must tend the remaining livestock, but most of the stock has been taken to feed their husbands and brothers in the army. One knows only that the weak winter light will soon be gone completely. There will be no welcoming fire glow from those windows where wood fuel must be conserved and where the blinds are drawn against the war. It is almost a relief to go back into the boxcar where at least we are warm when pressed so tightly together. We arrived at our camp close to midnight, but it was many hours more before we were organized enough to erect our tents and sleep.

By late February he wrote, "Whatever strength we had lost by our forced shipboard inactivity has been restored by our endless marching through the countryside, ten or twenty miles in a day with full packs. I don't really tire of it though; I've always liked to hike and I prefer a day of marching to a day spent idling in camp."

In March the headlines told of new German offensives, which drew large numbers of American soldiers into combat for the first time. The casualty lists began to appear and, at home, we all became more committed to support the troops in whatever way we could by helping in hospitals and factories and by following the government's directives to forgo meat on Mondays and wheat on Wednesdays. By April and May, Matt's animated letters reflected the vibrancy of spring.

When our unit was given a one week leave, some of us retired to a small village about twenty miles from our encampment. For a few francs Hezekiah and I secured a room and meals with an elderly French couple. It is difficult to describe the delight of a real bed with sheets and quilt and, most glorious of all, a soft pillow in which my head remains snuggled as long as I like each morning as I drift from one pleasant dream to another. Finally, my hunger pangs driven wild by the beckoning smells of coffee and bread, I leave my chamber, dressed as I please, to be served breakfast in a tiny courtyard surrounded by stone walls six feet in height connecting to the matching stone house. Hezekiah and I sit there in the courtyard, filling our stomachs with the most pleasant food and gazing through an arched gateway across several fields to low hills covered in the wild yellows, reds, and violets of spring. It reminds me of home when we would sit on the knoll surrounded by the bright wildflowers and bask in the sunlight and look out to the opposite hills where the same colors would summon us to explore each field and hill, knowing that if we arrived at a distant hill there would be countless more beyond. Remember how we could see plows working the fields by the river? Did we imagine it or could we actually smell that damp pungent upturned earth? It was a scent which would ask us to explore the spring countryside. But we did not leave that one spot. We were content to gaze on the scene below as we stretched out among the grass and flowers and soaked up the sun's warmth. Or we would perch in a tree, hidden and endlessly patient, spying on others and telling our tales. Do you remember?

Well, it is the same here now. We sit in this snug courtyard as the flowers and hills and new plowed fields call to us; yet we do not go. We are content to stay here, watching and thinking and composing letters. The smell of the fields and the colors of the flowers are the same, but there are differences of course. The fields are plowed not by men but by woman and girls or by boys not yet fourteen years of age. And there is general dismay at the slow progress of cultivation; you see, the horses and draft animals have gone off to war with the men, so the soil must be tilled by hand.

The stone work is rustically elegant and the homes and walls blend with the natural landscape. Someday I should like such a solid and pleasing dwelling. But their welcoming appearance is deceitful; with the men gone, a worried melancholy remains. The people are pleased to have us here; we provide them a measure of security.

We are content to stay in the courtyard, limiting our forays to late afternoon when we cannot resist the light which seems to focus on the old church steeple and the hills beyond. Then we climb to a knoll to watch the sunset when the sky is lit up with red, orange, pink, and gold, and we talk of our friends and family over there in the west. But, once the sun is gone, the cool dampness descends to the earth and we retreat to our courtyard. And I think that I would never want to leave this place . . .

But a letter, only ten days later, offered a different sentiment.

Those days off were pleasant and restful, but I am glad to be back to our camp. We have heard that many American divisions have seen action now and we are fearful we may miss the war. Rumors circulate daily that we will march to the front soon or that we will stay here for two more months. No one seems to know. It is grand to see us on the march, hundreds of men, sometimes thousands—we are full of energy and enthusiasm and spirit. It reminds me of the stories I've heard of Teddy Roosevelt and his exuberant leadership, and then I think of Father and San Juan Hill, though of course I know he feels differently now. Sometimes I catch a view of the marching lines ahead curving into a wood or up over a hill and it is just the most splendid thing to see. I feel so fortunate to be part of it. We feel fit and strong and ready for action . . .

And by midsummer, he had seen action as his unit rotated to the front line and back several times.

It is good we had heard so much about the squalor of the trenches; I think we would have been disappointed had they not lived up to our fears. And yet, when we express admiration for those who have survived among the rats and mud, we are advised that current summer conditions are quite luxurious compared to winter's torment of storms when icy muck can reach up over the knees. One Brit disagreed though, saying that in winter the heavy aromas produced by unclean men, both living and dead, are muted in the frosty air. And I have to say that there are times when the stench of sweat, moldering garbage, and human waste are so overpowering that I cannot eat. The dead and wounded are removed quickly so we do not have to contend with that type of odor (although the veterans tell of times when corpses have lain rotting for weeks in the no-man's-land between the trenches before they could be retrieved).

In spite of it all, it is rather glorious being at the front. This is what we have been training for and our spirits are grand. Much of the time there is an eerie quiet with lots of time for thought. I often have only a view of the trench muck below and the sky above and a few of my comrades (including Hezekiah) to the sides. Although it is tempting to rise up and stare about, the exposure is risky and the view is hardly pleasing. Out in front of us are two hundred yards of barren land pockmarked by shell craters and crisscrossed with barbed wire, and beyond are the German trenches.

The landscapes to the sides and rear are not much better. I retain an image of a stark tree collapsed grotesquely onto an abandoned roofless barn from which the animals had fled, all save a plaintive, scrawny, black and white cat mewing at the doorframe. And another memory of a home missing an entire sidewall, floor covered in plaster, dust and rubble, furniture all gone for fuel, cupboards open and long since emptied by the fleeing family or troops. And strewn everywhere over the landscape, there are shell craters, waste, and wreckage. We see these things when we rotate to the rear. We spend eight days at the front followed by four days in the remnants of a town, three miles back, where we are relatively safe except for the occasional shell. Here we catch up on sleep and the rations are more predictably supplied. At the front I don't sleep much, perhaps only a few hours each night; I am surprised by my lack of fatigue, but when we are relieved Hezekiah and I and others bivouac in the small village church (which is missing the steeple and half the roof) where we collapse and sleep for an entire day. Yet only twenty miles away is the cozy village which kept us for that lovely week.

I may have already said more than the censors allow. And we are not to discuss battle details. Suffice it to say that I have fired my rifle and been fired upon. But I am well and I feel so fortunate not to have missed this adventure. Every day is memorable and magnificent: the marching troops, the playing of the Marseillaise, the hours of quiet in the trenches, the camaraderie of friends, and even the thundering shells and the chaos of battle for they remind us of the noble and just cause we are pursuing.

Hezekiah asks if you would mind checking on his wife and daughter. It has been some time since he has heard from them; it is probably just the mail delays—your letters often take two months to arrive. His family receives his paycheck, but he worries about them with the shortages and rations . . .

There were large gaps of time between Matt's letters, too. My worry about him became a vague sort of fear, something restless and irritable in the back of my mind, like a constant whine which by its continual presence becomes more muted and less noticed. At times I felt guilty that I was not more worried, but really I could do nothing for him. I could only help the general cause with my volunteer efforts. I continued my education, but I also took instruction to become a nurse's aide. I helped with the usual nursing chores, delivering care to a surprising number of wounded veterans, men with missing limbs or eyes. I most enjoyed sitting with these men, offering comfort and conversation and reading to them.

And I needed time for Marshall. His recruitment duties had subsided; the vast majority of men now entered through the draft. I was surprised that he was not drafted, but I suppose he was more valuable to the government as an effective speaker, a Four Minute Man, where he could explain why pacifists and socialists remained a danger, and why it had become a crime to speak against the government, and why it was beneficial to the country to observe "meatless Mondays" and "wheatless Wednesdays."

I had a lovely visit with Hezekiah's wife and child. They lived in a small house with his mother and seemed comfortable and happy. I think they were embarrassed that I brought them a grocery bag with cheese, fruit, vegetables, and a small cut of beef. The child had grown so much in the past few months that I thought it a shame that Hezekiah was missing it all. She had quite a vocabulary, repeating everything she heard and laughing at her own mispronunciations in unison with her grandmother. As she peeked out from behind her mother's dress folds, her luminous brown eyes sparkled. She tugged at her dark curls before charging into the next room to retrieve her favorite book, *Peter Rabbit*, which she confidently brought to me. "Read me this," she demanded. So I lifted her onto my lap to oblige.

Chapter 19
1918–19

In late August of 1918, Father was released. He agreed to a plea bargain in which he admitted guilt for seditious speech in return for a sentence of fifteen months in prison, the time he had already served. It was only through his father's intervention that he was not barred from the practice of law, but he worried that his clients would shun him. He returned to Birkett Ferry to open the house and to try to reestablish his practice. Mother remained in the beach house considering his appeal for a reunion.

And then our tenuous stability was destroyed when Jonathan, my first boyfriend and my cousin's husband, was killed in France. Slaughtered really, but we only learned that a year later when some of his companions returned from France and stopped in Birkett Ferry for a sympathy visit with Anna. They had been ordered up an embankment to disarm several nests of German machine guns. And they finally succeeded but only because of the sheer volume of men sent up that embankment—only after more than one hundred men had fallen, mowed down in front of their charging comrades.

I was numb with grief. I could not believe Jonathan was really gone.

At the service he was memorialized as the hero he was. Anna sat up straight in the first pew dressed in black, holding the child that he had never seen, supported by our large family. As the last hymn faded, the child batted at Anna's tears and restlessly squirmed about to smile at anyone who dared to catch her eye. Jonathan's young body remained in France, nestled among his friends in the endless straight rows of white crosses. He was the first casualty from Birkett Ferry and, for many of us, the first casualty we had personally known. In spite of the lists of casualties published daily in the newspapers, in spite of my work in the hospital, in spite of the letters from Kevin and Matt, or maybe because of these things, my mind had become hardened against the possibility of true personal tragedy, and it took the hammer blow of Jonathan's death to shatter my shield.

Mother came home for the funeral but it was unclear if she would remain. With the three of us in the house for ten days, the tension became so thick that each day I sought refuge outside, wandering along the river or sometimes up to the knoll. I thought it might be easier to heal with just the two of them in the house. So far they had barely spoken. They slept separately but that was the easy part. It was more difficult to pass in the kitchen with averted eyes, to sit at the table in uncomfortable silence, and to pretend to be absorbed in evening reading. We took turns preparing functional meals and ate dinner with Grandmother and Grandfather a couple of times. But it was hard to find a safe subject. Every topic related to the war, which we discussed gingerly, fearful of deepening the family rift. But Matt was our common thread. The shock of Jonathan's death combined with the family reunion—all of us except Matt—made us ache for his safety. My parents must have imagined, as I did, the worst that could happen to him. It was as though by imagining his death we could negate the possibility of its occurrence.

As I walked through the familiar fields and along the river, Matt was a constant presence. We had canoed the river a hundred times; we knew every ripple, current, and eddy. We had basked on the beach of the island, devouring our picnic lunch and teasing the jays with our leftover bread. We had skated on the river when the ice was black and snowshoed across when the snows came.

In those early September days following Jonathan's funeral, I didn't see another person up on the knoll, and I thought how cruel it was to relegate children to musty classrooms when the air was the clearest, the sky the brightest, the sunlight the most welcome, and the clouds the most playful. How cruel to relegate men and women to dark offices, stores and homes. And how cruel to relegate men to war. I sat on the stone foundations where we had read for hours as the sun sparkled across the sky, and I sat by the lake where we warmed our bodies between icy swims and where we could see the fields and river and the eastern hills, their ridges highlighted by the clearest blue sky.

And once, in that lonely September sun, I stripped and swam out to the middle of the lake, stopping there, feeling the chilly water deaden my muscles, wondering how long I could bear it. But I began to shiver uncontrollably and made my way back to shore to dry and rest. Then, looking up into our tree, I could see my eight-year-old brother Matt and next to him my ten-year-old self, perched on a limb telling our tales. But when I dressed and climbed up to our branch, we were gone and it was just me looking out at the sparkling pond, the abandoned orchard, and the moss growing over the old foundations. The wild apples had ripened, but when I climbed down to pick one and bit through the red skin, the stunning tartness finally forced the tears that had nearly spilled so many times that week. And I cried and cried. I cried for all of us, for Jonathan and Anna and their child, for Mother and Father, for me and Matt. Why did I not stop him from going to war? And why was Mother so weak as to allow it? And why was Father so foolish in his behavior? And why could not my parents find enough reason to reunite—for Matt and me.

I climbed up on the highest point of the foundation and managed to finish the bitter apple. I always thought that this spot afforded the best view of the valley, but now my misty eyes blurred the contours of the hills and exaggerated the sweep of the river along the tree-lined banks. And then there was a single sign of hope. I quickly blotted my eyes to be sure, and yes, there it was on the river: a red canoe. And did it carry both of my parents? I couldn't tell because the canoe remained in the shade of the trees on the western bank until it disappeared around the corner of the island. I had to wait while it was hidden by the island, my hope building with each minute. And then, with delight, I thought that maybe it would not reappear for hours and that maybe my family had turned a difficult corner. But after twenty minutes it came round the upper end of the island, and now my tears had cleared, and the western sun silhouetted the canoe. And my heart sank for there was but one occupant fighting both the current and the north wind and making slow progress on his homeward journey.

Mother returned with me on the train to Cambridge and quickly went on to the beach house. She said she found autumn to be a delightful time there. The weather and light were perfect for painting. And in winter she would enjoy the bracing beach walks and the warmth of the cottage where she would work to complete her landscapes.

I returned to college and my volunteer hospital work where the wards were busier than ever. The number of patients suffering from the influenza epidemic now exceeded the number being treated for war injuries. I left myself scant time to worry, filling every moment with duty: classroom time, study, hospital work, bookstore shifts, and Marshall.

Our relationship had settled into an easy familiarity, an evolution that I suppose was natural and expected. There seemed never a morning when my free hour intersected his free hour, and I missed our simple pastime of taking coffee in a café as the world bustled by. There was no time for lounging by the riverbank on a Sunday afternoon, watching as the autumn trees attained the miracle of red and gold and marveling at their reflection as a crew clad in crimson jerseys glided past, leaving a gentle wake to commingle the colors. And there was no time, on a pleasantly crisp night, to wander hand in hand under the moon and stars past the darkened shops and the quieting streets back to the river, where we would have playfully kicked at the dry leaves to see them scuttle and flutter in the wind and where we would have no concern for past or future.

It was quite difficult when weeks passed in September and October without a letter from Matt. But then there was a brief note which said his unit had, at least temporarily, been stationed toward the rear; they were helping with supply lines. I wondered how much he heard about the course of the war. By late October, some news reports suggested the Germans were pulling back to defensive positions, while others stated they were in full retreat and the end of the war was near.

And then in November, quite suddenly, it was over. Marshall and I joined the throngs that celebrated in the streets of Boston and Cambridge; we cheered and yelled and hugged strangers and slapped each other on the back. And we literally danced in the streets. I prayed that Matt was still safely to the rear and not among the isolated combatants of both sides who, unaware of the armistice, continued to fight and die.

Now there was just the matter of waiting, for us, and for over a million other American families, for our boy to come home. I gradually learned that my men were safe. Douglas wrote from Chicago that he had finally been drafted in August, but the war was over before he had finished training and he was quickly discharged. The government had no desire to keep extra men on the payroll and Douglas was pleased to resume his job with the Northern Pacific.

Kevin's ambulance duties ended, and he was fortunate to find quick passage back to Boston in early December just a few weeks after the armistice. He came to the bookstore, eager to see me, but was disappointed, I think, when I told him of my close relationship with Marshall. I said I hoped we could remain friends and he agreed, saying that would be easy now that I lived in Cambridge. He was excited about resuming his classics studies.

And then a letter from Matt. He and Hezekiah were both fine. Oh, they could use better rations and it would have been nice to sleep in a bed, but their only real worry was how long it would take to ship home. When this letter arrived, I was so relieved. I went to Hezekiah's home to be sure they had heard the boys were safe, and then Marshall and I went out for a celebratory dinner. We toasted Matt and Hezekiah and we toasted many others.

The servicemen were forced to linger in Europe waiting for available shipping to take them home. Time tables for return were published and then retracted and then repeatedly changed so that finally we gave little credence to each rumor of imminent homecoming.

So none of us were at the pier in New Jersey when the crowded ship arrived. The troops had suffered once again, not only from being stacked atop one another in coffin-sized berths, from seasickness, from the stench of vomit and human waste, and from inedible meals, but also from the contagion of the horrendous influenza epidemic. That year the flu disproportionately affected the young and killed at a much higher rate than the usual strain. On Matt's ship alone, we learned, at least three hundred men had been infected and thirty-seven had died, all buried at sea. The chance of infection was increased by the crowded conditions on the ship. And the chance of survival was decreased by physical and mental fatigue from the war, by weight loss from the poor rations, and by exposure to the constant damp mud and vermin of the trenches. And the chance of survival was further decreased by the weakening effects of injuries and wounds, wounds such as Matt had suffered.

That was the real reason he had been at the rear; he just didn't want to alarm us because it was such a minor thing, just a flesh wound. A bullet had grazed his thigh as they overtook some German trenches. His unit had been sent to the rear at that point—they had suffered so many deaths and wounds that they needed to regroup. Hezekiah had not been injured and Matt's wound was so minor that they were able to stay together. Hezekiah learned to change the dressing, and when the wound began to fester he insisted Matt return to the medic. The pus was drained, but the wound continued to seep a thick, foul, yellow fluid. And as they boarded the ship the infection seemed to spread deeper into his skin, ascending toward his hip. And then the flu struck, confining Matt to his berth. There were uncontrollable shaking chills followed by fever which made him throw off the covers to gain relief for his sweat-drenched body. A wet mucousy cough prevented sleep and made breathing difficult. With so many sick men on board, he was fortunate to have a friend to nurse him and Hezekiah never left his bedside.

When the men disembarked on that gray December day, some made their way across the New Jersey docks to find the ferry bound for Manhattan. Most of the men sought shelter and warmth in the ferry's interior. But one man ventured out on deck. I doubt he was much bothered by the constant cold drizzle or by the numbing north wind which drove the moisture under his coat. He'd been through too much for that to matter, so he stayed outside hoping, perhaps, to catch a view of the Statue of Liberty. From the ferry landing in New York, he walked through the dingy streets, the low gray clouds forcing an early end to the dreary afternoon light. But it must have been a relief to use his legs after so many cramped, ship-bound days. When he found he wouldn't be able to board a train until late that night, he entered a lonely diner and ordered coffee and eggs while he tried to read a newspaper.

I don't think he slept much on the train, even though there were repeated delays. There was so much extra traffic on the tracks with all the returning servicemen that the train did not arrive in Boston until late the next afternoon. The weather had not changed: the same gray drizzly clouds dampened the world and deadened the light. The few remaining brown leaves, long-dead remnants clinging to their twigs, were now loosened by the icy rain and fell against his chest and face. The very pavement slipped away underfoot with spots of ice. But I don't think any of this bothered him as he walked from the station out along the deserted river paths, under the stark, barren trees, toward Cambridge. He was almost home now.

And I suppose it was best that I was working the bookstore counter when he came in from the dark afternoon, chilled, damp, unshaven, and tired. For the minute he walked in alone and I saw the look on his face, I knew what had happened. Hezekiah did not need to say a word.

Chapter 20
1919–20

I needed to escape after Matt died. I blamed everyone else for his death, Father for his affair and politics, Mother for passivity and desertion, the Compston grandparents for honoring war, even Becky and Michael for not intervening. And of course I blamed Marshall. But really I blamed myself.

I tried to rationalize that the flu would have killed him anyway, war or no war. But I know, here at home, he could have survived the flu; he would not have been so worn down by the weight loss, the wound, the trenches, and the loneliness.

I could barely face Marshall. How could I stay with the man who had sent my brother to war? I asked Marshall not to come to Matt's memorial service. I couldn't bear the thought of telling my parents that he was Cindy's brother. Not now. How could I add to their misery?

I didn't return to Radcliffe for the spring term. I stayed at home with Father—and Mother. They began to live together again but it was not the same. The tense formality in their relationship never eased. Soon she divided her time between Birkett Ferry and her parents' home in Cambridge.

It was when I was alone that Matt would most haunt me. I'd look through the window to see him resting on the porch, reading his books, but when I came round the corner I'd find only a worn brown blanket, crumpled in a heap. As I walked the forest trails he'd drift ahead, staying in the thickets where I could not follow. He'd scamper up a tree on the knoll but when I looked, I'd see only the fresh green leaves waving in the spring breeze. And then, hearing a splash in the lake, I'd turn to see his shadow disappear under the water and I'd wait. But he could stay under a long time.

I needed complete escape from all of this. I spoke with my

parents—told them I needed to leave. I said I would suffocate if I stayed in Birkett Ferry. I asked Father about Labrador.

"There is no place more remote," he said. "Such a remarkable place, isolated and beautiful." But he also must have sensed that I needed more than escape. "It is a way to be useful," he continued, "a way to help people on a very basic level. And the nursing training you've had—there is such a dreadful need of it."

I wrote Kevin about this conversation and he responded that he knew about Labrador, too. Some of his Harvard friends were now serving there, staffing schools and medical clinics. He had no desire to leave Cambridge again, but he could understand my interest and my need to feel useful. He remembered how I had envied his war time service in Europe.

With Father's encouragement the idea took hold that spring and, after a series of letters, I secured a position as a volunteer nurse. Mother didn't want me to leave, but she was too grief-stricken to protest my plans. I would not have listened anyway.

The trip was long: the train to Boston, then one ship to Halifax, another to St. John's in Newfoundland, and finally a third ship to Labrador.

It was the sound of the wind that drew me out on deck that night. It was the emptiest sound I'd ever heard. The rushing air sped across the ocean, barreled into the hull, and ricocheted between the railings resulting in a hollow hum. That lonely pitch invited every sad memory. I stood out on deck allowing the wind to tangle my hair and flap my skirt. I knew the reassuring presence of the summer wind through the hardwoods, the leaves flapping and fluttering, directing the warm air into my bedroom, bringing dreams of peaceful picnics. And I knew the noise of the winter wind through the creaking leafless limbs, reminding me of the fireside comfort of home. But this ship-borne drone was like a barren echo, somewhat akin to a train whistle heard ten miles up a river valley but far more forlorn than that.

The daytime blanket of gray clouds must have persisted into that bleak night and, without star or moon, I had to guess our bearing. But south must be behind us. The northern wind picked up as I moved to the stern holding on to the railings. I pulled my coat across my chest and gazed out over the black waters. Somewhere off in that direction, to the south, in the depths of the ocean, lay my brother, Matt. Dead of influenza . . . buried at sea . . . only six months ago. I would always carry the guilt of his death.

The wind streamed my hair around my face, strands whipping across my cheeks and into my eyes. There was no one on deck to hear my words as I whispered a quiet prayer for him, and asked the wind to carry it to him there in the south. Then I leaned far out over the railing and I screamed his name, "Matt . . . Matt . . . MATT." Across the empty water, surely he would hear. I let the tears stream down my face and stood in the stern for a long time, watching our wake separate the ocean waves.

Finally, as I turned away, I saw an older woman, standing at a distance of twenty yards, watching me. Had she heard my cries? Witnessed my grief? I could have walked the other way around the deck but something drew me to her.

"Are you sick, child?" She looked at my tear-stained face and my chaotic hair. Maybe she thought I'd been seasick, leaning out over the ocean.

"No, I feel better now. Thank you."

"Why don't you come back inside with me?"

I followed her back through the inner corridor. I balanced back and forth against the sides of the narrow passage, jostled by the ship's swaying motion. We passed to the galley where a small room served as a mess hall to crew and passengers.

I could better see my new companion in this light. She stood less than five feet tall with a weathered face that looked as if she had watched out over the ocean for decades. Wrinkle lines came from forehead and cheeks to coalesce near her mouth. Her dark, leathery skin and her stocky frame gave the appearance of steadfast strength. Her silky gray hair was elegantly braided and looped up the sides of her head.

She had adopted the English name, Hannah, but she was a full-blooded Inuit, an Eskimo. Unexpected Scottish inflections and phrases peppered her words, lending a delightful brogue to her speech.

Perhaps she was only trying to distract me from the misery she had just witnessed, but she helped me pass the lonesome hours of that night by telling me her life's story. She thought herself to be about forty-five years old. She had been born into an Inuit band which traveled the northern coast of Labrador. They followed game, harvesting seal, walrus, caribou, salmon, and trout. At times, her clan would pass a season at Okkak, a settlement founded by missionaries. There was no town, just the mission buildings and whatever temporary dwellings the Inuit were occupying. But the missionaries ran a school, and during their sporadic stays she received bits of an education and exposure to English.

One mid-September day when Hannah was perhaps fifteen years old, the family was camped in a bay, fifty miles north of Okkak, fishing and trapping, when two men arrived at their camp, coming from the north. Their clothing was torn and not warm enough for the cold autumn nights. They were hungry and tired. Their ship had wrecked several days before along the desolate northern coast. There were no other survivors. They were walking south, hoping to reach Okkak. They knew only that the settlement was somewhere ahead along the coast. They never would have made it.

The family took them in for the winter, fed them, and gave them warm clothing of caribou and seal. And the clan gave them much more than that. Hannah smiled at the memory. These men were exotic with their light skin, their facial hair, and their foreign customs. Hannah welcomed one of them, Donald Macleod, to her bed. By June, she was heavy with child, and soon after the clan arrived in Okkak, she gave birth to a blustering boy with coppery tan skin and dark hair.

Donald considered himself married to her. When a ship came to the mission that summer to deliver supplies and trade in furs, he asked her to take passage with him. The ship was bound for St. John's, Newfoundland. They settled there and built a small sturdy home on a cove just outside of town.

Donald signed on to a series of seasonal jobs—fishing for cod, harvesting fur seals, lumbering—and they patched together a happy existence. She bore three children, two boys and a girl, all grown now; she thought the girl must be about my age. She took a job as a nursing assistant when her children left home. Donald had been killed three years before when his fishing boat sank in a horrible August storm.

She had always wanted to go back north to see her family. From time to time her husband, fishing for cod off the Labrador coast, would hear news of her family passed from the crew of another ship. The tales had likely been retold several times and were impossible to verify. They usually involved disaster: two cousins had left in kayaks and were never seen again. Or heroism: a brother had killed a polar bear, nine feet tall. But what she longed to know was much simpler: how many children had her sisters borne? And what were their names? Did her mother still live? She had hoped to return sooner, but this was to be her first trip back since she left nearly thirty years before.

This trip was motivated not only by the desire to see her family. Other news had filtered south that spring. Dreadful news. News that the flu epidemic had arrived in Labrador, brought home by returning servicemen, scouring the coastal settlements with death.

It was said that the native peoples had less natural resistance than Europeans, that the devastation was monstrous. Hannah could only hope the stories were exaggerated. It was, of course, the same flu epidemic that had claimed Matt.

The sky was brilliant as we approached the town of Battle Harbor, visible from sixty miles in the clear air. There were a smattering of small homes on the barren, rocky island, and a couple of larger buildings: the hospital and the orphanage. I disembarked here, planning to transfer to a ship bound for Northwest River, the town where I had been assigned to spend the year. And Hannah would wait for the coastal ferry to take her farther north to Okkak.

But there was a change in plans. In response to the flu reports, the clinic was sending a ship up the Labrador coast to assess the damage and help the victims. I was to go on this ship, and when the doctor heard of Hannah's nursing training, he recruited her for the voyage as well.

It was in Battle Harbor that we heard firsthand reports of the epidemic. In nearby Cartwright, one-quarter of the people had died, leaving forty orphans; half of them had come to this orphanage. Most were dressed in ill-fitting, ragged clothing, but they were in high spirits, romping about a rough field of grass and rocks, kicking a ball back and forth. It was a game reminiscent of soccer but with a different set of rules, difficult to decipher. There were several boulders, as big as cars, that provided strategic points to duck behind, the opponent unsure from which direction the ball would emerge.

Some of the orphans were pure Inuit, sturdy-framed children with brown skin and dark hair. Others had European blood; their fathers or grandfathers were fishermen or traders from Scotland, Ireland, England, or France. Most of the men had stayed on, legitimizing their relationship with the native women with a marriage, sanctioned by the church when this could be arranged, common law when it could not. These mixed-blood families were called settlers; it was these families that suffered most from the harsh climate and from the vagaries of hunting and fishing. The men lacked the native skills of survival, gleaned through thousands of years of experience. Their efforts to replicate a European lifestyle were rebuffed by the harsh climate. They built tiny log homes with rough-hewn boards for floors. Gaps between logs were chinked with moss and paper against the winter wind. Wood stoves and mattresses stuffed with bird feathers provided a measure of warmth. The men would be gone during the winter several months at a time, trapping inland, leaving the women to tend the children and the home. In spring, they would hunt seals, ducks, and geese. And, in summer, they fished for cod and salmon and harvested logs for winter warmth.

Our medical team included Hannah and me and a young English doctor. He'd been attracted to the exotic coast of Labrador for travel and adventure and to be useful in his profession.

On a clear morning in early July we sailed out of the harbor. The sun sent sparkles across our bow, the reflections bouncing off each wave crest all the way to the horizon, pulling us northward.

We generally stayed within sight of the coast. The captain knew the location of each settlement and each homestead. That first night out, we sat on deck, watching the red glow fade from the western horizon. It was a grand night, the sky high and arched with a few stars visible even before daylight was gone. We were sheltered in the horseshoe bay of a small island a few miles off the coast. The wind barely rippled the flag and the waves lapped against our hull with a quiet hesitation. The gulls, screeching and cantankerous only an hour before, had settled onto a rocky shoal. It felt good to be finally under way.

The captain tapped his pipe into the water, then refilled it.

"What we find up north may not be a good business. In Northwest River," he paused to look at me, "That's where you'll be this winter—in the hospital there?"

I nodded.

"Well, in Northwest River even Dr. Padden, the settlement doctor, got the flu. Everybody did. I don't know how anyone survived. There was no one to get food or keep the fires going. No one to care for the sick."

He looked out over the water. He used his pipe to point to a seal passing close to the ship; its gray round head turned to look at us.

"Dr. Padden recovered." The captain glanced at the young doctor. "He's back at full strength now. Is that not right, lad?"

"Yes, sir. That's correct."

"I understand Dr. Padden is a fine medical man. Dedicated. Before he was halfway well, he had his snowshoes on, making the rounds of the village homes. There was one place, two miles outside of town, isolated spot on a pretty little cove. A family lived there, mother and father and four children all less than ten years old. As Doc Padden came across the ice with his dog team he became alarmed. There was no smoke from the chimney. When he approached the door he was even more worried. The only tracks in the snow were canine. Then the curtain fluttered and he saw a haggard, ghostly woman's face. He said the sight made him take three steps backward. But then she opened the door. She was not an old woman, not yet thirty years old, but her hair was tangled and gray, her eyes were red and vacant, her face was creased. She wore layers and layers of clothes and skins but still she shivered. When she finally spoke, she seemed to have trouble making her tongue work right; her voice was hollow: 'My children, my babies, they are all gone, all dead.'"

We gasped.

The captain looked us each in the eye and continued quietly. "They all died of the flu, one after the other. All four children and the father, too. The last had died eleven days before Doc Padden came to the door. She said the bodies had begun to smell and after the last one died, she simply let the fire go out so they would freeze. Even so, there were dogs stalking the cabin and rattling the door in the night. She was afraid to go outside, afraid of the dogs. She had arranged the bodies, all together over by the bed wrapped in blankets and clothing."

We were quiet, speechless.

The captain studied us. "I just thought you should know. I suppose that's the type of thing we might find."

I rose and walked to the rail to gaze east where a faint glow gave hint of the moon about to rise. I thought of Matt's ship, what his illness and his death had been like. The fever drenching his clothes, the chills shaking his body, the fluid filling his lungs. The gasping breaths. His body slipping downward, downward, through the cold waters.

211

Of the four thousand men on board, three hundred had the flu, and thirty-seven had died. Here in Labrador, the rates of infection and death were much higher.

The log home was nestled into a grove of black spruce on a bluff, perhaps thirty feet above the ocean. The hills behind rose steeply, the forest giving way to a succession of low brush, alpine tundra, and rocky summits.

Even at a distance, we could see there was some matter of interest on the shore below the house. There were three eagles and several hawks, each swooping down to feed for a moment before flying off. Gulls, thirty or forty, stood to the side waiting for an opening. A husky or a wolf, it was hard to say which, suddenly appeared out of the shadows and the birds squawked and flew. He stood next to the kill for a minute, but then, perhaps not liking the heat of the day, retreated back into the shade.

The captain was unsure of the depth here and anchored a half mile out. Four of us came toward shore in a punt. Soon we were close enough to see it was a human carcass that the dogs and eagles were feeding on. Skin had been ripped from the chest, limbs, and face. Patches of dark hair remained on the scalp. I felt like I would vomit. I brought my head over the side of the punt, dry stomach spasms shuddering my body. When I looked up, I saw that four dogs had come out on shore. We could now see they were huskies, not wolves. They stood near the body watching our approach, growling and snapping at us.

"Protecting their kill," the captain said. "I think those dogs must be owned by the family—their dog team." He paused and squinted toward shore. "Oh my God. Look!"

From out of the shadows came a young girl, four or five years of age, wearing a dirty, torn frock. She stood just behind the dogs, looking at us.

We called, "Hello," but she did not respond.

When we were just twenty feet from shore the dogs charged closer to us, nipping and yapping and growling. The captain aimed his rifle at the head of one husky and fired, killing it instantly. The others fled into the brush and the girl followed. We signaled to the crew that we would need help and we did not feel safe splitting our party until reinforcements had arrived.

Three men went in search of the dogs—and the girl. The rest of us went to the house. The door stood open. Inside were more bodies, seven in all, four adults and three children. Some had been dragged across the floor and partially eaten. Others remained in bed untouched. The odor was unbearable.

Rocks and shallow soil made the digging of graves nearly impossible. But we found a marshy spot one hundred yards behind the house and dug out swampy graves which we thought might give protection from the dogs. One of the dead had kept brief medical notes that spoke of high fevers, worsening coughs, and death.

The men returned from the woods unable to find the girl or the dogs. They had discovered a spot beneath an overhanging rock where the dogs had rested. The packed ground was covered in tracks. And there they found things the girl must have carried from the house: a pillow partially chewed apart, a rag doll, and a hair brush. Why had the dogs not attacked her?

We went back to the ship, leaving two men in the house and two more hidden near the den site. When, the next day, there was still no sign of the girl or the dogs, the men posted near the den withdrew. Late that afternoon, the girl came through the shrubbery, pausing only a moment to glance toward the ship before walking toward the house. One of the men grabbed her, and even from the ship we could hear her scream, and see her struggle. Her cries continued as they rowed her out to us. Once on board she was so frantic that we feared she would go overboard.

"Bring her to me," said Hannah. The girl continued to struggle but Hannah held her firmly, preventing most of her scratches, bites, slaps, and kicks.

The captain shook his head, "We may need to tie her down."

"Captain, I don't think that will be necessary," Hannah murmured.

The captain turned away and began preparation for departure.

"Captain," Hannah spoke again. "Send two of your men back to shore with Gwen." She nodded to me. "Look through the house, Gwen, and bring back some of her things."

I found a small pair of moccasins made from caribou hide, a cup, and a bowl. And I retrieved the pillow, the doll, and the brush from the den site.

Her sobs had subsided by the time of my return, but her body was still tense and her eyes open wide. She clutched the remnants of the pillow and the clawed-up doll and held them close to her chest.

Hannah looked down at the pillow. "We can sew that for you, child."

We didn't know her name. There was no mention of names in the medical notes we had found, though it was reassuring that the notes were in English, and, by that night, it was clear she understood some of our words. But she would not speak. At first she ate ravenously; and she hoarded food, bringing hunks of bread back to our cabin to hide beneath the pillow.

She had wavy, thick hair that came to her shoulders and shone with black brilliance after we washed it and combed out the tangles. Her skin was a light coppery color. Gradually, she was more comfortable, eating with us and sleeping in our cabin, nestled against Hannah. And she began to speak, cautiously at first, but soon it seemed she was only quiet when she slept.

She ran about on deck from one end of the ship to the other. The crew played with her, lifting her into the air and turning her upside down while her laughter echoed in the salty air. We no longer worried that she would jump overboard; she was quicker, nimbler, more sure-footed than anyone else on board.

I began to call her Best Beloved but Hannah shortened this name to Lovely. One day when I called to her, "Lovely, come look at this book," she approached me with a hard scowl, stopped a foot away, stomped her foot, and looked me straight in the eye.

"You call me Flora, FLORA!"

Then she climbed onto my lap. I don't think she had ever seen a book, much less a picture book. She liked them all, but her favorites were *Just So Stories* and *Peter Rabbit*. I wondered how she could relate to English rabbits, dressed in funny clothes, eating vegetables she had never seen.

"It must be so foreign to her," I said to Hannah.

"Perhaps not so strange, not compared to what she has been through."

A couple of days later, one of the crew called to her, "Lovely, come see what I've got: a big old wiggling cod fish."

Hannah spoke immediately. "You must call her Flora now."

"But . . ."

"Please. It's all she has left."

But at night, when she would snuggle into my lap for a bedtime story, I'd whisper into her ear, "Lovely, my Best Beloved." And she didn't seem to mind.

With Flora on board, our ship seemed to dance to the north under blue skies and thin wispy clouds. There were other settlements where the flu had struck, but the effects were more isolated as we traveled up the coast. Some homesteads had been completely spared. So we hoped for better news as we approached Okkak, the spot where Hannah separated from her family thirty years before.

We had not planned to venture beyond Okkak. "Not much more up there," the captain gestured north. "And we need time to get back south before winter sets in." It was now early August.

I suppose we should have been better prepared for the disaster of

Okkak. Of the two hundred and seventy inhabitants, only thirty-nine survived the epidemic, all women and children. Not a single adult male lived. Hannah found one of her sisters still alive, and two nieces.

Her sister described the horror. "We were all sick at once. Fever, cough." As she spoke, more people gathered round. "And then so many died. There was no one to bring food or water. No one to care for the sick. No one to take away the dead. Some who burned with fever finally froze to death; there was no one to keep the fires going."

We were stunned and for several moments no one spoke. There was only the sound of the waves lapping into the rocky shore, the water pulling the stones forward and back, a monotonous scraping of rock against rock.

Hannah's sister had maintained her composure during her speech. But now she looked into our eyes and realized, I think, that there was no way to relate the scope of the horror. When her eyes met Hannah's, they began to sob, and then it turned into a wail. We knew not to try to comfort them at that moment. Hannah cried for three days and ate little. But, even in her grief, she began to help the survivors.

We took seven of the orphans with us. Our ship was small and we had no room for more. They needed to be Flora's age or older; we could not watch their every movement. In her sweet way Flora welcomed them on board, taking one small girl by the hand, leading the others, showing them where they would eat, where they would sleep. We all knew, and I think they knew too, that they would never again see Okkak.

We promised help for the survivors and, as we sailed south along the barren coast, we soon met the fleet of fishing boats. Two vessels quickly left—they needed no persuasion to rescue the marooned people. Okkak was soon abandoned.

We made steady progress south, having no time to explore the inviting bays and islands. In six days we arrived at the entrance to Hamilton Inlet, a huge bay which cuts two hundred miles into the center of

Labrador. As we progressed up the bay, we passed into more sheltered areas where the spruce, birch, and tamarack grew thickly enough to be called forests. We reached our destination near the head of the bay. The town of Northwest River had a few large buildings: trading post, hospital, school, and orphanage; and perhaps thirty small log homes.

It was late August, autumn already evident in the chilled night air, and soon we saw migrations of ducks and geese flapping and honking overhead; at times they filled the sky. We had snow by late September, and the men worked to lay in the cords of wood needed for the winter.

Flora and the seven others moved into the orphanage. Only a few were ever adopted; there was such a surplus of children. Hannah decided to stay on and help in the orphanage. She and three other women cooked meals, cleaned floors, and washed clothes—and children. They conducted a rudimentary school and cared for the children when they were ill. They helped me at the hospital, too.

I had settled into a tiny room on the second floor of the hospital, the nurse's room. There were two wards of six beds each, an examination room, and a small surgical area. I cleaned the floors, carried bedpans, sterilized equipment, and cared for patients. Dr. Padden, who had lived in Northwest River for years, did all of this too, and he was advisor, theologian, and undertaker. And he was Santa Claus for the orphans at Christmas.

The doctor and I alternated in making home visits, my favorite part of the job. The information was always sketchy when word came of an injury, illness, or childbirth. But if Dr. Padden judged the problem to be within my ability, I was sent on the mission.

It was grand to be out of the building. I'd give last-minute instructions to Hannah, "Don't forget to check Mr. Marston; he's been running a fever every afternoon. Mrs. McLachlan will need help with the bedpan." And then I was off, out the door, into the winter of Labrador. It might be sunny with a high blue sky and a frigid wind; it might be snowing with blowing drifts migrating hither and yon. I didn't care, for I was outside where the sea-freshened air was filtered by spruce and snow, free of the hospital smells of urine, pus, and feces—scents that overpowered our weapons of soap and bleach.

Many of my patient visits were in town. The eight-year-old boy with the skin sores: I wanted to be sure his mother understood how to clean the sores and keep them bandaged. The elderly man with a history of heart problems: he'd sent word that his breathing had become worse overnight. And I could check his neighbor's knee: the swelling had increased. I liked that I would have time with each person, without interruption. In the hospital, I'd often be pulled in three different directions.

But if the home was more than a couple of miles from Northwest River, we traveled by dogsled. Joseph, a man about my age, an Inuit, came with me. It was these longer trips that I most welcomed. While Joseph harnessed the dogs, I stood at the hospital gate, medical bag in hand, inhaling one long cleansing breath after another. We filled the sled with gear and provisions and then we angled off across the bay. On the clear days, we could see forty miles, the eye following the low, spruce-covered hills along the shore until the land blended with the horizon. On many days, the temperature was twenty or thirty below, and we spent much of our time walking alongside the sled, moving our muscles to stay warm. But when there was sun, the light bounced off the ice and snow seeming to double the heat, and we loosened our clothing, removing layers and hats.

If our journey took more than a couple of hours, we'd move into a protected cove and stop for a boil-up. Joseph would claim the dogs needed rest, but they always seemed so eager to run that I wondered if the stops were more for him. At first, I thought it a grand waste of time, but he'd find some dead spruce boughs and, within twenty minutes, he'd have a pot of water boiling for our tea. I'd fashion chairs using one snowshoe as a seat and the other as a backrest, and I had to admit there was nothing better than sitting there, sipping the steaming broth. I'd look past the dogs, where they lay nestled in the snow, out along our tracks of sled and snowshoe leading through the miles of quiet ice, and I'd wonder if there were any other living person in that vast territory.

One January day, we'd traveled fifteen miles to an isolated home where a woman was in labor. Her eight-year-old son had snowshoed alone to the nearest neighbor, a mile away, to ask for help. The neighbor left immediately to carry the news to us.

"I'm not sure I can handle a delivery," I had worried to Dr. Padden.

"You've helped with quite a few. There's usually not much to it."

"But..."

"Besides, by the time you arrive, it will all be over."

"How do you know that?"

"She's got three other children. She knows what to expect. She'll have a short labor, most likely, and she'll be able to deliver the baby herself. But she's alone with the children. Her husband must be a hundred miles away on his traplines."

He was right. She had been helped by her two older children, aged seven and eight. The baby had been cleaned and swaddled, and was feeding contentedly when we arrived, about six hours after the birth. There was not much for me to do.

"The afterbirth seemed okay, I think." She looked down, embarrassed. But she'd saved it, knowing I would want to examine it. "It's out there—it must be frozen by now." She pointed to the porch. She had some mild bleeding, probably normal. The baby kicked awake and opened her mouth and let loose a howl. Her mother clucked and put her to the breast where she latched on, taking three or four quick sucks before falling back into sleep.

As I boiled water to clean the blood from beddings and floor, I took stock. There was a cozy feel to the small home, but it was difficult to imagine the family, now numbering six, passing the winter in so small a space. Built of logs, the spaces chinked with mud and moss, the roof of sod, the one-room house could not have been larger than fourteen by fourteen feet. Their furniture was handmade: a crude bed in the corner, covered with animal skins, a table, and three chairs.

I checked the food stores. There was half a barrel of flour, salt, tea, and small amounts of dried berries, molasses, and oleo.

"Better than most," I thought to myself.

"There's some fish and caribou meat frozen outside." The mother had noticed my survey. "My boy," she smiled at her eight-year-old son, "he got two ptarmigan yesterday. Last week he got a rabbit."

I could not quite picture this small child holding a gun.

We always carried extra food, often finding families in severe need. I baked bread and made a soup of potato, carrot, and caribou meat. In some homes, the children had never eaten carrots, but these children didn't act surprised to see me slicing them into the broth.

There was a good deal of firewood, piled in a heap off to the side of the house. Joseph spent the afternoon cutting more. He and the two older children carried load after load to stack close to the door.

That evening, after dinner, and after the children and I cleaned the kitchen, we settled in close to the stove. The mother stayed under the covers of the bed, nursing the baby. The children unrolled bedding skins across the floor.

Joseph scratched his head. "Ah, I nearly forgot." The children watched eagerly, as he unlatched our storage box. I wondered if they had heard of this ritual. They each selected one hard candy from Joseph's hand, and the girl took one to her mother. As they settled back into their skins, I opened a book, *Just So Stories* by Kipling. I remember that the three children jumped up from their bedding to come to my side, to touch the book, to hold it.

"What is it?" the girl asked.

They had never seen a book.

The mother averted her eyes, looking down to the baby. "We've got no money for that."

"I understand," I said. And I began to read. I read for two hours before the last one slept. Joseph put more wood in the stove, and we unrolled our covers to sleep next to the children.

We ate pancakes the next morning. I cooked one after another until they could eat no more. We left them most of our extra provisions. I wished we had extra books to leave; no one could read, but they would have enjoyed the pictures and they could have created stories.

On our homeward journey, alternately sitting on the sled bundled in furs and walking to regain warmth, I considered the success of my plan. The novelty of my new life blocked, most of the time, the memories of my old life. But as I traveled behind the trotting dogs across the sun-glared ice, the vista of low, spruce-covered hills barely changing, there was too much time to think about why I was there, escaping my past, creating a new present.

Matt had been dead just over a year and I still thought of him every day. Sometimes I felt guilty, as if I should be spending more time remembering him. And there would be other times when my thoughts would skitter through a series of pasts: events in Cambridge, or Birkett Ferry, or Hastings Beach, and my mind would stop in shock at a scene involving Matt. He's dead, I'd remind myself. He's really dead. This reality still caused a jolt of surprise and disbelief. Over a year after his death, I still expected a letter from Mother saying it was all a mistake; it was another boy who had died of the flu; Matt had been delayed in France but now was home.

Yet, how could I pity myself in comparison with the grief of others? Flora and the other orphans. And Hannah, who returned home to Okkak after thirty years to find most of her relatives had died the previous winter. I should be the one to comfort her, but it was more often that she would find me alone, gazing from a hospital window, my eyes misty. She'd put her arm around me, and pull me close.

"It's a part of life," she'd say. "We can't control it or change it. And all this worry does no good. Come drink tea with me."

She buried her grief in her work: school, orphanage, hospital. She was always busy; she had no time to think or cry. I did the same,

I suppose, but at night, alone in my tiny hospital room, or on these homeward treks, there was lots of time for the past.

Joseph stopped for a boil-up and again it seemed like a miracle to sip hot tea, the steam billowing about my face as I held the mug just under my chin. After his tea, Joseph moved among the dogs. He had detected a limp in one and he lifted its paw. He stroked the dog's head and spoke a few words. The sun was behind us, highlighting Joseph's coppery face, his sharp chin. The warmth had allowed him to remove his hat, and his coal black hair sparkled in the sunlight.

He glanced up to catch me looking at him and smiled. "His paw is a little swollen and tender but not too bad."

"He can go on?"

"Oh sure. We'll keep an eye on him."

As we set off, I was struck again by the grandeur of it all. I thought how we must look from high above, a tiny speck of life moving across a continent of white, heading—for where? For home? Or was it just some way station I had come to, a place to escape my reality?

On our return to the hospital, I was pulled further into the past. The mail had arrived. It came from Quebec City, nearly fifteen hundred miles away, carried by a series of dog teams. Letters from my parents and grandparents, which were chatty, upbeat, and without any real news. Three letters from Marshall: he missed me; he would visit if Labrador were not so far away. He was working for a Massachusetts congressman and very much enjoying it. He wondered who would be nominated this summer, to replace President Wilson.

And from Kevin: he was trying to work on his classics dissertation, but his other academic responsibilities and his translating job occupied most of his time. We still wrote back and forth about poetry. He'd given me Carl Sandburg's *Chicago Poems* when I departed Boston. We studied various sections of the volume, studiously avoiding mention of Sandburg's haunting war poems. In fact, I read those poems over and over again, poems of senseless death and slaughter. Perhaps Kevin suspected this, for now he asked if I had read the poem, Wars. "We can only hope," Kevin wrote, "these prophecies will not come to pass."

Wars

In the old wars drum of hoofs and the beat of shod feet.
In the new wars hum of motors and the tread of rubber tires.
In the wars yet to come silent wheels and whirr of rods not yet
dreamed out in the heads of men.

In the old wars clutches of short swords and jabs into faces with
spears.
In the new wars long range guns and smashed walls, guns
running a spit of metal and men falling in tens and twenties.
In the wars to come new silent deaths, new silent hurlers not
yet dreamed out in the heads of men.

In the old wars kings quarreling and thousands of men
following.
In the new wars kings quarrelling and millions of men
following.
In the wars to come kings kicked under the dust and millions
of men following great causes not yet dreamed out in the heads
of men.

My eyes blurred each time I read that verse. But then I'd try to convince myself to release my war memories; they were so foreign to my new life. Those tentacles from the past, trying to pull me backward, when I just wanted to forget.

There was also a letter from Cindy and Nick, just a short note which basically said, "I wish I had more time to write, but . . ." And she must have forced Nick to write something ("Nick, just anything—write anything—just do it"). Nick reluctantly scrawled across the bottom in his ten year old hand, "I hope you like Labrador. Is it fun? Love, Nick." Cindy had enclosed a photo of Nick; his light hair and his freckled cheeks gave him an uncanny resemblance to Matt. Somehow I did not mind this memory, and I placed the photo into my mirror frame and the card beside it.

February brought a string of storms, drifting deep snow against buildings and bending the spruce boughs to the ground. The snow continued for five days, the flakes obliterating horizons and obscuring landmarks. And even when the snow tapered, the low clouds limited the light, blending the grayness of sky and bay together. The storm kept us homebound by our fires, consuming hot tea and stews, insulated from the world.

But the clear days and nights that followed were glorious. The sunlight bounced up the endless bay, nothing but ice and snow for forty miles, the eye relieved only by hints of green where the shoreline spruce poked through the drifts. The clarity of the night sky prismed each star's brightness so that every inch of the heavens shimmered. And with the insulating cloud layer gone, the arctic air funneled down, plunging the temperature to negative fifty or negative sixty degrees.

But by midmorning the temperature would rise thirty or forty degrees, and my heart leapt at the chance to head out, traveling toward the sun and the distant shore. The dogs, and Joseph, always found a way around the jumbled blocks of ice that had been shoved up from the layers below. In some spots the dogs floundered up to their bellies in drifts, legs wiggling forward, struggling for each inch as Joseph and I pushed the sleigh from behind. But then we'd hit a stretch of ice and hard-packed snow and we'd skim across the surface, the dogs galloping, and Joseph would claim that we covered three miles in fifteen minutes.

One day we traveled to see a family whose three children were "laid up with a nasty cough; they can hardly breathe." This was the report relayed to us from twenty-five miles down the bay. To reach them, we had to travel over the bay ice and then move several miles up a river valley. Their mean cabin sat on a bluff where the river widened into a lake, twenty miles long. The good trapping drew them there; the father could string his traplines along the lake and back into the nearby wilderness, allowing more frequent winter visits with his family. Somehow, the rough-hewn timbers and the uneven, snow-drifted roof seemed welcoming—I suppose it was the smoke curling from the stove-pipe, and the path freshly cleared of snow, and the appearance in the doorway of the couple, stocky and smiling, the man already in hat and coat, hurrying down to help Joseph unleash the dogs and give them food. As I walked to the door, I was greeted by the aroma of fresh bread and another smell of meat and onion, simmering in a bubbly stew. I knew they didn't eat like this every night.

The children had only mild coughs and stuffy noses when we arrived. But the mother was quick to say, "It's at night that it gets worse; none of us sleep."

And that night, it was easy to see how the children's barking coughs and gasping breaths had frightened their parents. I asked them to keep water boiling on the stove and to bring the children near, to have them inhale the steamy vapors. And if that failed, they were to bundle them up and take them outside. Breathing that icy night air for a few minutes nearly always worked against the croup.

Clouds hung heavy and low the next morning, only dismal light penetrating. We left early, just after breakfast. We wanted to return to Northwest River via an overland route, stopping at a small settlement where an extended family inhabited three houses. The elderly grand-mother's emphysema had worsened that winter.

Joseph was less familiar with the inland terrain and, as snowfall started and thickened, his sense of direction, usually reliable, became confused. At one point he gave the dogs their head, but they were indecisive, it seemed to me, pulling us first in one direction and then on an opposite path.

We stopped for a boil-up, to fortify ourselves with strong tea and thick slabs of fresh bread which the mother had insisted we take.

"Are we lost?"

"Let's follow the dogs a while longer." Joseph shrugged.

"They don't seem to know where to go. Maybe we should head back to our croupy family."

"I'm not sure which direction that is," he confessed. He looked up at the swirling snowflakes and the drooping spruce boughs. "I think we're all turned about."

The dogs led us in a senseless zigzag route, but after another hour we saw a faint depression in the snow.

"They've found a trail." Joseph was relieved, but I wasn't so sure we'd discovered anything but a path used by animals.

The trail soon led out to a wide, treeless expanse, presumably a lake, though it was hard to make much sense of anything, out in the open where there was no protection from the wind and the flakes came at us horizontally.

The dogs saw it before Joseph, a snowy mound set under a cluster of spruce. We were right next to it before I realized there was a tiny log structure under the snow—a tilt, one of a series of structures built along a trapper's route for nightly shelter. This one was only about five by four with a roof so low we couldn't stand upright. Joseph unhitched the dogs and fed them frozen fish heads while I started a fire in the stove using the dry wood which had been stored inside the tilt against just such a need. Then it seemed cozy enough. I was able to prepare a hot meal of cornbread and broth. The trapper kept some food there, and when I needed to borrow some salt, I left a measure of flour to replace it.

As we prepared for bed, I wondered how we would fit into the small space, designed for one inhabitant. I went out to relieve myself but was soon back for my hat and coat.

"Joseph, come out. You've got to see this."

The sky had cleared to reveal a million distant suns and a spectacular display of northern lights. As we propped our snowshoes into seats on the shore of the lake, I wondered if the display had any interest for him. Was this event common enough to bore him? This suspicion was magnified when, after looking to the stars, his first comment was, "No trouble with direction now." After he had surveyed the lake shore for a moment, he continued, "I wonder if this could be the lake of our croupy family. I think we've doubled back somehow."

The lights shimmered green from the northern horizon, extending, at times, all the way to the sky's apex. It was as if thousands of translucent butterflies fluttered about, backlit by pale, penetrating light. And then, as if we were in a large auditorium, a curtain of red and gold pulsated slowly across the sky from west to east. A narrow shaft of green appeared at the horizon, like a searchlight to center stage, and slowly lengthened, penetrating through all the other colors to reach the apex where it lingered for a long time before dissolving. And then we heard the eerie howls of wolves, also from the north, and also far away, but I shivered with each of their cries.

We must have watched for an hour, but the cold, attracted by our immobility, worked its way through our layers. As we retreated to the tilt, we again heard the wolves. The sound carried easily across the lake expanse, making them seem closer than they probably were. Our dogs, ears perked and wide awake, heard them, too.

We lay diagonally in the warmth of that narrow space, carefully avoiding contact with the stove, and with one another. We held our arms and legs stiffly; it was impossible to roll or turn without touching the other. An hour later, I was still wide awake, and so was Joseph. He sat up to put more wood into the stove.

"That should keep it for a few hours." His voice was deeper than usual, throaty, and I knew he was just as tense as I was. I rolled to my side, my back to him. But this left him no option but to move into a similar position, his front to my back. He brushed against me, then pulled back, scrunching his middle away while bringing his knees up against my thighs. This could not have been comfortable and soon he sat up, leaning into a corner of the tilt.

I turned to look at him as he explained, "Maybe I'll just sit up for a while and keep an eye on the fire. You'll have more space."

It had been so long since I had slept with Marshall. I tried to relax, to dismiss the thought, but my mind kept whirling away. Maybe it was the northern lights, or the wolves, or the cozy warmth of the tilt. I did know that neither of us would sleep that night.

Later, I thought it my turn to sit and, in exchanging places, we brushed against each other, became entangled, then paused, allowing our hands and eyes to linger. I knew I should excuse myself and go outside. But my mind wasn't working. I couldn't stop his touching or mine, and soon we were kissing and making love.

Afterward, we lay quietly, embarrassed.

"I'm sorry," he whispered. "I didn't mean . . ."

"Joseph, I know. I'm sorry, too. There's nothing we can do now."

Joseph stoked more wood into the stove. We both lay awake far into the night.

In the morning, Joseph split some wood to replace the stores in the tilt. Then he packed the sled and hitched the dogs and we were off.

Back at the hospital, things returned to normal, almost. Of course I saw Joseph frequently, caring for the dogs, shoveling the hospital entrance, splitting wood, eating his meals. We never talked of our night together. There were times I wanted him but I tried to divert my mind with work. The hospital and the orphanage could consume every available minute. I knew he had a girl in Nain, and that he was returning to her that summer. I could not allow myself to give in.

I told no one I was pregnant. I was suspicious in April and certain in May. I wanted no one to know, not until Joseph left. It was mid-June when the first boat of the season arrived. That day, Joseph shook my hand along with those of all the hospital staff gathered on the dock to see him off. And soon he was headed up the bay, eventually to take the ferry north to Nain.

The mail went out on the same boat; three of the letters were mine. I couldn't confide in my parents or grandparents, but I needed help from someone. I wrote to Marshall and to Kevin. And I wrote to Cindy, thinking of her similar experience. I forbade each of them from telling others.

And I told Hannah. I had felt a spiritual connection with her ever since we met on the Labrador-bound ship that windy night a year before. And we shared the heavy losses from the flu: Matt, and her Okkak relatives.

She hugged me immediately. "That's wonderful, child!" There was no condemnation from her, but she had lived long enough in St. John's, with Europeans, to know that my culture would not see this as a blessing.

"I won't be able to hide it much longer." I looked doubtfully at my abdomen.

In July, I received two letters back. Marshall tried to comfort me. He offered condolences, support, and money. He assumed I might want an abortion "if you can get to Boston, or Portland, or even to St. John's in Newfoundland. Just go to a reputable place . . ."

Cindy offered to help in any way she could, with abortion or adoption, if that was what I wanted. But she also knew I might want to keep the baby. "If you do keep the baby, you will encounter unimagined difficulty—and unimagined joy. I, more than anyone, know what you are going through. I wish I could come to you. Let me know how I can help."

Hannah never considered that I might want an abortion. "We'll have to tell the others, and Dr. Padden. Sometime soon. Don't you think?"

And then the arrival of a schooner, in late July, brought a profound and most-welcome surprise.

Chapter 21
1920–26

Kevin was on that ship. I watched in disbelief as he stepped down the gangplank, his smiling face scanning the crowd below. I was at the dock as I often was when a ship arrived; there'd be medical supplies on board and I'd direct their transport to the hospital. And it was always exciting to see the ship come in, to see the passengers, and to wait for the mailbag.

"Kevin?" I was speaking to myself—he was too far away to hear. But, as he came closer, I could only repeat myself. "Kevin?" I could not believe I was seeing him. It was so incongruous, a collision of my lives: Kevin in Labrador.

"Kevin? What in the world?"

He smiled for a moment, watching my face and my eyes. And then he put down his suitcase, pulled me toward him, and kissed me hard—right there on the dock with everyone looking on.

When he had received my letter, he'd written back—several times. But nothing he wrote seemed right and he tore up each letter. He said his love for me gnawed at his soul; he couldn't stand the thought of me, alone and pregnant. His only choice, he said, was to come to Labrador.

He was prepared to stay the winter, or to take me back to Massachusetts, whatever I thought best. I would need to decide quickly; soon it would be unwise to travel—we'd be trapped by the late stages of pregnancy and by winter weather. But when I seriously considered the prospect of leaving, I knew I wanted to stay.

I had announced my pregnancy to Dr. Padden and the hospital staff a few weeks earlier. It wasn't long before the whole town knew. There was surprise, but no one was openly critical. Dr. Padden said I could continue to work as long as I felt up to it. And I could stay in my hospital room where there was heat and food, and where care for babies and mothers was instantly available.

Kevin's arrival changed all of this. He was able to rent a small cabin, a one-room affair, perhaps fifteen by fifteen feet. Kevin worked for three days to clean and stock it. No one was surprised when I moved in. But, at times, it was difficult for me to believe we were really doing this. Kevin was not handy. Whenever he split wood, I worried that he would collapse into the room, spurting blood from his knee or foot. He had no common sense about patching a leaky roof or sealing a drafty doorframe. On the village paths he'd trip over rocks and roots and his feet would tangle in the ropes of the dock.

But he could teach. He worked in the school, where a third of the students were the children of the orphanage. In return, timber was delivered to our cabin for Kevin to saw and split. And we could take meals at the hospital or the orphanage. And he was paid a little cash, enough to supplement what he had brought, and what I had saved, enough for basic supplies.

I stopped working in the middle of September. Hannah came regularly, to gossip and laugh, and to reassure me about my pregnancy. She gave me cooking tips so I could produce passable bread and delicious stews—or so Kevin said.

It was often dark by the time Kevin returned from school. Leaving his briefcase of papers and books just inside the door, he'd make several trips to the woodpile, stacking the logs next to the stove, before removing his winter clothes. The ice and snow melted from the logs, soaking into the floorboards.

We had but two chairs and, after dinner, we'd sit on either side of the table sharing the glow of a lantern. He would sift through the student papers and prepare for the next day. I would read or knit and listen to the logs crackle and shift. Sometimes, when he was absorbed in his work, I'd gaze at him, his thin frame, his deep-set blue eyes, his thick black hair. But he'd always catch me at it and he'd look back and smile.

Then he would get up to make tea. He'd always manage to spill some water onto the stove where the drops would sizzle and sputter. I loved that sound. He'd return to his work and I'd return to mine, but soon my eyes would wander to the table where the mugs sent steam drifting up into the soft glow of the lamp. Later, he would rise again and stand behind my chair, massaging my shoulders. Then he'd bend, placing his cheek next to mine, and slip his hands over my breasts to my abdomen.

He'd pause like that before speaking. "I can feel the baby's heartbeat."

"Maybe it's just my pulse."

"I don't think so. I'm so lucky to be here with you," he'd say. And my smile would exceed the glow of the lantern.

I was able to walk to the hospital in early December when the contractions started. Twenty-four hours later, Ruth came into the world. Moments after her birth, Hannah went to find Kevin, who'd been walking in circles from the hospital to the school to our cabin.

Once Ruth and I returned home, Hannah came each day, a perfect grandmother. She stayed for hours, cleaning, cooking, and talking. She'd check each time Ruth blinked an eye or kicked a leg, her obsession nearly equaling my own.

One afternoon in March when Kevin was at school and Ruth was napping, Hannah and I sat at the table, patching an old quilt. A stew bubbled on the stove and, from time to time, Hannah would rise to stir the pot.

"I've got news," she said.

I looked up to her happy face. But then I felt a tinge of shame. Something about the way she spoke made me wonder how long it had been since I had asked about her life. I'd been so absorbed with Ruth and Kevin and myself. I put down the quilt, looked into her eyes, and waited.

"I spoke with Doc Padden. He says it's fine. I'm going to adopt Flora."

I rose and we hugged.

"I'll take her to Newfoundland this summer. I miss my children. And my son has written. He says I'll be a grandmother soon."

I could do nothing but hug her again.

In the first seven months of her life, I doubt I had been away from Ruth for more than an hour at a time. Kevin insisted we go on an outing.

"Here I am in Labrador," he said, "and I've been confined to an area less than one square mile."

"What do you have in mind?"

"Let's take a canoe. We can go up the bay and explore."

"What about Ruth?" I did not want to leave her.

"Hannah will watch her. They'll both love it."

"We can't be gone more than a couple of hours. She'll need to nurse."

"She's good for three hours, at least."

We stayed close to shore, heading up the bay. I kept looking back to the dock at Ruth and Hannah. Hannah waved happily each time I turned around.

"Have fun!" She called.

Forty minutes later, I pointed to a pebbly beach nestled in a small cove. We landed and spread a blanket.

"I don't want to go too far," I apologized.

"This is fine; I just wanted to be out of town."

"I suppose we do have a decision to make." I paused to watch his face, but he knew what I meant. We'd skirted around the issue of whether to return home this summer. It was already mid-July. We'd have to decide soon. "I still have trouble imagining the scene: Returning to Birkett Ferry, my beautiful Eskimo girl in tow. I'm not sure I'm ready to face it."

"I doubt it will be all that bad. But I'm happy to stay, or go, as long as I can be with you."

I picked up his hand and kissed his fingers.

"Let's stay then, one more year. Then we'll go back."

"Okay with me. But I have one request." He turned to look into my eyes. "I want to marry you."

Tears started down my cheeks as I murmured, "I accept, of course." And then I smiled. "I thought you'd never ask."

We had an August wedding, our cake garnished with blueberries and raspberries. My matron of honor, Hannah, held Ruth, who remained mercifully quiet.

Dr. Padden officiated. "I think it's legal," he said. "I've married a number of others, anyway."

In late August, we all cried on the dock when we said good-bye to Hannah and Flora. And then we settled back into our home to watch Ruth crawl, stand, toddle, and walk. Kevin still felt out of place much of the time. He had no experience in fishing, trapping, hunting, or lumbering. No practical skills at all. He was a poor fit with Labrador, as, I suppose, I was. We only fit with each other. And, each night, I thanked the heavens that he seemed to fit with Ruth too, accepting her as if she were his child.

The next summer, the summer of 1922, I brought them home with me: Ruth, my beautiful daughter with long, black hair and deeply tanned skin, and Kevin, my husband. Ruth was a terror. At eighteen months, she would not be still on the ship or train, too young to be much distracted by toys and books. One of us was with her every second, of course. She'd crawl up the train aisles and that was safe enough, but then she'd try to stand. She'd pick a random leg and pull herself up on some businessman's trousers, flashing him her irresistible grin, digging her fingers into his thigh, balancing as the train lurched her from side to side. Mostly the men didn't mind, not the first time anyway.

It was good to be back in New England. After my time in Labrador where my vistas were of endless rocky coastline, icy bays, and snowy hills, it now felt as if the train was floating through a canopy of luxuriant green, the forests overwhelming in their thick tangle of diversity. And I was awed by the abundance from the farmland: corn, bean, carrot, lettuce, potato, tobacco, tomato; everything grew here without worry of a June freeze. And the soil had such depth. For every inch of Labrador dirt, barely held fast by the roots of a precariously placed spruce, here in Massachusetts there was a foot, or three feet, of dark, nutritious loam.

Diversity of the farmland crops and forests: yes. Diversity in humans: no. Ruth would not be fully accepted in western Massachusetts. In Labrador, such a racial mixture was commonplace, nearly the norm. But not here. Our path was eased by the presence of Kevin, but it was clear he was not her father.

Even knowing all this, I'd been ready to return home. I had come to realize that the distance of Labrador and the chill of its winters would not separate me from my past. In coming home, I was acknowledging to myself that I would never fully recover from Matt's death. The memory would always haunt me whether I was in Labrador or Birkett Ferry.

My grandmother, Joan Compston, had died of a stroke the year after I left. News of her death did not reach me for six weeks; I was so far away and so isolated, but that was what I had wanted. By the time of our return to Birkett Ferry, my grandfather was aging and withdrawn. So it was natural that we move in with him, into the grand mansion. Ruth's laughter filled the house, and her dolls and books covered the living room floor. The old man was fond of reading to her, and I thought his great-granddaughter had eased his depression.

It would have been easier if we had claimed Ruth was adopted. But this child was born of mixed race and out of wedlock. Some whispered that it must be in our genes: after all, look at Father's past behavior. I was glad for the frequent company of my widowed cousin, Anna. She always brought her daughter, Barbara, who was three years older than Ruth. Barbara relished her role, demonstrating the proper technique with a toy and showing Ruth where to hide from the grown-ups. And Ruth loved the attention.

The other townsfolk were a mix. Some parents bent over backward to include Ruth, in such an artificial display of acceptance that it was almost as bad as the parents who quickly left the playground, toddlers in tow, as we approached.

My mother and father still lived next door in the old family saltbox. It seemed to me that they were never fully reconciled, and Mother spent large blocks of time in Cambridge and at the beach. But then, in December 1923, she developed a high fever and pneumonia. She died three days later, her family gathered round. I was heartbroken. Michael and Becky came west to see their only child buried next to the marker we had erected for Matt. For days, I couldn't stop crying, and I believe it was only because of Ruth and Kevin that I avoided prolonged depression. I knew I should be grateful we had returned from Labrador in time for her to know my daughter and husband, but if she had lived just three more months she would have also seen her grandson, my Matthew, born in March 1924.

I wondered how Becky and Michael, and Father, would be able to go on. Father had lost his son, his mother, and his wife in a span of five years. Once, I found him at the mantel, staring into the painting of the island, the painting that celebrated the day of their wedding, the day of my conception.

By the summer of 1926 we were well settled. Kevin taught classics at Smith College, an easy commute by train. Sometimes Ruth and I would go with him to Northampton, leaving Matthew with his grandfather. While Kevin taught, we'd wander through the shops and drink tea in a café.

We saw Becky and Michael every summer. Michael rearranged the lower bookshelf for Ruth; it was her favorite spot to hide from us or to curl up with a book. She liked to hear how her Uncle Matt had loved the same spot at just her age. And when the family gathered for a week at the beach, Michael joked that they could have bought the house for all the rent they'd paid over the years. Ruth and Matthew played in the sand, and ran through the shallow surf, and ate Becky's oatmeal cookies, just as Matt and I had done.

Occasionally we'd see Marshall in Cambridge but he never had much time to visit—he was always checking his watch, needing to be on time for his next appointment. He'd been elected to the Massachusetts legislature and it was said that this very eligible young bachelor had a bright future in politics.

It promised to be pleasant for our July Fourth celebration. A light north wind had moderated the heat of the week before. The clarity of the air sharpened the contrast of the fluffy white clouds against the deep blue summer sky. Grandfather had stopped hosting these parties in 1917, first because of the war and then because of the string of family tragedies. But now, in 1926, more than two years after my mother's death, he found the spirit to resume the festivities. He claimed it was all for Ruth and Matthew.

"It's important the children know what life is supposed to be like. How else will they be able to continue the tradition?"

By July third, preparations were complete. A multitude of tables and chairs had been positioned in the shade of the large tent that stood on the stone terrace. The caterer and waiters would arrive early the next morning. We had the day free. Ruth and I had taken the red canoe out that morning. We explored south, stopping at the island beach for sandwiches and lemonade. And even though the day was cool, we swam briefly. I watched my thin, five-year-old child, silhouetted against the sun sparkles which danced on the water's surface. She'd dash in, running until the water stopped her progress, and then fall forward gleefully. And then she'd do it again. When she began to shiver, I fluffed her with a towel. While she dried, we picked wildflowers for her grandfather. On the way home, she leaned over the bow, watching for turtles and fish.

Once home, Ruth would not nap. The day was just so inviting, we could not resist going back outside. We walked across the lawn to the riverbank into the shade of the willow. I steadied the hammock while Ruth climbed in. I sat next to her and used my legs to propel us. We swayed gently back and forth and watched the tips of the willow branches moving in the river current. My father saw us and came to say he was off to town. Did we want to come too? I declined, pleading fatigue. Then he said, for the thousandth time, how grateful he was to have us next door. Ruth pulled from her pocket the crushed bouquet of wildflowers and gave it to him. I apologized for forgetting about the flowers but he said it was the nicest present he had received in years.

Before leaving for town, Father took the flowers back to his house, and I pictured him placing them in a small vase on his desk. And there he'd linger for a moment, to read the letter from Matt. Matt mailed it from France at the end of the war but the letter did not arrive until weeks after his death. Father had framed it and kept it by his desk. There was one passage he often read. "While I am proud of my military service, I wonder if we have accomplished anything of lasting value. Now I have seen war as you saw it. And now I understand why you opposed it."

Ruth and I settled back in the hammock to read her favorite book, Kipling's *Just So Stories*. At bedtime she still wanted to hear *Peter Rabbit*, but Kipling was perfect for a summer afternoon. And she loved that everyone—grandparents, great-grandparents, and friends—everyone called her Best Beloved.

The slanting sun took the shadows of the riverbank trees across the water, but the golden fields on the other side and the green hills beyond were still in perfect light. Soon Ruth had dozed off. I drowsily laid the open book across my chest and listened to the river murmurs.

Mine was a light sleep. I dreamed of Matt as I often did. And by 1926, most of the dreams were pleasant. We'd be exploring the woods or sitting on the knoll or ice-skating at the cove. In my dream of that day, it was summer and we had just returned from canoeing to the island and back. I lay in the hammock while he took the paddles up to the house. Now he was walking back with a tray of lemonade. And it was all so pleasant. It was one of those times that I knew I was asleep and dreaming and the dream was so nice that I did not want to wake. As he walked across the yard, the slanting light came from behind him, making his thin frame wispy. Within that sharp light he quivered in and out of existence, a dream within a dream. I was content to lie there and smile as he cautiously approached, trying to judge if I was asleep.

When he was close enough to see my open eyes, he whispered, "I've brought some lemonade for you both."

I felt Ruth stir beside me. She opened her eyes and smiled up to this stranger.

It was Matt.

Except it was Nick. Gazing dreamily into that slanted light, he could have been the Matt of my dream. And even now, as he sat on the grass at my feet and I could see him clearly, the resemblance was uncanny. He was the Matt of 1916.

"Who's he?" Ruth woke more quickly than I had. She hopped down from the hammock to grab her lemonade and to study Nick more closely.

"He's . . ." I paused. Still in my sleepy fog, I was trying to make sense of Nick's appearance. "He's your cousin." That seemed easiest.

"Uncle," Nick corrected.

"Uncle," I agreed.

"Uncle-cousin!" declared Ruth. She danced around the tree singing, "Uncle-cousin, uncle-cousin."

By the time she ran to the riverbank and back, I was awake enough to make sensible conversation. "How is your mother?"

"She's here with me." He smiled at my surprise. "It worked then."

"What?"

"The secret. Your grandfather." Nick paused to correct himself, "Our grandfather. He wanted to keep it secret. He invited us for the picnic tomorrow. Mom was hesitant but he insisted. He said it was high time he got to know me, his other grandchild."

I had seen Nick and Cindy several times since I returned from Labrador. But this was the first time Grandfather had seen Cindy since she taught me in sixth grade. And it was the first time he had seen his grandson, Nick.

The screen door thumped shut and I turned to watch Grandfather carry a tray of lemonade across the terrace. Father sat in the shade of the tent, bent across a table in close conversation with Cindy.

"Did Father know you were coming?"

"No, he was just as surprised as you."

Probably more surprised, I thought.

Grandfather set the tray on the table and sat beside Cindy. The sun had dipped lower, sending shadows across the lawn, but the top of the white tent was tinged with a warm, golden glow.

Nick picked a dandelion puffball. He rose and handed it to Ruth, grandly bowing from the waist as if he were offering the most valuable gift ever given. She accepted it with a bow in return. And then she held it above her head and raced round us in circles. The seeds followed in her wake as if drawn along by her gay laughter and, when she stopped running, a few seeds sparkled in her dark hair.

Nick turned back to me. "And where is Matthew?"

"He's napping but he should wake soon. Kevin is inside, finishing some work and listening for him."

Just after I spoke, the screen door banged shut again. Grandfather rose to greet them. Kevin held Matthew in his arms. Kevin looked uncertainly toward me, waved once, and then joined the group on the terrace. I could hear the oohs and aahs as Matthew squirmed out of his father's lap to amble about the terrace, going from one chair to the next, greeting and exploring. Then he noticed us. It took just one wave from Ruth for his stumpy legs to begin pumping ahead. As he neared, he leaned so far forward that he might have plunged face first into the grass had not Nick grabbed him and twirled him high up into the air, landing him into my arms. Matthew grabbed my glass of lemonade and, squealing happily, he turned it upside down across my lap.

"Matthew! No!" I scolded, jumping to my feet.

Matthew might have cried had not Ruth distracted him. "Matthew, try to catch me," she said.

He grinned and took chase. Ruth stayed just ahead of him, at times pretending to trip and fall, rising just before he could grasp her. He shouted happily each time he was close. She led him in a big circle, back to us, where she scrambled up into the hammock. I lifted him up too and tickled them both as I swung them back and forth.

The entire sky was brilliant orange, pink, and red. We lingered by the river, watching the color. But soon a cool breeze started off the water, rippling through my damp skirt.

"I should have thought to bring a sweater." I reluctantly stood. "Time for us to head up." As Nick replaced the glasses on the tray, I looked across the lawn to the group on the terrace where Cindy, Father, Kevin, and Grandfather were laughing about something. Ruth skipped ahead, still singing about her uncle-cousin. And Matthew stumped gamely after her.

But Nick called them back. "Wait a moment. I almost forgot. I have a present here for you." They were back to the hammock in a second. "Just one thing. You must share this with each other. I've always treasured it and I hope you will, too."

Matthew watched, wide-eyed, as Ruth ripped off the paper to find Matt's tattered old trainman's cap. Ruth put it on Matthew's head. It slipped down over his ears and nose. She quickly moved it to her head.

"Come on, Matthew," she yelled. She used one hand to hold the cap back from her brow so she could see ahead as she dashed up to the terrace to show off her present.

I followed them more slowly, hand in hand with my brother.

But they will never do it again, Best Beloved.
They are quite contented as they are.

Rudyard Kipling
Just So Stories

Acknowledgements

I am most grateful to my family: wife Janet, and children, Amanda and Aaron, for giving me the encouragement and support to write this book. Janet is the only person to have read more than one draft, each time offering exquisite advice.

I am indebted to friends and relatives who read early drafts and gave invaluable advice including Sue Bissell, Pat McDonagh, Marisa Labozzetta, Esther Cohen, Sharon Fiffer, Steve Fiffer, Diana Larkin and Andy Larkin. Members of my writing group including Rita Bleiman, Fred Contrada, Joan Cenedella, Bill Newman, Harriet Rodgers and Susanne Dunlop were extraordinarily helpful with their precise suggestions for improvement.

For offering the encouragement to continue the publishing process, I thank Marty Wohl and Jon Schwab.

Professional editor Connie Parks meticulously read the novel, saving me from several plot inconsistencies and a multitude of grammatical errors. Every writer needs such an editor.

I was also the beneficiary of professional help from James Madden of On the Button; Rachel Myers and Ruth Greenstein of Greenline Publishing Consultants; Linda McCullough Moore; and Irene Zahava. Each carefully read the manuscript and offered detailed ideas.

I also thank artist Walter Cudnohufsky of Ashfield Massachusetts. Based on my vague description, he painted the perfect cover illustration.

This book would not have been published without the professional guidance given by Caleb Wetmore along with the rest of the staff at Collective Copies of Florence and Amherst Massachusetts. It was Caleb's idea to connect the front and back covers in such an effective way.

Robert Bissell, a retired pediatrician, lives in Northampton, Massachusetts with his wife, Janet. He is the author of *Stock Market: You Can Do It.* This is his first novel.